The Curious Case of Benjamin Button

F. Scott Fitzgerald was born in 1896 in St Paul, Minnesota, and went to Princeton University, which he left in 1917 to join the army. He was said to have epitomized the Jazz Age, which he himself defined as 'a generation grown up to find all Gods dead, all wars fought, all faiths in man shaken'. In 1920 he married Zelda Sayre. Their traumatic marriage and her subsequent breakdowns became the leading influence on his writing. Among his publications were five novels, *This Side of Paradise*, *The Great Gatsby*, *The Beautiful and Damned*, *Tender is the Night* and *The Last Tycoon* (his last and unfinished work); six volumes of short stories and *The Crack-Up*, a selection of autobiographical pieces. Fitzgerald died suddenly in 1940. After his death *The New York Times* said of him that 'He was better than he knew, for in fact and in the literary sense he invented a "generation" . . . he might have interpreted and even guided them, as in their middle years they saw a different and nobler freedom threatened with destruction.'

F. SCOTT FITZGERALD

The Curious Case of Benjamin Button

AND SIX OTHER STORIES

PENGUIN BOOKS

PENGUIN CLASSICS

Published by the Penguin Group
Penguin Books Ltd, 80 Strand, London WC2R 0RL, England
Penguin Group (USA) Inc., 375 Hudson Street, New York, New York 10014, USA
Penguin Group (Canada), 90 Eglinton Avenue East, Suite 700, Toronto, Ontario, Canada M4P 2Y3
(a division of Pearson Penguin Canada Inc.)
Penguin Ireland, 25 St Stephen's Green, Dublin 2, Ireland
(a division of Penguin Books Ltd)
Penguin Group (Australia), 250 Camberwell Road,
Camberwell, Victoria 3124, Australia (a division of Pearson Australia Group Pty Ltd)
Penguin Books India Pvt Ltd, 11 Community Centre,
Panchsheel Park, New Delhi – 110 017, India
Penguin Group (NZ), 67 Apollo Drive, Rosedale, North Shore 0632, New Zealand
(a division of Pearson New Zealand Ltd)
Penguin Books (South Africa) (Pty) Ltd, 24 Sturdee Avenue, Rosebank, Johannesburg 2196,
South Africa

Penguin Books Ltd. Registered Offices: 80 Strand, London WC2R 0RL, England

www.penguin.com

'The Curious Case of Benjamin Button', 'May Day' and 'O Russet Witch' taken from
Tales of the Jazz Age first published by Charles Scribner's Sons 1922
'Head and Shoulders', 'The Cut-Glass Bowl' and 'The Four Fists'
taken from *Flappers and Philosophers* first published by
Charles Scribner's Sons 1920
'Crazy Sunday' first published 1932
This selection published in Penguin Classics 2008
16

Typeset by Palimpsest Book Production Limited,
Grangemouth, Stirlingshire
Printed in England by Clays Ltd, St Ives plc

978-0-141-19019-8

www.greenpenguin.co.uk

Mixed Sources
Product group from well-managed
forests and other controlled sources
www.fsc.org Cert no. SA-COC-1592
© 1996 Forest Stewardship Council

FSC

Penguin Books is committed to a sustainable future
for our business, our readers and our planet.
The book in your hands is made from paper
certified by the Forest Stewardship Council.

Contents

The Curious Case of Benjamin Button 1
Head and Shoulders 29
The Cut-Glass Bowl 56
The Four Fists 78
May Day 96
'O Russet Witch!' 151
Crazy Sunday 184

The Curious Case of Benjamin Button

I

As long ago as 1860 it was the proper thing to be born at home. At present, so I am told, the high gods of medicine have decreed that the first cries of the young shall be uttered upon the anesthetic air of a hospital, preferably a fashionable one. So young Mr and Mrs Roger Button were fifty years ahead of style when they decided, one day in the summer of 1860, that their first baby should be born in a hospital. Whether this anachronism had any bearing upon the astonishing history I am about to set down will never be known.

I shall tell you what occurred, and let you judge for yourself.

The Roger Buttons held an enviable position, both social and financial, in ante-bellum Baltimore. They were related to the This Family and the That Family, which, as every Southerner knew, entitled them to membership in that enormous peerage which largely populated the Confederacy. This was their first experience with the charming old custom of having babies – Mr Button was naturally nervous. He hoped it would be a boy so that he could be sent to Yale College in Connecticut, at which institution Mr Button himself had been known for four years by the somewhat obvious nickname of 'Cuff.'

On the September morning consecrated to the enormous event he arose nervously at six o'clock, dressed himself, adjusted an impeccable stock, and hurried forth through the streets of Baltimore to the hospital, to determine whether the darkness of the night had borne in new life upon its bosom.

When he was approximately a hundred yards from the Maryland Private Hospital for Ladies and Gentlemen he saw Doctor Keene, the family physician, descending the front steps, rubbing his hands together with a washing movement – as all doctors are required to do by the unwritten ethics of their profession.

Mr Roger Button, the president of Roger Button & Co., Wholesale Hardware, began to run toward Doctor Keene with much less dignity than was expected from a Southern gentleman of that picturesque period. 'Doctor Keene!' he called. 'Oh, Doctor Keene!'

The doctor heard him, faced around, and stood waiting, a curious expression settling on his harsh, medicinal face as Mr Button drew near.

'What happened?' demanded Mr Button, as he came up in a gasping rush. 'What was it? How is she? A boy? Who is it? What—'

'Talk sense!' said Doctor Keene sharply. He appeared somewhat irritated.

'Is the child born?' begged Mr Button.

Doctor Keene frowned. 'Why, yes, I suppose so – after a fashion.' Again he threw a curious glance at Mr Button.

'Is my wife all right?'

'Yes.'

'Is it a boy or a girl?'

'Here now!' cried Doctor Keene in a perfect passion of irritation, 'I'll ask you to go and see for yourself. Outrageous!' He snapped the last word out in almost one syllable, then he turned away muttering: 'Do you imagine a case like this will help my professional reputation? One more would ruin me – ruin anybody.'

'What's the matter?' demanded Mr Button, appalled. 'Triplets?'

'No, not triplets!' answered the doctor cuttingly. 'What's more, you can go and see for yourself. And get another doctor. I brought you into the world, young man, and I've been physician to your family for forty years, but I'm through with you! I don't want to see you or any of your relatives ever again! Good-by!'

Then he turned sharply, and without another word climbed into his phaeton, which was waiting at the curbstone, and drove severely away.

Mr Button stood there upon the sidewalk, stupefied and trembling from head to foot. What horrible mishap had occurred? He had suddenly lost all desire to go into the Maryland Private Hospital for Ladies and Gentlemen – it was with the greatest difficulty that, a moment later, he forced himself to mount the steps and enter the front door.

A nurse was sitting behind a desk in the opaque gloom of the hall. Swallowing his shame, Mr Button approached her.

'Good-morning,' she remarked, looking up at him pleasantly.

'Good-morning. I – I am Mr Button.'

At this a look of utter terror spread itself over the girl's face. She rose to her feet and seemed about to fly from the hall, restraining herself only with the most apparent difficulty.

'I want to see my child,' said Mr Button.

The nurse gave a little scream. 'Oh – of course!' she cried hysterically. 'Up-stairs. Right up-stairs. Go – *up!*'

She pointed the direction, and Mr Button, bathed in a cool perspiration, turned falteringly, and began to mount to the second floor. In the upper hall he addressed another nurse who approached him, basin in hand. 'I'm Mr Button,' he managed to articulate. 'I want to see my—'

Clank! The basin clattered to the floor and rolled in the direction of the stairs. Clank! Clank! It began a methodical descent as if sharing in the general terror which this gentleman provoked.

'I want to see my child!' Mr Button almost shrieked. He was on the verge of collapse.

Clank! The basin had reached the first floor. The nurse regained control of herself, and threw Mr Button a look of hearty contempt.

'All *right*, Mr Button,' she agreed in a hushed voice. 'Very *well!* But if you *knew* what state it's put us all in this morning! It's perfectly outrageous! The hospital will never have the ghost of a reputation after—'

'Hurry!' he cried hoarsely. 'I can't stand this!'

'Come this way, then, Mr Button.'

He dragged himself after her. At the end of a long hall they reached a room from which proceeded a variety of howls – indeed, a room which, in later parlance, would have been known as the 'crying-room.' They entered. Ranged around the walls were half a dozen white-enameled rolling cribs, each with a tag tied at the head.

'Well,' gasped Mr Button, 'which is mine?'

'There!' said the nurse.

Mr Button's eyes followed her pointing finger, and this is what he saw. Wrapped in a voluminous white blanket, and partially crammed into one of the cribs, there sat an old man apparently about seventy years of age. His sparse hair was almost white, and from his chin dripped a long smoke-colored beard, which waved absurdly back and forth, fanned by the breeze coming in at the window. He looked up at Mr Button with dim, faded eyes in which lurked a puzzled question.

'Am I mad?' thundered Mr Button, his terror resolving into rage. 'Is this some ghastly hospital joke?'

'It doesn't seem like a joke to us,' replied the nurse severely. 'And I don't know whether you're mad or not – but that is most certainly your child.'

The cool perspiration redoubled on Mr Button's forehead. He closed his eyes, and then, opening them, looked again. There was no mistake – he was gazing at a man of threescore and ten – a *baby* of threescore and ten, a baby whose feet hung over the sides of the crib in which it was reposing.

The old man looked placidly from one to the other for a moment, and then suddenly spoke in a cracked and ancient voice. 'Are you my father?' he demanded.

Mr Button and the nurse started violently.

'Because if you are,' went on the old man querulously, 'I wish you'd get me out of this place – or, at least, get them to put a comfortable rocker in here.'

'Where in God's name did you come from? Who are you?' burst out Mr Button frantically.

'I can't tell you *exactly* who I am,' replied the querulous whine, 'because I've only been born a few hours – but my last name is certainly Button.'

'You lie! You're an impostor!'

The old man turned wearily to the nurse. 'Nice way to welcome a new-born child,' he complained in a weak voice. 'Tell him he's wrong, why don't you?'

'You're wrong, Mr Button,' said the nurse severely. 'This is your child, and you'll have to make the best of it. We're going to ask you to take him home with you as soon as possible – some time today.'

'Home?' repeated Mr Button incredulously.

'Yes, we can't have him here. We really can't, you know?'

'I'm right glad of it,' whined the old man. 'This is a fine place to keep a youngster of quiet tastes. With all this yelling and howling, I haven't been able to get a wink of sleep. I asked for something to eat' – here his voice rose to a shrill note of protest – 'and they brought me a bottle of milk!'

Mr Button sank down upon a chair near his son and concealed his face in his hands. 'My heavens!' he murmured, in an ecstasy of horror. 'What will people say? What must I do?'

'You'll have to take him home,' insisted the nurse – 'immediately!'

A grotesque picture formed itself with dreadful clarity before the eyes of the tortured man – a picture of himself walking through the crowded streets of the city with this appalling apparition stalking by his side. 'I can't. I can't,' he moaned.

People would stop to speak to him, and what was he going to say? He would have to introduce this – this septuagenarian: 'This is my son, born early this morning.' And then the old man would gather his blanket around him and they would plod on, past the bustling stores, the slave market – for a dark instant Mr Button wished passionately that his son was black – past the luxurious houses of the residential district, past the home for the aged . . .

'Come! Pull yourself together,' commanded the nurse.

'See here,' the old man announced suddenly, 'if you think I'm going to walk home in this blanket, you're entirely mistaken.'

'Babies always have blankets.'

With a malicious crackle the old man held up a small white swaddling garment. 'Look!' he quavered. '*This* is what they had ready for me.'

'Babies always wear those,' said the nurse primly.

'Well,' said the old man, 'this baby's not going to wear anything in about two minutes. This blanket itches. They might at least have given me a sheet.'

'Keep it on! Keep it on!' said Mr Button hurriedly. He turned to the nurse. 'What'll I do?'

'Go down town and buy your son some clothes.'

Mr Button's son's voice followed him down into the hall: 'And a cane, father. I want to have a cane.'

Mr Button banged the outer door savagely . . .

II

'Good-morning,' Mr Button said, nervously, to the clerk in the Chesapeake Dry Goods Company. 'I want to buy some clothes for my child.'

'How old is your child, sir?'

'About six hours,' answered Mr Button, without due consideration.

'Babies' supply department in the rear.'

'Why, I don't think – I'm not sure that's what I want. It's – he's an unusually large-size child. Ecceptionally – ah – large.'

'They have the largest child's sizes.'

'Where is the boys' department?' inquired Mr Button, shifting his ground desperately. He felt that the clerk must surely scent his shameful secret.

'Right here.'

'Well—' He hesitated. The notion of dressing his son in men's clothes was repugnant to him. If, say, he could only find a *very* large boy's suit, he might cut off that long and awful beard, dye the white hair brown, and thus manage to conceal the worst, and to retain something of his own self-respect – not to mention his position in Baltimore society.

But a frantic inspection of the boys' department revealed no suits to fit the new-born Button. He blamed the store, of course – in such cases it is the thing to blame the store.

'How old did you say that boy of yours was?' demanded the clerk curiously.

'He's – sixteen.'

'Oh, I beg your pardon. I thought you said six *hours*. You'll find the youths' department in the next aisle.'

Mr Button turned miserably away. Then he stopped, brightened, and pointed his finger toward a dressed dummy in the window display. 'There!' he exclaimed.

'I'll take that suit, out there on the dummy.'

The clerk stared. 'Why,' he protested, 'that's not a child's suit. At least it *is*, but it's for fancy dress. You could wear it yourself!'

'Wrap it up,' insisted his customer nervously.

'That's what I want.'

The astonished clerk obeyed.

Back at the hospital Mr Button entered the nursery and almost threw the package at his son, 'Here's your clothes,' he snapped out.

The old man untied the package and viewed the contents with a quizzical eye.

'They look sort of funny to me,' he complained. 'I don't want to be made a monkey of—'

'You've made a monkey of me!' retorted Mr Button fiercely. 'Never you mind how funny you look. Put them on – or I'll – or I'll *spank* you.' He swallowed uneasily at the penultimate word, feeling nevertheless that it was the proper thing to say.

'All right, father' – this with a grotesque simulation of filial respect – 'you've lived longer; you know best. Just as you say.'

As before, the sound of the word 'father' caused Mr Button to start violently.

'And hurry.'

'I'm hurrying, father.'

When his son was dressed Mr Button regarded him with depression. The costume consisted of dotted socks, pink pants, and a belted blouse with a wide white collar. Over the latter waved the long whitish beard, drooping almost to the waist. The effect was not good.

'Wait!'

Mr Button seized a hospital shears and with three quick snaps amputated a large section of the beard. But even with this improvement the ensemble fell far short of perfection. The remaining brush of scraggly hair; the watery eyes, the ancient teeth, seemed oddly out of tone with the gayety of the costume. Mr Button, however, was obdurate – he held out his hand. 'Come along!' he said sternly.

His son took the hand trustingly. 'What are you going to call me, dad?' he quavered as they walked from the nursery – 'just "baby" for a while? till you think of a better name?'

Mr Button grunted. 'I don't know,' he answered harshly. 'I think we'll call you Methuselah.'

III

Even after the new addition to the Button family had had his hair cut short and then dyed to a sparse unnatural black, had had his face shaved so close that it glistened, and had been attired in small-boy clothes made to order by a flabbergasted tailor, it was impossible for Mr Button to ignore the fact that his son was a poor excuse for a first family baby. Despite his aged stoop, Benjamin Button – for it was by this name they called him instead of by the appropriate but invidious Methuselah – was five feet eight inches tall. His clothes did not conceal this, nor did the clipping and dyeing of his eyebrows disguise the fact that the eyes underneath were faded and watery and tired. In fact, the baby-nurse who had been engaged in advance left the house after one look, in a state of considerable indignation.

But Mr Button persisted in his unwavering purpose. Benjamin was a baby, and a baby he should remain. At first he declared that if Benjamin didn't like warm milk he could go without food altogether, but he was finally prevailed upon to allow his son bread and butter, and even oatmeal by way of a compromise. One day he brought home a rattle and, giving it to Benjamin, insisted in no uncertain terms that he should 'play with it,' whereupon the old man took it with a weary expression and could be heard jingling it obediently at intervals throughout the day.

There can be no doubt, though, that the rattle bored him, and that he found other and more soothing amusements when he was left alone. For instance, Mr Button discovered one day that during the preceding week he had smoked more cigars than ever before – a phenomenon which was explained a few days later when, entering the nursery unexpectedly, he found the room full of faint blue haze and Benjamin, with a guilty expression on his face, trying to conceal the butt of a dark Havana. This, of course, called for a severe spanking, but Mr Button found that he could not bring himself to administer it. He merely warned his son that he would 'stunt his growth.'

Nevertheless he persisted in his attitude. He brought home lead soldiers, he brought toy trains, he brought large pleasant animals made of cotton, and, to perfect the illusion which he was creating – for himself at least – he passionately demanded of the clerk in the toy-store whether 'the paint would come off the pink duck if the baby put it in his mouth.' But, despite all his father's efforts, Benjamin refused to be interested. He would steal down the back stairs and return to the nursery with a volume of the 'Encyclopaedia Britannica,' over which he would pore through an afternoon, while his cotton cows and his Noah's ark were left neglected on the floor. Against such a stubbornness Mr Button's efforts were of little avail.

The sensation created in Baltimore was, at first, prodigious. What the mishap would have cost the Buttons and their kinsfolk socially cannot be determined, for the outbreak of the Civil War drew the city's attention to other things. A few people who were unfailingly polite racked their brains for compliments to give to the parents – and finally hit upon the ingenious device of declaring that the baby resembled his grandfather, a fact which, due to the standard state of decay common to all men of seventy, could not be denied. Mr and Mrs Roger Button were not pleased, and Benjamin's grandfather was furiously insulted.

Benjamin, once he left the hospital, took life as he found it. Several small boys were brought to see him, and he spent a stiff-jointed afternoon trying to work up an interest in tops and marbles – he even managed, quite accidentally, to break a kitchen window with a stone from a sling shot, a feat which secretly delighted his father.

Thereafter Benjamin contrived to break something every day, but he did these things only because they were expected of him, and because he was by nature obliging.

When his grandfather's initial antagonism wore off, Benjamin and that gentleman took enormous pleasure in one another's company. They would sit for hours, these two so far apart in age and experience, and, like old cronies, discuss with tireless monotony the slow events of the day. Benjamin felt more at ease in his grandfather's presence than in his parents' – they seemed always somewhat in awe of him and, despite the dictatorial authority they exercised over him, frequently addressed him as 'Mr.'

He was as puzzled as any one else at the apparently advanced age of his mind and body at birth. He read up on it in the medical journal, but found that no such case had been previously recorded. At his father's urging he made an honest attempt to play with other boys, and frequently he joined in the milder games – football shook him up too much, and he feared that in case of a fracture his ancient bones would refuse to knit.

When he was five he was sent to kindergarten, where he was initiated into the art of pasting green paper on orange paper, of weaving colored maps and manufacturing eternal cardboard necklaces. He was inclined to drowse off to sleep in the middle of these tasks, a habit which both irritated and frightened his young teacher. To his relief she complained to his parents, and he was removed from the school. The Roger Buttons told their friends that they felt he was too young.

By the time he was twelve years old his parents had grown used to him. Indeed, so strong is the force of custom that they no longer felt that he was different from any other child – except when some curious anomaly reminded them of the fact. But one day a few weeks after his twelfth birthday, while looking in the mirror, Benjamin made, or thought he made, an astonishing discovery. Did his eyes deceive him, or had his hair turned in the dozen years of his life from white to iron-gray under its concealing dye? Was the network of wrinkles on his face becoming less pronounced? Was his skin healthier and firmer, with even a touch of ruddy winter color? He could not tell. He knew that he no longer stooped and that his physical condition had improved since the early days of his life.

'Can it be—?' he thought to himself, or, rather, scarcely dared to think.

He went to his father. 'I am grown,' he announced determinedly. 'I want to put on long trousers.'

His father hesitated. 'Well,' he said finally, 'I don't know. Fourteen is the age for putting on long trousers – and you are only twelve.'

'But you'll have to admit,' protested Benjamin, 'that I'm big for my age.'

His father looked at him with illusory speculation. 'Oh, I'm not so sure of that,' he said. 'I was as big as you when I was twelve.'

This was not true – it was all part of Roger Button's silent agreement with himself to believe in his son's normality.

Finally a compromise was reached. Benjamin was to continue to dye his hair. He was to make a better attempt to play with boys of his own age. He was not to wear his spectacles or carry a cane in the street. In return for these concessions he was allowed his first suit of long trousers . . .

IV

Of the life of Benjamin Button between his twelfth and twenty-first year I intend to say little. Suffice to record that they were years of normal ungrowth. When Benjamin was eighteen he was erect as a man of fifty; he had more hair and it was of a dark gray; his step was firm, his voice had lost its cracked quaver and descended to a healthy baritone. So his father sent him up to Connecticut to take examinations for entrance to Yale College. Benjamin passed his examination and became a member of the freshman class.

On the third day following his matriculation he received a notification from Mr Hart, the college registrar, to call at his office and arrange his schedule. Benjamin, glancing in the mirror, decided that his hair needed a new application of its brown dye, but an anxious inspection of his bureau drawer disclosed that the dye bottle was not there. Then he remembered – he had emptied it the day before and thrown it away.

He was in a dilemma. He was due at the registrar's in five minutes. There seemed to be no help for it – he must go as he was. He did.

'Good-morning,' said the registrar politely. 'You've come to inquire about your son.'

'Why, as a matter of fact, my name's Button—' began Benjamin, but Mr Hart cut him off.

'I'm very glad to meet you, Mr Button. I'm expecting your son here any minute.'

'That's me!' burst out Benjamin. 'I'm a freshman.'

'What!'

'I'm a freshman.'

'Surely you're joking.'

'Not at all.'

The registrar frowned and glanced at a card before him. 'Why, I have Mr Benjamin Button's age down here as eighteen.'

'That's my age,' asserted Benjamin, flushing slightly.

The registrar eyed him wearily. 'Now surely, Mr Button, you don't expect me to believe that.'

Benjamin smiled wearily. 'I am eighteen,' he repeated.

The registrar pointed sternly to the door. 'Get out,' he said. 'Get out of college and get out of town. You are a dangerous lunatic.'

'I am eighteen.'

Mr Hart opened the door. 'The idea!' he shouted. 'A man of your age trying to enter here as a freshman. Eighteen years old, are you? Well, I'll give you eighteen minutes to get out of town.'

Benjamin Button walked with dignity from the room, and half a dozen undergraduates, who were waiting in the hall, followed him curiously with their eyes. When he had gone a little way he turned around, faced the infuriated registrar, who was still standing in the doorway, and repeated in a firm voice: 'I am eighteen years old.'

To a chorus of titters which went up from the group of undergraduates, Benjamin walked away.

But he was not fated to escape so easily. On his melancholy walk to the railroad station he found that he was being followed by a group, then by a swarm, and finally by a dense mass of undergraduates. The word had gone around that a lunatic had passed the entrance examinations for Yale and attempted to palm himself off as a youth of eighteen. A fever of excitement permeated the college. Men ran hatless out of classes, the football team abandoned its practice and joined the mob, professors' wives with bonnets awry and bustles out of position, ran shouting after the procession, from which proceeded a continual succession of remarks aimed at the tender sensibilities of Benjamin Button.

'He must be the Wandering Jew!'

'He ought to go to prep school at his age!'

'Look at the infant prodigy!'

'He thought this was the old men's home.'

'Go up to Harvard!'

Benjamin increased his gait, and soon he was running. He would show them! He *would* go to Harvard, and then they would regret these ill-considered taunts!

Safely on board the train for Baltimore, he put his head from the window. 'You'll regret this!' he shouted.

'Ha-ha!' the undergraduates laughed. 'Ha-ha-ha!' It was the biggest mistake that Yale College had ever made . . .

V

In 1880 Benjamin Button was twenty years old, and he signalized his birthday by going to work for his father in Roger Button & Co., Wholesale Hardware. It was in that same year that he began 'going out socially' – that is, his father insisted on taking him to several fashionable dances. Roger Button was now fifty, and he and his son were more and more companionable – in fact, since Benjamin had ceased to dye his hair (which was still grayish) they appeared about the same age, and could have passed for brothers.

One night in August they got into the phaeton attired in their full-dress suits and drove out to a dance at the Shevlins' country house, situated just outside of Baltimore. It was a gorgeous evening. A full moon drenched the road to the lustreless color of platinum, and late-blooming harvest flowers breathed into the motionless air aromas that were like low, half-heard laughter. The open country, carpeted for rods around with bright wheat, was translucent as in the day. It was almost impossible not to be affected by the sheer beauty of the sky – almost.

'There's a great future in the dry-goods business,' Roger Button was saying. He was not a spiritual man – his esthetic sense was rudimentary.

'Old fellows like me can't learn new tricks,' he observed profoundly. 'It's you youngsters with energy and vitality that have the great future before you.'

Far up the road the lights of the Shevlins' country house drifted into view, and presently there was a sighing sound that crept persistently toward them – it might have been the fine plaint of violins or the rustle of the silver wheat under the moon.

They pulled up behind a handsome brougham whose passengers were disembarking at the door. A lady got out, then an elderly gentleman, then another young lady, beautiful as sin. Benjamin started; an almost chemical change seemed to dissolve and recompose the very elements of his body. A rigor passed over him, blood rose into his cheeks, his forehead, and there was a steady thumping in his ears. It was first love.

The girl was slender and frail, with hair that was ashen under the moon and honey-colored under the sputtering gas-lamps of the porch. Over her shoulders was thrown a Spanish mantilla of softest yellow, butterflied in black; her feet were glittering buttons at the hem of her bustled dress.

Roger Button leaned over to his son. 'That,' he said, 'is young Hildegarde Moncrief, the daughter of General Moncrief.'

Benjamin nodded coldly. 'Pretty little thing,' he said indifferently. But when the negro boy had led the buggy away, he added: 'Dad, you might introduce me to her.'

They approached a group of which Miss Moncrief was the center. Reared in the old tradition, she courtesied low before Benjamin. Yes, he might have a dance. He thanked her and walked away – staggered away.

The interval until the time for his turn should arrive dragged itself out interminably. He stood close to the wall, silent, inscrutable, watching with murderous eyes the young bloods of Baltimore as they eddied around Hildegarde Moncrief, passionate admiration in their faces. How obnoxious they seemed to Benjamin; how intolerably rosy! Their curling brown whiskers aroused in him a feeling equivalent to indigestion.

But when his own time came, and he drifted with her out upon the changing floor to the music of the latest waltz from Paris, his jealousies and anxieties melted from him like a mantle of snow. Blind with enchantment, he felt that life was just beginning.

'You and your brother got here just as we did, didn't you?' asked Hildegarde, looking up at him with eyes that were like bright blue enamel.

Benjamin hesitated. If she took him for his father's brother, would it be best to enlighten her? He remembered his experience at Yale, so he decided against it. It would be rude to contradict a lady; it would be criminal to mar this exquisite occasion with the grotesque story of his origin. Later, perhaps. So he nodded, smiled, listened, was happy.

'I like men of your age,' Hildegarde told him. 'Young boys are so idiotic. They tell me how much champagne they drink at college, and how much money they lose playing cards. Men of your age know how to appreciate women.'

Benjamin felt himself on the verge of a proposal – with an effort he choked back the impulse.

'You're just the romantic age,' she continued – 'fifty. Twenty-five is too worldly-wise; thirty is apt to be pale from overwork; forty is the age of long stories that take a whole cigar to tell; sixty is – oh, sixty is too near seventy; but fifty is the mellow age. I love fifty.'

Fifty seemed to Benjamin a glorious age. He longed passionately to be fifty.

'I've always said,' went on Hildegarde, 'that I'd rather marry a man of fifty and be taken care of than marry a man of thirty and take care of *him*.'

For Benjamin the rest of the evening was bathed in a honey-colored mist. Hildegarde gave him two more dances, and they discovered that they were marvellously in accord on all the questions of the day. She was to go driving with him on the following Sunday, and then they would discuss all these questions further.

Going home in the phaeton just before the crack of dawn, when the first bees were humming and the fading moon glimmered in the cool dew, Benjamin knew vaguely that his father was discussing wholesale hardware.

'. . . And what do you think should merit our biggest attention after hammers and nails?' the elder Button was saying.

'Love,' replied Benjamin absent-mindedly.

'Lugs?' exclaimed Roger Button. 'Why, I've just covered the question of lugs.'

Benjamin regarded him with dazed eyes just as the eastern sky was suddenly cracked with light, and an oriole yawned piercingly in the quickening trees . . .

VI

When, six months later, the engagement of Miss Hildegarde Moncrief to Mr Benjamin Button was made known (I say 'made known,' for General Moncrief declared he would rather fall upon his sword than announce it), the excitement in Baltimore society reached a feverish pitch. The almost forgotten story of Benjamin's birth was remembered and sent out upon the winds of scandal in picaresque and incredible forms. It was said that Benjamin was really the father of Roger Button, that he was his brother who had been in prison for forty years, that he was John Wilkes Booth in disguise – and, finally, that he had two small conical horns sprouting from his head.

The Sunday supplements of the New York papers played up the case with fascinating sketches which showed the head of Benjamin Button attached to a fish, to a snake, and, finally, to a body of solid brass. He became known, journalistically, as the Mystery Man of Maryland. But the true story, as is usually the case, had a very small circulation.

However, every one agreed with General Moncrief that it was 'criminal' for a lovely girl who could have married any beau in Baltimore to throw herself into the arms of a man who was assuredly fifty. In vain Mr Roger Button published his son's birth certificate in large type in the Baltimore *Blaze*. No one believed it. You had only to look at Benjamin and see.

On the part of the two people most concerned there was no wavering. So many of the stories about her fiancé were false that Hildegarde refused stubbornly to believe even the true one. In vain General Moncrief pointed out to her the high mortality among men of fifty – or, at least, among men who looked fifty; in vain he told her of the instability of the wholesale hardware business. Hildegarde had chosen to marry for mellowness – and marry she did . . .

VII

In one particular, at least, the friends of Hildegarde Moncrief were mistaken. The wholesale hardware business prospered amazingly. In the fifteen years between Benjamin Button's marriage in 1880 and his father's retirement in 1895, the family fortune was doubled – and this was due largely to the younger member of the firm.

Needless to say, Baltimore eventually received the couple to its bosom. Even old General Moncrief became reconciled to his son-in-law when Benjamin gave him the money to bring out his 'History of the Civil War' in twenty volumes, which had been refused by nine prominent publishers.

In Benjamin himself fifteen years had wrought many changes. It seemed to him that the blood flowed with new vigor through his veins. It began to be a pleasure to rise in the morning, to walk with an active step along the busy, sunny street, to work untiringly with his shipments of hammers and his cargoes of nails. It was in 1890 that he executed his famous business coup: he brought up the suggestion that *all nails used in nailing up the boxes in which nails are shipped are the property of the shippee*, a proposal which became a statute, was approved by Chief Justice Fossile, and saved Roger Button and Company, Wholesale Hardware, more than *six hundred nails every year*.

In addition, Benjamin discovered that he was becoming more and more attracted by the gay side of life. It was typical of his growing enthusiasm for pleasure that he was the first man in the city of Baltimore to own and run an automobile. Meeting him on the street, his contemporaries would stare enviously at the picture he made of health and vitality.

'He seems to grow younger every year,' they would remark. And if old Roger Button, now sixty-five years old, had failed at first to give a proper welcome to his son he atoned at last by bestowing on him what amounted to adulation.

And here we come to an unpleasant subject which it will be well to pass over as quickly as possible. There was only one thing that worried Benjamin Button: his wife had ceased to attract him.

At that time Hildegarde was a woman of thirty-five, with a son, Roscoe, fourteen years old. In the early days of their marriage Benjamin had worshipped her. But, as the years passed, her honey-colored hair became an unexciting brown, the blue enamel of her eyes assumed the aspect of cheap crockery – moreover, and most of all, she had become too settled in her ways, too placid, too content, too anemic in her excitements, and too sober in her taste. As a bride it had been she who had 'dragged' Benjamin to dances and dinners – now conditions were reversed. She went out socially with him, but without enthusiasm, devoured already by that eternal inertia which comes to live with each of us one day and stays with us to the end.

Benjamin's discontent waxed stronger. At the outbreak of the Spanish-American War in 1898 his home had for him so little charm that he decided to join the army. With his business influence he obtained a commission as captain, and proved so adaptable to the work that he was made a major, and finally a lieutenant-colonel just in time to participate in the celebrated charge up San Juan Hill. He was slightly wounded, and received a medal.

Benjamin had become so attached to the activity and excitement of army life that he regretted to give it up, but his business required attention, so he resigned his commission and came home. He was met at the station by a brass band and escorted to his house.

VIII

Hildegarde, waving a large silk flag, greeted him on the porch, and even as he kissed her he felt with a sinking of the heart that these three years had taken their toll. She was a woman of forty now, with a faint skirmish line of gray hairs in her head. The sight depressed him.

Up in his room he saw his reflection in the familiar mirror – he went closer and examined his own face with anxiety, comparing it after a moment with a photograph of himself in uniform taken just before the war.

'Good Lord!' he said aloud. The process was continuing. There was no doubt of it – he looked now like a man of thirty. Instead of being delighted, he was uneasy – he was growing younger. He had hitherto hoped that once he reached a bodily age equivalent to his age in years, the grotesque phenomenon which had marked his birth would cease to function. He shuddered. His destiny seemed to him awful, incredible.

When he came down-stairs Hildegarde was waiting for him. She appeared annoyed, and he wondered if she had at last discovered that there was something amiss. It was with an effort to relieve the tension between them that he broached the matter at dinner in what he considered a delicate way.

'Well,' he remarked lightly, 'everybody says I look younger than ever.'

Hildegarde regarded him with scorn. She sniffed. 'Do you think it's anything to boast about?'

'I'm not boasting,' he asserted uncomfortably.

She sniffed again. 'The idea,' she said, and after a moment: 'I should think you'd have enough pride to stop it.'

'How can I?' he demanded.

'I'm not going to argue with you,' she retorted. 'But there's a right way of doing things and a wrong way. If you've made up your mind to be different from everybody else, I don't suppose I can stop you, but I really don't think it's very considerate.'

'But, Hildegarde, I can't help it.'

'You can too. You're simply stubborn. You think you don't want to be like any one else. You always have been that way, and you always will be. But just think how it would be if every one else looked at things as you do – what would the world be like?'

As this was an inane and unanswerable argument Benjamin made no reply, and from that time on a chasm began to widen between them. He wondered what possible fascination she had ever exercised over him.

To add to the breach, he found, as the new century gathered headway, that his thirst for gayety grew stronger. Never a party of any kind in the city of Baltimore but he was there, dancing with the prettiest of the young married women, chatting with the most popular of the débutantes, and finding their company charming, while his wife, a dowager of evil omen, sat among the chaperons, now in haughty disapproval, and now following him with solemn, puzzled, and reproachful eyes.

'Look!' people would remark. 'What a pity! A young fellow that age tied to a woman of forty-five. He must be twenty years younger than his wife.' They had forgotten – as people inevitably forget – that back in 1880 their mammas and papas had also remarked about this same ill-matched pair.

Benjamin's growing unhappiness at home was compensated for by his many new interests. He took up golf and made a great success of it. He went in for dancing: in 1906 he was an expert at 'The Boston,' and in 1908 he was considered proficient at the 'Maxixe,' while in 1909 his 'Castle Walk' was the envy of every young man in town.

His social activities, of course, interfered to some extent with his business, but then he had worked hard at wholesale hardware for twenty-five years and felt that he could soon hand it on to his son, Roscoe, who had recently graduated from Harvard.

He and his son were, in fact, often mistaken for each other. This pleased Benjamin – he soon forgot the insidious fear which had come over him on his return from the Spanish-American War, and grew to take a naïve pleasure in his appearance. There was only one fly in the delicious ointment – he hated to appear in public with his wife. Hildegarde was almost fifty, and the sight of her made him feel absurd . . .

IX

One September day in 1910 – a few years after Roger Button & Co., Wholesale Hardware, had been handed over to young Roscoe Button – a man, apparently about twenty years old, entered himself as a freshman at Harvard University in Cambridge. He did not make the mistake of announcing that he would never see fifty again nor did he mention the fact that his son had been graduated from the same institution ten years before.

He was admitted, and almost immediately attained a prominent position in the class, partly because he seemed a little older than the other freshmen, whose average age was about eighteen.

But his success was largely due to the fact that in the football game with Yale he played so brilliantly, with so much dash and with such a cold, remorseless anger that he scored seven touchdowns and fourteen field goals for Harvard, and caused one entire eleven of Yale men to be carried singly from the field, unconscious. He was the most celebrated man in college.

Strange to say, in his third or junior year he was scarcely able to 'make' the team. The coaches said that he had lost weight, and it seemed to the more observant among them that he was not quite as tall as before. He made no touchdowns – indeed, he was retained on the team chiefly in hope that his enormous reputation would bring terror and disorganization to the Yale team.

In his senior year he did not make the team at all. He had grown so slight and frail that one day he was taken by some sophomores for a freshman, an incident which humiliated him terribly. He became known as something of a prodigy – a senior who was surely no more than sixteen – and he was often shocked at the worldliness of some of his classmates. His studies seemed harder to him – he felt that they were too advanced. He had heard his classmates speak of St Midas', the famous preparatory school, at which so many of them had prepared for college, and he determined after his graduation to enter himself at St Midas', where the sheltered life among boys his own size would be more congenial to him.

Upon his graduation in 1914 he went home to Baltimore with his Harvard diploma in his pocket. Hildegarde was now residing in Italy, so Benjamin went to live with his son, Roscoe. But though he was welcomed in a general way, there was obviously no heartiness in Roscoe's feeling toward him – there was even perceptible a tendency on his son's part to think that Benjamin, as he moped about the house in adolescent mooniness, was somewhat in the way. Roscoe was married now and prominent in Baltimore life, and he wanted no scandal to creep out in connection with his family.

Benjamin, no longer persona grata with the débutantes and younger college set, found himself left much alone, except for the companionship of three or four fifteen-year-old boys in the neighborhood. His idea of going to St Midas' school recurred to him.

'Say,' he said to Roscoe one day, 'I've told you over and over that I want to go to prep school.'

'Well, go, then,' replied Roscoe shortly. The matter was distasteful to him, and he wished to avoid a discussion.

'I can't go alone,' said Benjamin helplessly. 'You'll have to enter me and take me up there.'

'I haven't got time,' declared Roscoe abruptly. His eyes narrowed and he looked uneasily at his father. 'As a matter of fact,' he added, 'you'd better not go on with this business much longer. You better pull up short. You better – you better' – he paused and his face crimsoned as he sought for words – 'you better turn right around and start back the other way. This has gone too far to be a joke. It isn't funny any longer. You – you behave yourself!'

Benjamin looked at him, on the verge of tears.

'And another thing,' continued Roscoe, 'when visitors are in the house I want you to call me "Uncle" – not "Roscoe," but "Uncle," do you understand? It looks absurd for a boy of fifteen to call me by my first name. Perhaps you'd better call me "Uncle" *all* the time, so you'll get used to it.'

With a harsh look at his father, Roscoe turned away . . .

X

At the termination of this interview, Benjamin wandered dismally upstairs and stared at himself in the mirror. He had not shaved for three months, but he could find nothing on his face but a faint white down with which it seemed unnecessary to meddle. When he had first come home from Harvard, Roscoe had approached him with the proposition that he should wear eye-glasses and imitation whiskers glued to his cheeks, and it had seemed for a moment that the farce of his early years was to be repeated. But whiskers had itched and made him ashamed. He wept and Roscoe had reluctantly relented.

Benjamin opened a book of boys' stories, 'The Boy Scouts in

Bimini Bay,' and began to read. But he found himself thinking persistently about the war. America had joined the Allied cause during the preceding month, and Benjamin wanted to enlist, but, alas, sixteen was the minimum age, and he did not look that old. His true age, which was fifty-seven, would have disqualified him, anyway.

There was a knock at his door, and the butler appeared with a letter bearing a large official legend in the corner and addressed to Mr Benjamin Button. Benjamin tore it open eagerly, and read the enclosure with delight. It informed him that many reserve officers who had served in the Spanish-American War were being called back into service with a higher rank, and it enclosed his commission as brigadier-general in the United States army with orders to report immediately.

Benjamin jumped to his feet fairly quivering with enthusiasm. This was what he had wanted. He seized his cap and ten minutes later he had entered a large tailoring establishment on Charles Street, and asked in his uncertain treble to be measured for a uniform.

'Want to play soldier, sonny?' demanded a clerk, casually.

Benjamin flushed. 'Say! Never mind what I want!' he retorted angrily. 'My name's Button and I live on Mt. Vernon Place, so you know I'm good for it.'

'Well,' admitted the clerk, hesitantly, 'if you're not, I guess your daddy is, all right.'

Benjamin was measured, and a week later his uniform was completed. He had difficulty in obtaining the proper general's insignia because the dealer kept insisting to Benjamin that a nice Y. W. C. A. badge would look just as well and be much more fun to play with.

Saying nothing to Roscoe, he left the house one night and proceeded by train to Camp Mosby, in South Carolina, where he was to command an infantry brigade. On a sultry April day he approached the entrance to the camp, paid off the taxicab which had brought him from the station, and turned to the sentry on guard.

'Get some one to handle my luggage!' he said briskly.

The sentry eyed him reproachfully. 'Say,' he remarked, 'where you goin' with the general's duds, sonny?'

Benjamin, veteran of the Spanish-American War, whirled upon him with fire in his eye, but with, alas, a changing treble voice.

'Come to attention!' he tried to thunder; he paused for breath – then suddenly he saw the sentry snap his heels together and bring his rifle to the present. Benjamin concealed a smile of gratification, but when he glanced around his smile faded. It was not he who had inspired obedience, but an imposing artillery colonel who was approaching on horseback.

'Colonel!' called Benjamin shrilly.

The colonel came up, drew rein, and looked coolly down at him with a twinkle in his eyes. 'Whose little boy are you?' he demanded kindly.

'I'll soon darn well show you whose little boy I am!' retorted Benjamin in a ferocious voice. 'Get down off that horse!'

The colonel roared with laughter.

'You want him, eh, general?'

'Here!' cried Benjamin desperately. 'Read this.' And he thrust his commission toward the colonel.

The colonel read it, his eyes popping from their sockets.

'Where'd you get this?' he demanded, slipping the document into his own pocket.

'I got it from the Government, as you'll soon find out!'

'You come along with me,' said the colonel with a peculiar look. 'We'll go up to headquarters and talk this over. Come along.'

The colonel turned and began walking his horse in the direction of headquarters. There was nothing for Benjamin to do but follow with as much dignity as possible – meanwhile promising himself a stern revenge.

But this revenge did not materialize. Two days later, however, his son Roscoe materialized from Baltimore, hot and cross from a hasty trip, and escorted the weeping general, *sans* uniform, back to his home.

XI

In 1920 Roscoe Button's first child was born. During the attendant festivities, however, no one thought it 'the thing' to mention that the little grubby boy, apparently about ten years of age who played around the house with lead soldiers and a miniature circus, was the new baby's own grandfather.

No one disliked the little boy whose fresh, cheerful face was crossed with just a hint of sadness, but to Roscoe Button his presence was a source of torment. In the idiom of his generation Roscoe did not consider the matter 'efficient.' It seemed to him that his father, in refusing to look sixty, had not behaved like a 'red-blooded he-man' – this was Roscoe's favorite expression – but in a curious and perverse manner. Indeed, to think about the matter for as much as a half an hour drove him to the edge of insanity. Roscoe believed that 'live wires' should keep young, but carrying it out on such a scale was – was – was inefficient. And there Roscoe rested.

Five years later Roscoe's little boy had grown old enough to play childish games with little Benjamin under the supervision of the same nurse. Roscoe took them both to kindergarten on the same day and Benjamin found that playing with little strips of colored paper, making mats and chains and curious and beautiful designs, was the most fascinating game in the world. Once he was bad and had to stand in the corner – then he cried – but for the most part there were gay hours in the cheerful room, with the sunlight coming in the windows and Miss Bailey's kind hand resting for a moment now and then in his tousled hair.

Roscoe's son moved up into the first grade after a year, but Benjamin stayed on in the kindergarten. He was very happy. Sometimes when other tots talked about what they would do when they grew up a shadow would cross his little face as if in a dim, childish way he realized that those were things in which he was never to share.

The days flowed on in monotonous content. He went back a third year to the kindergarten, but he was too little now to understand what the bright shining strips of paper were for. He cried because the other boys were bigger than he and he was afraid of them. The teacher talked to him, but though he tried to understand he could not understand at all.

He was taken from the kindergarten. His nurse, Nana, in her starched gingham dress, became the center of his tiny world. On bright days they walked in the park; Nana would point at a great gray monster and say 'elephant,' and Benjamin would say it after her, and when he was being undressed for bed that night he would say it over and over aloud to her: 'Elyphant, elyphant, elyphant.' Sometimes Nana let him jump on the bed, which was fun, because if you sat down exactly right it would bounce you up on your feet again, and if you said 'Ah' for a long time while you jumped you got a very pleasing broken vocal effect.

He loved to take a big cane from the hatrack and go around hitting chairs and tables with it and saying: 'Fight, fight, fight.' When there were people there the old ladies would cluck at him, which interested him, and the young ladies would try to kiss him, which he submitted to with mild boredom. And when the long day was done at five o'clock he would go up-stairs with Nana and be fed oatmeal and nice soft mushy foods with a spoon.

There were no troublesome memories in his childish sleep; no token came to him of his brave days at college, of the glittering years when he flustered the hearts of many girls. There were only the white, safe walls of his crib and Nana and a man who came to see him sometimes, and a great big orange ball that Nana pointed at just before his twilight bed hour and called 'sun.' When the sun went his eyes were sleepy – there were no dreams, no dreams to haunt him.

The past – the wild charge at the head of his men up San Juan Hill; the first years of his marriage when he worked late into the summer dusk down in the busy city for young Hildegarde whom he loved; the days before that when he sat smoking far into the night in the gloomy old Button house on Monroe Street with his grandfather – all these had faded like unsubstantial dreams from his mind as though they had never been.

He did not remember. He did not remember clearly whether the milk was warm or cool at his last feeding or how the days passed – there was only his crib and Nana's familiar presence. And then he remembered nothing. When he was hungry he cried – that was all. Through the noons and nights he breathed and over him there were soft mumblings and murmurings that he scarcely heard, and faintly differentiated smells, and light and darkness.

Then it was all dark, and his white crib and the dim faces that moved above him, and the warm sweet aroma of the milk, faded out altogether from his mind.

Head and Shoulders

I

In 1915 Horace Tarbox was thirteen years old. In that year he took the examinations for entrance to Princeton University and received the Grade A – excellent – in Cæsar, Cicero, Vergil, Xenophon, Homer, Algebra, Plane Geometry, Solid Geometry, and Chemistry.

Two years later, while George M. Cohan was composing 'Over There,' Horace was leading the sophomore class by several lengths and digging out theses on 'The Syllogism as an Obsolete Scholastic Form,' and during the battle of Château-Thierry he was sitting at his desk deciding whether or not to wait until his seventeenth birthday before beginning his series of essays on 'The Pragmatic Bias of the New Realists.'

After a while some newsboy told him that the war was over, and he was glad, because it meant that Peat Brothers, publishers, would get out their new edition of 'Spinoza's Improvement of the Understanding.' Wars were all very well in their way, made young men self-reliant or something, but Horace felt that he could never forgive the President for allowing a brass band to play under his window on the night of the false armistice, causing him to leave three important sentences out of his thesis on 'German Idealism.'

The next year he went up to Yale to take his degree as Master of Arts.

He was seventeen then, tall and slender, with near-sighted gray eyes and an air of keeping himself utterly detached from the mere words he let drop.

'I never feel as though I'm talking to him,' expostulated Professor Dillinger to a sympathetic colleague. 'He makes me feel as though I were talking to his representative. I always expect him to say: "Well, I'll ask myself and find out."'

And then, just as nonchalantly as though Horace Tarbox had been Mr Beef the butcher or Mr Hat the haberdasher, life reached in, seized him, handled him, stretched him, and unrolled him like a piece of Irish lace on a Saturday-afternoon bargain-counter.

To move in the literary fashion I should say that this was all because when way back in colonial days the hardy pioneers had come to a bald place in Connecticut and asked of each other, 'Now, what shall we build here?' the hardiest one among 'em had answered: 'Let's build a town where theatrical managers can try out musical comedies!' How afterward they founded Yale College there, to try the musical comedies on, is a story every one knows. At any rate one December, 'Home James' opened at the Shubert, and all the students encored Marcia Meadow, who sang a song about the Blundering Blimp in the first act and did a shaky, shivery, celebrated dance in the last.

Marcia was nineteen. She didn't have wings, but audiences agreed generally that she didn't need them. She was a blonde by natural pigment, and she wore no paint on the streets at high noon. Outside of that she was no better than most women.

It was Charlie Moon who promised her five thousand Pall Malls if she would pay a call on Horace Tarbox, prodigy extraordinary. Charlie was a senior in Sheffield, and he and Horace were first cousins. They liked and pitied each other.

Horace had been particularly busy that night. The failure of the Frenchman Laurier to appreciate the significance of the new realists was preying on his mind. In fact, his only reaction to a low, clearcut rap at his study was to make him speculate as to whether any rap would have actual existence without an ear there to hear it. He fancied he was verging more and more toward pragmatism. But at that moment, though he did not know it, he was verging with astounding rapidity toward something quite different.

The rap sounded – three seconds leaked by – the rap sounded.

'Come in,' muttered Horace automatically.

He heard the door open and then close, but, bent over his book in the big armchair before the fire, he did not look up.

'Leave it on the bed in the other room,' he said absently.

'Leave what on the bed in the other room?'

Marcia Meadow had to talk her songs, but her speaking voice was like byplay on a harp.

'The laundry.'

'I can't.'

Horace stirred impatiently in his chair.

'Why can't you?'

'Why, because I haven't got it.'

'Hm!' he replied testily. 'Suppose you go back and get it.'

Across the fire from Horace was another easychair. He was accustomed to change to it in the course of an evening by way of exercise and variety. One chair he called Berkeley, the other he called Hume. He suddenly heard a sound as of a rustling, diaphanous form sinking into Hume. He glanced up.

'Well,' said Marcia with the sweet smile she used in Act Two ('Oh, so the Duke liked my dancing!') 'Well, Omar Khayyam, here I am beside you singing in the wilderness.'

Horace stared at her dazedly. The momentary suspicion came to him that she existed there only as a phantom of his imagination. Women didn't come into men's rooms and sink into men's Humes. Women brought laundry and took your seat in the street-car and married you later on when you were old enough to know fetters.

This woman had clearly materialized out of Hume. The very froth of her brown gauzy dress was an emanation from Hume's leather arm there! If he looked long enough he would see Hume right through her and then he would be alone again in the room. He passed his fist across his eyes. He really must take up those trapeze exercises again.

'For Pete's sake, don't look so critical!' objected the emanation pleasantly. 'I feel as if you were going to wish me away with that patent dome of yours. And then there wouldn't be anything left of me except my shadow in your eyes.'

Horace coughed. Coughing was one of his two gestures. When he talked you forgot he had a body at all. It was like hearing a phonograph record by a singer who had been dead a long time.

'What do you want?' he asked.

'I want them letters,' whined Marcia melodramatically – 'them letters of mine you bought from my grandsire in 1881.'

Horace considered.

'I haven't got your letters,' he said evenly. 'I am only seventeen years old. My father was not born until March 3, 1879. You evidently have me confused with some one else.'

'You're only seventeen?' repeated Marcia suspiciously.

'Only seventeen.'

'I knew a girl,' said Marcia reminiscently, 'who went on the ten-twenty-thirty when she was sixteen. She was so stuck on herself that she could never say "sixteen" without putting the "only" before it. We got to calling her "Only Jessie." And she's just where she was when she started – only worse. "Only" is a bad habit, Omar – it sounds like an alibi.'

'My name is not Omar.'

'I know,' agreed Marcia, nodding – 'your name's Horace. I just call you Omar because you remind me of a smoked cigarette.'

'And I haven't your letters. I doubt if I've ever met your grandfather. In fact, I think it very improbable that you yourself were alive in 1881.'

Marcia stared at him in wonder.

'Me – 1881? Why sure! I was second-line stuff when the Florodora Sextette was still in the convent. I was the original nurse to Mrs Sol Smith's Juliette. Why, Omar, I was a canteen singer during the War of 1812.'

Horace's mind made a sudden successful leap, and he grinned.

'Did Charlie Moon put you up to this?'

Marcia regarded him inscrutably.

'Who's Charlie Moon?'

'Small – wide nostrils – big ears.'

She grew several inches and sniffed.

'I'm not in the habit of noticing my friends' nostrils.'

'Then it was Charlie?'

Marcia bit her lip – and then yawned.

'Oh, let's change the subject, Omar. I'll pull a snore in this chair in a minute.'

'Yes,' replied Horace gravely, 'Hume has often been considered soporific.'

'Who's your friend – and will he die?'

Then of a sudden Horace Tarbox rose slenderly and began to pace the room with his hands in his pockets. This was his other gesture.

'I don't care for this,' he said as if he were talking to himself – 'at all. Not that I mind your being here – I don't. You're quite a pretty little thing, but I don't like Charlie Moon's sending you up here. Am I a laboratory experiment on which the janitors as well as the chemists can make experiments? Is my intellectual development humorous in any way? Do I look like the pictures of the little Boston boy in the comic magazines? Has that callow ass, Moon, with his eternal tales about his week in Paris, any right to—'

'No,' interrupted Marcia emphatically. 'And you're a sweet boy. Come here and kiss me.'

Horace stopped quickly in front of her.

'Why do you want me to kiss you?' he asked intently. 'Do you just go round kissing people?'

'Why, yes,' admitted Marcia, unruffled. '"At's all life is. Just going round kissing people.'

'Well,' replied Horace emphatically, 'I must say your ideas are horribly garbled! In the first place life isn't just that, and in the second place I won't kiss you. It might get to be a habit and I can't get rid of habits. This year I've got in the habit of lolling in bed until seven-thirty.'

Marcia nodded understandingly.

'Do you ever have any fun?' she asked.

'What do you mean by fun?'

'See here,' said Marcia sternly, 'I like you, Omar, but I wish you'd talk as if you had a line on what you were saying. You sound as if you were gargling a lot of words in your mouth and lost a bet every time you spilled a few. I asked you if you ever had any fun.'

Horace shook his head.

'Later, perhaps,' he answered. 'You see I'm a plan. I'm an experiment. I don't say that I don't get tired of it sometimes – I do. Yet – oh, I can't explain! But what you and Charlie Moon call fun wouldn't be fun to me.'

'Please explain.'

Horace stared at her, started to speak and then, changing his mind, resumed his walk. After an unsuccessful attempt to determine whether or not he was looking at her Marcia smiled at him.

'Please explain.'

Horace turned.

'If I do, will you promise to tell Charlie Moon that I wasn't in?'

'Uh-uh.'

'Very well, then. Here's my history: I was a "why" child. I wanted to see the wheels go round. My father was a young economics professor at Princeton. He brought me up on the system of answering every question I asked him to the best of his ability. My response to that gave him the idea of making an experiment in precocity. To aid in the massacre I had ear trouble – seven operations between the ages of nine and twelve. Of course this kept me apart from other boys and made me ripe for forcing. Anyway, while my generation was laboring through Uncle Remus I was honestly enjoying Catullus in the original.

'I passed off my college examinations when I was thirteen because I couldn't help it. My chief associates were professors, and I took a tremendous pride in knowing that I had a fine intelligence, for though I was unusually gifted I was not abnormal in other ways. When I was sixteen I got tired of being a freak; I decided that some one had made a bad mistake. Still as I'd gone that far I concluded to finish it up by taking my degree of Master of Arts. My chief interest in life is the study of modern philosophy. I am a realist of the School of Anton Laurier – with Bergsonian trimmings – and I'll be eighteen years old in two months. That's all.'

'Whew!' exclaimed Marcia. 'That's enough! You do a neat job with the parts of speech.'

'Satisfied?'

'No, you haven't kissed me.'

'It's not in my programme,' demurred Horace. 'Understand that I don't pretend to be above physical things. They have their place, but—'

'Oh, don't be so darned reasonable!'

'I can't help it.'

'I hate these slot-machine people.'

'I assure you I—' began Horace.

'Oh, shut up!'

'My own rationality—'

'I didn't say anything about your nationality. You're an Amurican, ar'n't you?'

'Yes.'

'Well, that's O.K. with me. I got a notion I want to see you do something that isn't in your highbrow programme. I want to see if a what-ch-call-em with Brazilian trimmings – that thing you said you were – can be a little human.'

Horace shook his head again

'I won't kiss you.'

'My life is blighted,' muttered Marcia tragically

'I'm a beaten woman. I'll go through life without ever having a kiss with Brazilian trimmings.' She sighed. 'Anyways, Omar, will you come and see my show?'

'What show?'

'I'm a wicked actress from "Home James"!'

'Light opera?'

'Yes – at a stretch. One of the characters is a Brazilian rice-planter. That might interest you.'

'I saw "The Bohemian Girl" once,' reflected Horace aloud. 'I enjoyed it – to some extent.'

'Then you'll come?'

'Well, I'm – I'm—'

'Oh, I know – you've got to run down to Brazil for the weekend.'

'Not at all. I'd be delighted to come.'

Marcia clapped her hands.

'Goodyforyou! I'll mail you a ticket – Thursday night?'

'Why, I—'

'Good! Thursday night it is.'

She stood up and walking close to him laid both hands on his shoulders.

'I like you, Omar. I'm sorry I tried to kid you. I thought you'd be sort of frozen, but you're a nice boy.'

He eyed her sardonically.

'I'm several thousand generations older than you are.'

'You carry your age well.'

They shook hands gravely.

'My name's Marcia Meadow,' she said emphatically. ''Member it – Marcia Meadow. And I won't tell Charlie Moon you were in.'

An instant later as she was skimming down the last flight of stairs three at a time she heard a voice call over the upper banister: 'Oh, say—'

She stopped and looked up – made out a vague form leaning over.

'Oh, say!' called the prodigy again. 'Can you hear me?'

'Here's your connection, Omar.'

'I hope I haven't given you the impression that I consider kissing intrinsically irrational.'

'Impression? Why, you didn't even give me the kiss! Never fret – so long.'

Two doors near her opened curiously at the sound of a feminine voice. A tentative cough sounded from above. Gathering her skirts, Marcia dived wildly down the last flight, and was swallowed up in the murky Connecticut air outside.

Up-stairs Horace paced the floor of his study. From time to time he glanced toward Berkeley waiting there in suave dark-red respectability, an open book lying suggestively on his cushions. And then he found that his circuit of the floor was bringing him each time nearer to Hume. There was something about Hume that was strangely and inexpressibly different. The diaphanous form still seemed hovering near, and had Horace sat there he would have felt as if he were sitting on a lady's lap. And though Horace couldn't have named the quality of difference, there was such a quality – quite intangible to the speculative mind, but real, nevertheless. Hume was radiating something that in all the two hundred years of his influence he had never radiated before.

Hume was radiating attar of roses.

II

On Thursday night Horace Tarbox sat in an aisle seat in the fifth row and witnessed 'Home James.' Oddly enough he found that he was enjoying himself. The cynical students near him were annoyed at his audible appreciation of time-honored jokes in the Hammerstein tradition. But Horace was waiting with anxiety for Marcia Meadow singing her song about a Jazz-bound Blundering Blimp. When she did appear, radiant under a floppity flower-faced hat, a warm glow settled over him, and when the song was over he did not join in the storm of applause. He felt somewhat numb.

In the intermission after the second act an usher materialized beside him, demanded to know if he were Mr Tarbox, and then handed him a note written in a round adolescent hand. Horace read it in some confusion, while the usher lingered with withering patience in the aisle.

'DEAR OMAR:

    After the show I always grow an awful hunger. If you want to satisfy it for me in the Taft Grill just communicate your answer to the big-timber guide that brought this and oblige.

    Your friend,

    MARCIA MEADOW.'

'Tell her' – he coughed – 'tell her that it will be quite all right. I'll meet her in front of the theatre.'

The big-timber guide smiled arrogantly.

'I giss she meant for you to come roun' t' the stage door.'

'Where – where is it?'

'Ou'side. Tunayulef. Down ee alley.'

'What?'

'Ou'side. Turn to y' left! Down ee alley!'

The arrogant person withdrew. A freshman behind Horace snickered.

Then half an hour later, sitting in the Taft Grill opposite the hair that was yellow by natural pigment, the prodigy was saying an odd thing.

'Do you have to do that dance in the last act?' he was asking earnestly – 'I mean, would they dismiss you if you refused to do it?'

Marcia grinned.

'It's fun to do it. I like to do it.'

And then Horace came out with a *faux pas*.

'I should think you'd detest it,' he remarked succinctly. 'The people behind me were making remarks about your bosom.'

Marcia blushed fiery red.

'I can't help that,' she said quickly. 'The dance to me is only a sort of acrobatic stunt. Lord, it's hard enough to do! I rub liniment into my shoulders for an hour every night.'

'Do you have – fun while you're on the stage?'

'Uh-huh – sure! I got in the habit of having people look at me, Omar, and I like it.'

'Hm!' Horace sank into a brownish study.

'How's the Brazilian trimmings?'

'Hm!' repeated Horace, and then after a pause: 'Where does the play go from here?'

'New York.'

'For how long?'

'All depends. Winter – maybe.'

'Oh!'

'Coming up to lay eyes on me, Omar, or aren't you int'rested? Not as nice here, is it, as it was up in your room? I wish we was there now.'

'I feel idiotic in this place,' confessed Horace, looking round him nervously.

'Too bad! We got along pretty well.'

At this he looked suddenly so melancholy that she changed her tone, and reaching over patted his hand.

'Ever take an actress out to supper before?'

'No,' said Horace miserably, 'and I never will again. I don't know why I came to-night. Here under all these lights and with all these people laughing and chattering I feel completely out of my sphere. I don't know what to talk to you about.'

'We'll talk about me. We talked about you last time.'

'Very well.'

'Well, my name really is Meadow, but my first name isn't Marcia – it's Veronica. I'm nineteen. Question – how did the girl make her leap to the footlights? Answer – she was born in Passaic, New Jersey, and up to a year ago she got the right to breathe by pushing Nabiscoes in Marcel's tea-room in Trenton. She started going with a guy named Robbins, a singer in the Trent House cabaret, and he got her to try a song and dance with him one evening. In a month we were filling the supper-room every night. Then we went to New York with meet-my-friend letters thick as a pile of napkins.

'In two days we'd landed a job at Divinerries', and I learned to shimmy from a kid at the Palais Royal. We stayed at Divinerries' six months until one night Peter Boyce Wendell, the columnist, ate his milk-toast there. Next morning a poem about Marvellous Marcia came out in his newspaper, and within two days I had three vaude-ville offers and a chance at the Midnight Frolic. I wrote Wendell a thank-you letter, and he printed it in his column – said that the style was like Carlyle's, only more rugged, and that I ought to quit dancing and do North American literature. This got me a coupla more vaudeville offers and a chance as an ingénue in a regular show. I took it – and here I am, Omar.'

When she finished they sat for a moment in silence, she draping the last skeins of a Welsh rabbit on her fork and waiting for him to speak.

'Let's get out of here,' he said suddenly.

Marcia's eyes hardened.

'What's the idea? Am I making you sick?'

'No, but I don't like it here. I don't like to be sitting here with you.'

Without another word Marcia signalled for the waiter.

'What's the check?' she demanded briskly. 'My part – the rabbit and the ginger ale.'

Horace watched blankly as the waiter figured it.

'See here,' he began, 'I intended to pay for yours too. You're my guest.'

With a half-sigh Marcia rose from the table and walked from the room. Horace, his face a document in bewilderment, laid a bill down and followed her out, up the stairs and into the lobby. He overtook her in front of the elevator and they faced each other.

'See here,' he repeated, 'you're my guest. Have I said something to offend you?'

After an instant of wonder Marcia's eyes softened.

'You're a rude fella,' she said slowly. 'Don't you know you're rude?'

'I can't help it,' said Horace with a directness she found quite disarming. 'You know I like you.'

'You said you didn't like being with me.'

'I didn't like it.'

'Why not?'

Fire blazed suddenly from the gray forests of his eyes.

'Because I didn't. I've formed the habit of liking you. I've been thinking of nothing much else for two days.'

'Well, if you—'

'Wait a minute,' he interrupted. 'I've got something to say. It's this: in six weeks I'll be eighteen years old. When I'm eighteen years old I'm coming up to New York to see you. Is there some place in New York where we can go and not have a lot of people in the room?'

'Sure!' smiled Marcia. 'You can come up to my 'partment. Sleep on the couch, if you want to.'

'I can't sleep on couches,' he said shortly. 'But I want to talk to you.'

'Why, sure,' repeated Marcia – 'in my 'partment.'

In his excitement Horace put his hands in his pockets.

'All right – just so I can see you alone. I want to talk to you as we talked up in my room.'

'Honey boy,' cried Marcia, laughing, 'is it that you want to kiss me?'

'Yes,' Horace almost shouted. 'I'll kiss you if you want me to.'

The elevator man was looking at them reproachfully. Marcia edged toward the grated door.

'I'll drop you a post-card,' she said.

Horace's eyes were quite wild.

'Send me a post-card! I'll come up any time after January first. I'll be eighteen then.'

And as she stepped into the elevator he coughed enigmatically, yet with a vague challenge, at the ceiling, and walked quickly away.

III

He was there again. She saw him when she took her first glance at the restless Manhattan audience – down in the front row with his head bent a bit forward and his gray eyes fixed on her. And she knew that to him they were alone together in a world where the high-rouged row of ballet faces and the massed whines of the violins were as imperceivable as powder on a marble Venus. An instinctive defiance rose within her.

'Silly boy!' she said to herself hurriedly, and she didn't take her encore.

'What do they expect for a hundred a week – perpetual motion?' she grumbled to herself in the wings.

'What's the trouble, Marcia?'

'Guy I don't like down in front.'

During the last act as she waited for her specialty she had an odd attack of stage fright. She had never sent Horace the promised post-card. Last night she had pretended not to see him – had hurried from the theatre immediately after her dance to pass a sleepless night in her apartment, thinking – as she had so often in the last month – of his pale, rather intent face, his slim, boyish figure, the merciless, unworldly abstraction that made him charming to her.

And now that he had come she felt vaguely sorry – as though an unwonted responsibility was being forced on her.

'Infant prodigy!' she said aloud.

'What?' demanded the negro comedian standing beside her.

'Nothing – just talking about myself.'

On the stage she felt better. This was her dance – and she always felt that the way she did it wasn't suggestive any more than to some men every pretty girl is suggestive. She made it a stunt.

> 'Uptown, downtown, jelly on a spoon,
> After sundown shiver by the moon.'

He was not watching her now. She saw that clearly. He was looking very deliberately at a castle on the back drop, wearing that expression he had worn in the Taft Grill. A wave of exasperation swept over her – he was criticising her.

> 'That's the vibration that thr-ills me,
> Funny how affection fi-lls me,
> Uptown, downtown—'

Unconquerable revulsion seized her. She was suddenly and horribly conscious of her audience as she had never been since her first appearance. Was that a leer on a pallid face in the front row, a droop of disgust on one young girl's mouth? These shoulders of hers – these shoulders shaking – were they hers? Were they real? Surely shoulders weren't made for this!

> *'Then – you'll see at a glance*
> *I'll need some funeral ushers with St. Vitus dance*
> *At the end of the world I'll—'*

The bassoon and two cellos crashed into a final chord. She paused and poised a moment on her toes with every muscle tense, her young face looking out dully at the audience in what one young girl afterward called 'such a curious, puzzled look,' and then without bowing rushed from the stage. Into the dressing-room she sped, kicked out of one dress and into another, and caught a taxi outside.

Her apartment was very warm – small, it was, with a row of professional pictures and sets of Kipling and O. Henry which she had bought once from a blue-eyed agent and read occasionally. And there were several chairs which matched, but were none of them comfortable, and a pink-shaded lamp with blackbirds painted on it and an atmosphere of rather stifled pink throughout. There were nice things in it – nice things unrelentingly hostile to each other, offsprings of a vicarious, impatient taste acting in stray moments. The worst was typified by a great picture framed in oak bark of Passaic as seen from the Eric Railroad – altogether a frantic, oddly extravagant, oddly penurious attempt to make a cheerful room. Marcia knew it was a failure.

Into this room came the prodigy and took her two hands awkwardly.

'I followed you this time,' he said.

'Oh!'

'I want you to marry me,' he said.

Her arms went out to him. She kissed his mouth with a sort of passionate wholesomeness.

'There!'

'I love you,' he said.

She kissed him again and then with a little sigh flung herself into an armchair and half lay there, shaken with absurd laughter.

'Why, you infant prodigy!' she cried.

'Very well, call me that if you want to. I once told you that I was ten thousand years older than you – I am.'

She laughed again.

'I don't like to be disapproved of.'

'No one's ever going to disapprove of you again.'

'Omar,' she asked, 'why do you want to marry me?'

The prodigy rose and put his hands in his pockets.

'Because I love you, Marcia Meadow.'

And then she stopped calling him Omar.

'Dear boy,' she said, 'you know I sort of love you. There's something about you – I can't tell what – that just puts my heart through the wringer every time I'm round you. But, honey—' She paused.

'But what?'

'But lots of things. But you're only just eighteen, and I'm nearly twenty.'

'Nonsense!' he interrupted. 'Put it this way – that I'm in my nineteenth year and you're nineteen. That makes us pretty close – without counting that other ten thousand years I mentioned.'

Marcia laughed.

'But there are some more "buts." Your people—'

'My people!' exclaimed the prodigy ferociously. 'My people tried to make a monstrosity out of me.' His face grew quite crimson at the enormity of what he was going to say. 'My people can go way back and sit down!'

'My heavens!' cried Marcia in alarm. 'All that? On tacks, I suppose.'

'Tacks – yes,' he agreed wildly – 'on anything. The more I think of how they allowed me to become a little dried-up mummy—'

'What makes you think you're that?' asked Marcia quietly – 'me?'

'Yes. Every person I've met on the streets since I met you has made me jealous because they knew what love was before I did. I used to call it the "sex impulse." Heavens!'

'There's more "buts,"' said Marcia.

'What are they?'

'How could we live?'

'I'll make a living.'

'You're in college.'

'Do you think I care anything about taking a Master of Arts degree?'

'You want to be Master of Me, hey?'

'Yes! What? I mean, no!'

Marcia laughed, and crossing swiftly over sat in his lap. He put his arm round her wildly and implanted the vestige of a kiss somewhere near her neck.

'There's something white about you,' mused Marcia, 'but it doesn't sound very logical.'

'Oh, don't be so darned reasonable!'

'I can't help it,' said Marcia.

'I hate these slot-machine people!'

'But we—'

'Oh, shut up!'

And as Marcia couldn't talk through her ears she had to.

IV

Horace and Marcia were married early in February. The sensation in academic circles both at Yale and Princeton was tremendous. Horace Tarbox, who at fourteen had been played up in the Sunday magazines sections of metropolitan newspapers, was throwing over his career, his chance of being a world authority on American philosophy, by marrying a chorus girl – they made Marcia a chorus girl. But like all modern stories it was a four-and-a-half-day wonder.

They took a flat in Harlem. After two weeks' search, during which his idea of the value of academic knowledge faded unmercifully, Horace took a position as clerk with a South American export company – some one had told him that exporting was the coming thing. Marcia was to stay in her show for a few months – anyway until he got on his feet. He was getting a hundred and twenty-five to start with, and though of course they told him it was only a question of months until he would be earning double that, Marcia refused even to consider giving up the hundred and fifty a week that she was getting at the time.

'We'll call ourselves Head and Shoulders, dear,' she said softly, 'and the shoulders'll have to keep shaking a little longer until the old head gets started.'

'I hate it,' he objected gloomily.

'Well,' she replied emphatically, 'your salary wouldn't keep us in a tenement. Don't think I want to be public – I don't. I want to be yours. But I'd be a half-wit to sit in one room and count the sunflowers on the wall-paper while I waited for you. When you pull down three hundred a month I'll quit.'

And much as it hurt his pride, Horace had to admit that hers was the wiser course.

March mellowed into April. May read a gorgeous riot act to the parks and waters of Manhattan, and they were very happy. Horace, who had no habits whatsoever – he had never had time to form any – proved the most adaptable of husbands, and as Marcia entirely lacked opinions on the subjects that engrossed him there were very few joltings and bumpings. Their minds moved in different spheres. Marcia acted as practical factotum, and Horace lived either in his old world of abstract ideas or in a sort of triumphantly earthy worship and adoration of his wife. She was a continual source of astonishment to him – the freshness and originality of her mind, her dynamic, clear-headed energy, and her unfailing good humor.

And Marcia's co-workers in the nine-o'clock show, whither she had transferred her talents, were impressed with her tremendous pride in her husband's mental powers. Horace they knew only as a very slim, tight-lipped, and immature-looking young man, who waited every night to take her home.

'Horace,' said Marcia one evening when she met him as usual at eleven, 'you looked like a ghost standing there against the street lights. You losing weight?'

He shook his head vaguely.

'I don't know. They raised me to a hundred and thirty-five dollars to-day, and—'

'I don't care,' said Marcia severely. 'You're killing yourself working at night. You read those big books on economy—'

'Economics,' corrected Horace.

'Well, you read 'em every night long after I'm asleep. And you're getting all stooped over like you were before we were married.'

'But, Marcia, I've got to—'

'No, you haven't, dear. I guess I'm running this shop for the present, and I won't let my fella ruin his health and eyes. You got to get some exercise.'

'I do. Every morning I—'

'Oh, I know! But those dumb-bells of yours wouldn't give a consumptive two degrees of fever. I mean real exercise. You've got to join a gymnasium. 'Member you told me you were such a trick gymnast once that they tried to get you out for the team in college and they couldn't because you had a standing date with Herb Spencer?'

'I used to enjoy it,' mused Horace, 'but it would take up too much time now.'

'All right,' said Marcia. 'I'll make a bargain with you. You join a gym and I'll read one of those books from the brown row of 'em.'

'"Pepys' Diary"? Why, that ought to be enjoyable. He's very light.'

'Not for me – he isn't. It'll be like digesting plate glass. But you been telling me how much it'd broaden my lookout. Well, you go to a gym three nights a week and I'll take one big dose of Sammy.'

Horace hesitated.

'Well—'

'Come on, now! You do some giant swings for me and I'll chase some culture for you.'

So Horace finally consented, and all through a baking summer he spent three and sometimes four evenings a week experimenting on the trapeze in Skipper's Gymnasium. And in August he admitted to Marcia that it made him capable of more mental work during the day.

'*Mens sana in corpore sano,*' he said.

'Don't believe in it,' replied Marcia. 'I tried one of those patent medicines once and they're all bunk. You stick to gymnastics.'

One night in early September while he was going through one of his contortions on the rings in the nearly deserted room he was addressed by a meditative fat man whom he had noticed watching him for several nights.

'Say, lad, do that stunt you were doin' last night.'

Horace grinned at him from his perch.

'I invented it,' he said. 'I got the idea from the fourth proposition of Euclid.'

'What circus he with?'

'He's dead.'

'Well, he must of broke his neck doin' that stunt. I set here last night thinkin' sure you was goin' to break yours.'

'Like this!' said Horace, and swinging onto the trapeze he did his stunt.

'Don't it kill your neck an' shoulder muscles?'

'It did at first, but inside of a week I wrote the *quod erat demonstrandum* on it.'

'Hm!'

Horace swung idly on the trapeze.

'Ever think of takin' it up professionally?' asked the fat man.

'Not I.'

'Good money in it if you're willin' to do stunts like 'at an' can get away with it.'

'Here's another,' chirped Horace eagerly, and the fat man's mouth dropped suddenly agape as he watched this pink-jerseyed Prometheus again defy the gods and Isaac Newton.

The night following this encounter Horace got home from work to find a rather pale Marcia stretched out on the sofa waiting for him.

'I fainted twice to-day,' she began without preliminaries.

'What?'

'Yep. You see baby's due in four months now. Doctor says I ought to have quit dancing two weeks ago.'

Horace sat down and thought it over.

'I'm glad, of course,' he said pensively – 'I mean glad that we're going to have a baby. But this means a lot of expense.'

'I've got two hundred and fifty in the bank,' said Marcia hopefully, 'and two weeks' pay coming.'

Horace computed quickly.

'Including my salary, that'll give us nearly fourteen hundred for the next six months.'

Marcia looked blue.

'That all? Course I can get a job singing somewhere this month. And I can go to work again in March.'

'Of course nothing!' said Horace gruffly. 'You'll stay right here. Let's see now – there'll be doctor's bills and a nurse, besides the maid. We've got to have some more money.'

'Well,' said Marcia wearily, 'I don't know where it's coming from. It's up to the old head now. Shoulders is out of business.'

Horace rose and pulled on his coat.

'Where are you going?'

'I've got an idea,' he answered. 'I'll be right back.'

Ten minutes later as he headed down the street toward Skipper's Gymnasium he felt a placid wonder, quite unmixed with humor, at what he was going to do. How he would have gaped at himself a year before! How every one would have gaped! But when you opened your door at the rap of life you let in many things.

The gymnasium was brightly lit, and when his eyes became accustomed to the glare he found the meditative fat man seated on a pile of canvas mats smoking a big cigar.

'Say,' began Horace directly, 'were you in earnest last night when you said I could make money on my trapeze stunts?'

'Why, yes,' said the fat man in surprise.

'Well, I've been thinking it over, and I believe I'd like to try it. I could work at night and on Saturday afternoons – and regularly if the pay is high enough.'

The fat man looked at his watch.

'Well,' he said, 'Charlie Paulson's the man to see. He'll book you inside of four days, once he sees you work out. He won't be in now, but I'll get hold of him for to-morrow night.'

The fat man was as good as his word. Charlie Paulson arrived next night and put in a wondrous hour watching the prodigy swoop through the air in amazing parabolas, and on the night following he brought two large men with him who looked as though they had been born smoking black cigars and talking about money in low, passionate voices. Then on the succeeding Saturday Horace Tarbox's torso made its first professional appearance in a gymnastic exhibition at the Coleman Street Gardens. But though the audience numbered nearly five thousand people, Horace felt no nervousness. From his childhood he had read papers to audiences – learned that trick of detaching himself.

'Marcia,' he said cheerfully later that same night, 'I think we're out of the woods. Paulson thinks he can get me an opening at the Hippodrome, and that means an all-winter engagement. The Hippodrome, you know, is a big—'

'Yes, I believe I've heard of it,' interrupted Marcia, 'but I want to know about this stunt you're doing. It isn't any spectacular suicide, is it?'

'It's nothing,' said Horace quietly. 'But if you can think of any nicer way of a man killing himself than taking a risk for you, why that's the way I want to die.'

Marcia reached up and wound both arms tightly round his neck.

'Kiss me,' she whispered, 'and call me "dear heart." I love to hear you say "dear heart." And bring me a book to read to-morrow. No more Sam Pepys, but something trick and trashy. I've been wild for something to do all day. I felt like writing letters, but I didn't have anybody to write to.'

'Write to me,' said Horace. 'I'll read them.'

'I wish I could,' breathed Marcia. 'If I knew words enough I could write you the longest love-letter in the world – and never get tired.'

But after two more months Marcia grew very tired indeed, and for a row of nights it was a very anxious, weary-looking young athlete who walked out before the Hippodrome crowd. Then there were two days when his place was taken by a young man who wore pale blue instead of white, and got very little applause. But after the two days Horace appeared again, and those who sat close to the stage remarked an expression of beatific happiness on that young acrobat's face, even when he was twisting breathlessly in the air in the middle of his amazing and original shoulder swing. After that performance he laughed at the elevator man and dashed up the stairs to the flat five steps at a time – and then tiptoed very carefully into a quiet room.

'Marcia,' he whispered.

'Hello!' She smiled up at him wanly. 'Horace, there's something I want you to do. Look in my top bureau drawer and you'll find a big stack of paper. It's a book – sort of – Horace. I wrote it down in these last three months while I've been laid up. I wish you'd take it to that Peter Boyce Wendell who put my letter in his paper. He could tell you whether it'd be a good book. I wrote it just the way I talk, just the way I wrote that letter to him. It's just a story about a lot of things that happened to me. Will you take it to him, Horace?'

'Yes, darling.'

He leaned over the bed until his head was beside her on the pillow, and began stroking back her yellow hair.

'Dearest Marcia,' he said softly.

'No,' she murmured, 'call me what I told you to call me.'

'Dear heart,' he whispered passionately – 'dearest, dearest heart.'

'What'll we call her?'

They rested a minute in happy, drowsy content, while Horace considered.

'We'll call her Marcia Hume Tarbox,' he said at length.

'Why the Hume?'

'Because he's the fellow who first introduced us.'

'That so?' she murmured, sleepily surprised. 'I thought his name was Moon.'

Her eyes closed, and after a moment the slow, lengthening surge of the bedclothes over her breast showed that she was asleep.

Horace tiptoed over to the bureau and opening the top drawer found a heap of closely scrawled, lead-smeared pages. He looked at the first sheet:

SANDRA PEPYS, SYNCOPATED
By Marcia Tarbox

He smiled. So Samuel Pepys had made an impression on her after all. He turned a page and began to read. His smile deepened – he read on. Half an hour passed and he became aware that Marcia had waked and was watching him from the bed.

'Honey,' came in a whisper.

'What, Marcia?'

'Do you like it?'

Horace coughed.

'I seem to be reading on. It's bright.'

'Take it to Peter Boyce Wendell. Tell him you got the highest marks in Princeton once and that you ought to know when a book's good. Tell him this one's a world beater.'

'All right, Marcia,' said Horace gently.

Her eyes closed again and Horace crossing over kissed her forehead – stood there for a moment with a look of tender pity. Then he left the room.

All that night the sprawly writing on the pages, the constant mistakes in spelling and grammar, and the weird punctuation danced before his eyes. He woke several times in the night, each time full of a welling chaotic sympathy for this desire of Marcia's soul to express itself in words. To him there was something infinitely pathetic about it, and for the first time in months he began to turn over in his mind his own half-forgotten dreams.

He had meant to write a series of books, to popularize the new realism as Schopenhauer had popularized pessimism and William James pragmatism.

But life hadn't come that way. Life took hold of people and forced them into flying rings. He laughed to think of that rap at his door, the diaphanous shadow in Hume, Marcia's threatened kiss.

'And it's still me,' he said aloud in wonder as he lay awake in the darkness. 'I'm the man who sat in Berkeley with temerity to wonder if that rap would have had actual existence had my ear not been there to hear it. I'm still that man. I could be electrocuted for the crimes he committed.

'Poor gauzy souls trying to express ourselves in something tangible. Marcia with her written book; I with my unwritten ones.

Trying to choose our mediums and then taking what we get – and being glad.'

V

'Sandra Pepys, Syncopated,' with an introduction by Peter Boyce Wendell, the columnist, appeared serially in *Jordan's Magazine*, and came out in book form in March. From its first published instalment it attracted attention far and wide. A trite enough subject – a girl from a small New Jersey town coming to New York to go on the stage – treated simply, with a peculiar vividness of phrasing and a haunting undertone of sadness in the very inadequacy of its vocabulary, it made an irresistible appeal.

Peter Boyce Wendell, who happened at that time to be advocating the enrichment of the American language by the immediate adoption of expressive vernacular words, stood as its sponsor and thundered his indorsement over the placid bromides of the conventional reviewers.

Marcia received three hundred dollars an instalment for the serial publication, which came at an opportune time, for though Horace's monthly salary at the Hippodrome was now more than Marcia's had ever been, young Marcia was emitting shrill cries which they interpreted as a demand for country air. So early April found them installed in a bungalow in Westchester Country, with a place for a lawn, a place for a garage, and a place for everything, including a sound-proof impregnable study, in which Marcia faithfully promised Mr Jordan she would shut herself up when her daughter's demands began to be abated, and compose immortally illiterate literature.

'It's not half bad,' thought Horace one night as he was on his way from the station to his house. He was considering several prospects that had opened up, a four months' vaudeville offer in five figures, a chance to go back to Princeton in charge of all gymnasium work. Odd! He had once intended to go back there in charge of all philosophic work, and now he had not even been stirred by the arrival in New York of Anton Laurier, his old idol.

The gravel crunched raucously under his heel. He saw the lights of his sitting-room gleaming and noticed a big car standing in the drive. Probably Mr Jordan again, come to persuade Marcia to settle down to work.

She had heard the sound of his approach and her form was silhouetted against the lighted door as she came out to meet him.

'There's some Frenchman here,' she whispered nervously. 'I can't pronounce his name, but he sounds awful deep. You'll have to jaw with him.'

'What Frenchman?'

'You can't prove it by me. He drove up an hour ago with Mr Jordan, and said he wanted to meet Sandra Pepys, and all that sort of thing.'

Two men rose from chairs as they went inside.

'Hello, Tarbox,' said Jordan. 'I've just been bringing together two celebrities. I've brought M'sieur Laurier out with me. M'sieur Laurier, let me present Mr Tarbox, Mrs Tarbox's husband.'

'Not Anton Laurier!' exclaimed Horace.

'But, yes. I must come. I have to come. I have read the book of Madame, and I have been charmed' – he fumbled in his pocket – 'ah, I have read of you too. In this newspaper which I read to-day it has your name.'

He finally produced a clipping from a magazine.

'Read it!' he said eagerly. 'It has about you too.'

Horace's eye skipped down the page.

'A distinct contribution to American dialect literature,' it said. 'No attempt at literary tone; the book derives its very quality from this fact, as did "Huckleberry Finn."'

Horace's eyes caught a passage lower down; he became suddenly aghast – read on hurriedly:

'Marcia Tarbox's connection with the stage is not only as a spectator but as the wife of a performer. She was married last year to Horace Tarbox, who every evening delights the children at the Hippodrome with his wondrous flying-ring performance. It is said that the young couple have dubbed themselves Head and Shoulders, referring doubtless to the fact that Mrs Tarbox supplies the literary and mental qualities, while the supple and agile shoulders of her husband contribute their share to the family fortunes.

'Mrs Tarbox seems to merit that much-abused title – "prodigy." Only twenty—'

Horace stopped reading, and with a very odd expression in his eyes gazed intently at Anton Laurier.

'I want to advise you—' he began hoarsely.

'What?'

'About raps. Don't answer them! Let them alone – have a padded door.'

The Cut-Glass Bowl

I

There was a rough stone age and a smooth stone age and a bronze age, and many years afterward a cut-glass age. In the cut-glass age, when young ladies had persuaded young men with long, curly mustaches to marry them, they sat down several months afterward and wrote thank-you notes for all sorts of cut-glass presents – punch-bowls, finger-bowls, dinner-glasses, wine-glasses, ice-cream dishes, bonbon dishes, decanters, and vases – for, though cut glass was nothing new in the nineties, it was then especially busy reflecting the dazzling light of fashion from the Back Bay to the fastnesses of the Middle West.

After the wedding the punch-bowls were arranged on the side-board with the big bowl in the center; the glasses were set up in the china-closet; the candlesticks were put at both ends of things – and then the struggle for existence began. The bonbon dish lost its little handle and became a pin-tray upstairs; a promenading cat knocked the little bowl off the sideboard, and the hired girl chipped the middle-sized one with the sugar-dish; then the wine-glasses succumbed to leg fractures, and even the dinner-glasses disappeared one by one like the ten little niggers, the last one ending up, scarred and maimed, as a tooth-brush holder among other shabby genteels on the bathroom shelf. But by the time all this had happened the cut-glass age was over, anyway.

It was well past its first glory on the day the curious Mrs Roger Fairboalt came to see the beautiful Mrs Harold Piper.

'My *dear*,' said the curious Mrs Roger Fairboalt, 'I *love* your house. I think it's *quite* artistic.'

'I'm *so* glad,' said the beautiful Mrs Harold Piper, lights appearing in her young, dark eyes; 'and you *must* come often. I'm almost *always* alone in the afternoon.'

Mrs Fairboalt would have liked to remark that she didn't believe this at all and couldn't see how she'd be expected to – it was all over town that Mr Freddy Gedney had been dropping in on Mrs Piper five afternoons a week for the past six months. Mrs Fairboalt was at that ripe age where she distrusted all beautiful women—

'I love the dining-room *most*,' she said, 'all that *marvellous* china, and that *huge* cut-glass bowl.'

Mrs Piper laughed, so prettily that Mrs Fairboalt's lingering reservations about the Freddy Gedney story quite vanished.

'Oh, that big bowl!' Mrs Piper's mouth forming the words was a vivid rose petal. 'There's a story about that bowl—'

'Oh—'

'You remember young Carleton Canby? Well, he was very attentive at one time, and the night I told him I was going to marry Harold, seven years ago, in ninety-two, he drew himself way up and said: "Evylyn, I'm going to give a present that's as hard as you are and as beautiful and as empty and as easy to see through." He frightened me a little – his eyes were so black. I thought he was going to deed me a haunted house or something that would explode when you opened it. That bowl came, and of course it's beautiful. Its diameter or circumference or something is two and a half feet – or perhaps it's three and a half. Anyway, the sideboard is really too small for it; it sticks way out.'

'My *dear*, wasn't that *odd!* And he left town about then, didn't he?' Mrs Fairboalt was scribbling italicized notes on her memory – 'hard, beautiful, empty, and easy to see through.'

'Yes, he went West – or South – or somewhere,' answered Mrs Piper, radiating that divine vagueness that helps to lift beauty out of time.

Mrs Fairboalt drew on her gloves, approving the effect of large-ness given by the open sweep from the spacious music-room through the library, disclosing a part of the dining-room beyond. It was really the nicest smaller house in town, and Mrs Piper had talked of moving to a larger one on Devereaux Avenue. Harold Piper must be *coining* money.

As she turned into the sidewalk under the gathering autumn dusk she assumed that disapproving, faintly unpleasant expression that almost all successful women of forty wear on the street.

If *I* were Harold Piper, she thought, I'd spend a *little* less time on business and a *little* more time at home. Some *friend* should speak to him.

But if Mrs Fairboalt had considered it a successful afternoon she would have named it a triumph had she waited two minutes longer. For while she was still a black receding figure a hundred yards down the street, a very good-looking distraught young man turned up the walk to the Piper house. Mrs Piper answered the door-bell herself, and with a rather dismayed expression led him quickly into the library.

'I had to see you,' he began wildly; 'your note played the devil with me. Did Harold frighten you into this?'

She shook her head.

'I'm through, Fred,' she said slowly, and her lips had never looked to him so much like tearings from a rose. 'He came home last night sick with it. Jessie Piper's sense of duty was too much for her, so she went down to his office and told him. He was hurt and – oh, I can't help seeing it his way, Fred. He says we've been club gossip all summer and he didn't know it, and now he understands snatches of conversation he's caught and veiled hints people have dropped about me. He's mighty angry, Fred, and he loves me and I love him – rather.'

Gedney nodded slowly and half closed his eyes.

'Yes,' he said, 'yes, my trouble's like yours. I can see other people's points of view too plainly.' His gray eyes met her dark ones frankly. 'The blessed thing's over. My God, Evylyn, I've been sitting down at the office all day looking at the outside of your letter, and looking at it and looking at it—'

'You've got to go, Fred,' she said steadily, and the slight emphasis of hurry in her voice was a new thrust for him. 'I gave him my word of honor I wouldn't see you. I know just how far I can go with Harold, and being here with you this evening is one of the things I can't do.'

They were still standing, and as she spoke she made a little movement toward the door. Gedney looked at her miserably, trying, here at the end, to treasure up a last picture of her – and then suddenly both of them were stiffened into marble at the sound of steps on the walk outside. Instantly her arm reached out grasping the lapel of his coat – half urged, half swung him through the big door into the dark dining-room.

'I'll make him go up-stairs,' she whispered close to his ear; 'don't move till you hear him on the stairs. Then go out the front way.'

Then he was alone listening as she greeted her husband in the hall.

Harold Piper was thirty-six, nine years older than his wife. He was handsome – with marginal notes: these being eyes that were too close together, and a certain woodenness when his face was in repose. His attitude toward this Gedney matter was typical of all his attitudes. He had told Evylyn that he considered the subject closed and would never reproach her nor allude to it in any form; and he told himself that this was rather a big way of looking at it – that she was not a little impressed. Yet, like all men who are preoccupied with their own broadness, he was exceptionally narrow.

He greeted Evylyn with emphasized cordiality this evening.

'You'll have to hurry and dress, Harold,' she said eagerly; 'we're going to the Bronsons'.'

He nodded.

'It doesn't take me long to dress, dear,' and, his words trailing off, he walked on into the library. Evylyn's heart clattered loudly.

'Harold—' she began, with a little catch in her voice, and followed him in. He was lighting a cigarette. 'You'll have to hurry, Harold,' she finished, standing in the doorway.

'Why?' he asked, a trifle impatiently; 'you're not dressed yourself yet, Evie.'

He stretched out in a Morris chair and unfolded a newspaper. With a sinking sensation Evylyn saw that this meant at least ten minutes – and Gedney was standing breathless in the next room. Supposing Harold decided that before he went upstairs he wanted a drink from the decanter on the sideboard. Then it occurred to her to forestall this contingency by bringing him the decanter and a glass. She dreaded calling his attention to the dining-room in any way, but she couldn't risk the other chance.

But at the same moment Harold rose and, throwing his paper down, came toward her.

'Evie, dear,' he said, bending and putting his arms about her, 'I hope you're not thinking about last night—' She moved close to him, trembling. 'I know,' he continued, 'it was just an imprudent friendship on your part. We all make mistakes.'

Evylyn hardly heard him. She was wondering if by sheer clinging to him she could draw him out and up the stairs. She thought of playing sick, asking to be carried up – unfortunately, she knew he would lay her on the couch and bring her whiskey.

Suddenly her nervous tension moved up a last impossible notch. She had heard a very faint but quite unmistakable creak from the floor of the dining-room. Fred was trying to get out the back way.

Then her heart took a flying leap as a hollow ringing note like a gong echoed and re-echoed through the house. Gedney's arm had struck the big cut-glass bowl.

'What's that!' cried Harold. 'Who's there?'

She clung to him but he broke away, and the room seemed to crash about her ears. She heard the pantry-door swing open, a scuffle, the rattle of a tin pan, and in wild despair she rushed into the kitchen and pulled up the gas. Her husband's arm slowly unwound from Gedney's neck, and he stood there very still, first in amazement, then with pain dawning in his face.

'My golly!' he said in bewilderment, and then repeated: 'My golly!'

He turned as if to jump again at Gedney, stopped, his muscles visibly relaxed, and he gave a bitter little laugh.

'You people – you people—' Evylyn's arms were around him and her eyes were pleading with him frantically, but he pushed her away and sank dazed into a kitchen chair, his face like porcelain. 'You've been doing things to me, Evylyn. Why, you little devil! You little *devil!*'

She had never felt so sorry for him; she had never loved him so much.

'It wasn't her fault,' said Gedney rather humbly. 'I just came.' But Piper shook his head, and his expression when he started up was as if some physical accident had jarred his mind into a temporary inability to function. His eyes, grown suddenly pitiful, struck a deep, unsounded chord in Evylyn – and simultaneously a furious anger surged in her. She felt her eyelids burning; she stamped her foot violently; her hands scurried nervously over the table as if searching for a weapon, and then she flung herself wildly at Gedney.

'Get out!' she screamed, dark eyes blazing, little fists beating helplessly on his outstretched arm. 'You did this! Get out of here – get out – get *out! Get out!*'

II

Concerning Mrs Harold Piper at thirty-five, opinion was divided – women said she was still handsome; men said she was pretty no longer. And this was probably because the qualities in her beauty that women had feared and men had followed had vanished. Her eyes were still as large and as dark and as sad, but the mystery had departed; their sadness was no longer eternal, only human, and she had developed a habit, when she was startled or annoyed, of twitching her brows together and blinking several times. Her mouth also had lost: the red had receded and the faint down-turning of its corners when she smiled, that had added to the sadness of the eyes and been vaguely mocking and beautiful, was quite gone. When she smiled now the corners of her lips turned up. Back in the days when she revelled in her own beauty Evylyn had enjoyed that smile of hers – she had accentuated it. When she stopped accentuating it, it faded out and the last of her mystery with it.

Evylyn had ceased accentuating her smile within a month after the Freddy Gedney affair. Externally things had gone on very much as they had before. But in those few minutes during which she had discovered how much she loved her husband Evylyn had realized how indelibly she had hurt him. For a month she struggled against aching silences, wild reproaches and accusations – she pled with him, made quiet, pitiful little love to him, and he laughed at her bitterly – and then she, too, slipped gradually into silence and a shadowy, unpenetrable barrier dropped between them. The surge of love that had risen in her she lavished on Donald, her little boy, realizing him almost wonderingly as a part of her life.

The next year a piling up of mutual interests and responsibilities and some stray flicker from the past brought husband and wife together again – but after a rather pathetic flood of passion Evylyn realized that her great opportunity was gone. There simply wasn't anything left. She might have been youth and love for both – but that time of silence had slowly dried up the springs of affection and her own desire to drink again of them was dead.

She began for the first time to seek women friends, to prefer books she had read before, to sew a little where she could watch her two children to whom she was devoted. She worried about little things – if she saw crumbs on the dinner-table her mind drifted off the conversation: she was receding gradually into middle age.

Her thirty-fifth birthday had been an exceptionally busy one, for they were entertaining on short notice that night, and as she stood in her bedroom window in the late afternoon she discovered that she was quite tired. Ten years before she would have lain down and slept, but now she had a feeling that things needed watching: maids were cleaning down-stairs, bric-à-brac was all over the floor, and there were sure to be grocery-men that had to be talked to imperatively – and then there was a letter to write Donald, who was fourteen and in his first year away at school.

She had nearly decided to lie down, nevertheless, when she heard a sudden familiar signal from little Julie down-stairs. She compressed her lips, her brows twitched together, and she blinked.

'Julie!' she called.

'Ah-h-h-ow!' prolonged Julie plaintively. Then the voice of Hilda, the second maid, floated up the stairs.

'She cut herself a little, Mis' Piper.'

Evylyn flew to her sewing-basket, rummaged until she found a torn handkerchief, and hurried down-stairs. In a moment Julie was crying in her arms as she searched for the cut, faint, disparaging evidences of which appeared on Julie's dress!

'My *thu*-umb!' explained Julie. 'Oh-h-h-h, t'urts.'

'It was the bowl here, the he one,' said Hilda apologetically. 'It was waitin' on the floor while I polished the sideboard, and Julie come along an' went to foolin' with it. She yust scratch herself.'

Evylyn frowned heavily at Hilda, and twisting Julie decisively in her lap, began tearing strips off the handkerchief.

'Now – let's see it, dear.'

Julie held it up and Evylyn pounced.

'There!'

Julie surveyed her swathed thumb doubtfully. She crooked it; it waggled. A pleased, interested look appeared in her tear-stained face. She sniffled and waggled it again.

'You *precious!*' cried Evylyn and kissed her, but before she left the room she levelled another frown at Hilda. Careless! Servants all that way nowadays. If she could get a good Irishwoman – but you couldn't any more – and these Swedes—

At five o'clock Harold arrived and, coming up to her room, threatened in a suspiciously jovial tone to kiss her thirty five times for her birthday. Evylyn resisted.

'You've been drinking,' she said shortly, and then added qualitatively, 'a little. You know I loathe the smell of it.'

'Evie,' he said, after a pause, seating himself in a chair by the window, 'I can tell you something now. I guess you've known things haven't been going quite right down-town.'

She was standing at the window combing her hair, but at these words she turned and looked at him.

'How do you mean? You've always said there was room for more than one wholesale hardware house in town.' Her voice expressed some alarm.

'There *was*,' said Harold significantly, 'but this Clarence Ahearn is a smart man.'

'I was surprised when you said he was coming to dinner.'

'Evie,' he went on, with another slap at his knee, 'after January first "The Clarence Ahearn Company" becomes "The Ahearn, Piper Company" – and "Piper Brothers" as a company ceases to exist.'

Evylyn was startled. The sound of his name in second place was somehow hostile to her; still he appeared jubilant.

'I don't understand, Harold.'

'Well, Evie, Ahearn has been fooling around with Marx. If those two had combined we'd have been the little fellow, struggling along, picking up smaller orders, hanging back on risks. It's a question of capital, Evie, and "Ahearn and Marx" would have had the business just like "Ahearn and Piper" is going to now.' He paused and coughed and a little cloud of whiskey floated up to her nostrils. 'Tell you the truth, Evie, I've suspected that Ahearn's wife had something to do with it. Ambitious little lady, I'm told. Guess she knew the Marxes couldn't help her much here.'

'Is she – common?' asked Evie.

'Never met her, I'm sure – but I don't doubt it. Clarence Ahearn's name's been up at the Country Club five months – no action taken.' He waved his hand disparagingly. 'Ahearn and I had lunch together to-day and just about clinched it, so I thought it'd be nice to have him and his wife up to-night – just have nine, mostly family. After all, it's a big thing for me, and of course we'll have to see something of them, Evie.'

'Yes,' said Evie thoughtfully, 'I suppose we will.'

Evylyn was not disturbed over the social end of it – but the idea of 'Piper Brothers' becoming 'The Ahearn, Piper Company' startled her. It seemed like going down in the world.

Half an hour later, as she began to dress for dinner, she heard his voice from down-stairs.

'Oh, Evie, come down!'

She went out into the hall and called over the banister:

'What is it?'

'I want you to help me make some of that punch before dinner.'

Hurriedly rehooking her dress, she descended the stairs and found him grouping the essentials on the dining-room table. She went to the sideboard and, lifting one of the bowls, carried it over.

'Oh, no,' he protested, 'let's use the big one. There'll be Ahearn and his wife and you and I and Milton, that's five, and Tom and Jessie, that's seven, and your sister and Joe Ambler, that's nine. You don't know how quick that stuff goes when *you* make it.'

'We'll use this bowl,' she insisted. 'It'll hold plenty. You know how Tom is.'

Tom Lowrie, husband to Jessie, Harold's first cousin, was rather inclined to finish anything in a liquid way that he began.

Harold shook his head.

'Don't be foolish. That one holds only about three quarts and there's nine of us, and the servants'll want some – and it isn't strong punch. It's so much more cheerful to have a lot, Evie; we don't have to drink all of it.'

'I say the small one.'

Again he shook his head obstinately.

'No; be reasonable.'

'I *am* reasonable,' she said shortly. 'I don't want any drunken men in the house.'

'Who said you did?'

'Then use the small bowl.'

'Now, Evie—'

He grasped the smaller bowl to lift it back. Instantly her hands were on it, holding it down. There was a momentary struggle, and then, with a little exasperated grunt, he raised his side, slipped it from her fingers, and carried it to the sideboard.

She looked at him and tried to make her expression contemptuous, but he only laughed. Acknowledging her defeat but disclaiming all future interest in the punch, she left the room.

III

At seven-thirty, her cheeks glowing and her high-piled hair gleaming with a suspicion of brilliantine, Evylyn descended the stairs. Mrs Ahearn, a little woman concealing a slight nervousness under red hair and an extreme Empire gown, greeted her volubly. Evylyn disliked her on the spot, but the husband she rather approved of. He had keen blue eyes and a natural gift of pleasing people that might have made him, socially, had he not so obviously committed the blunder of marrying too early in his career.

'I'm glad to know Piper's wife,' he said simply. 'It looks as though your husband and I are going to see a lot of each other in the future.'

She bowed, smiled graciously, and turned to greet the others: Milton Piper, Harold's quiet, unassertive younger brother; the two Lowries, Jessie and Tom; Irene, her own unmarried sister; and finally Joe Ambler, a confirmed bachelor and Irene's perennial beau.

Harold led the way into dinner.

'We're having a punch evening,' he announced jovially – Evylyn saw that he had already sampled his concoction – 'so there won't be any cocktails except the punch. It's m' wife's greatest achievement, Mrs Ahearn; she'll give you the recipe if you want it; but owing to a slight' – he caught his wife's eye and paused – 'to a slight indisposition, I'm responsible for this batch. Here's how!'

All through dinner there was punch, and Evylyn, noticing that Ahearn and Milton Piper and all the women were shaking their heads negatively at the maid, knew she had been right about the bowl; it was still half full. She resolved to caution Harold directly afterward, but when the women left the table Mrs Ahearn cornered her, and she found herself talking cities and dressmakers with a polite show of interest.

'We've moved around a lot,' chattered Mrs Ahearn, her red head nodding violently. 'Oh, yes, we've never stayed so long in a town before – but I do hope we're here for good. I like it here; don't you?'

'Well, you see, I've always lived here, so, naturally—'

'Oh, that's true,' said Mrs Ahearn and laughed. 'Clarence always used to tell me he had to have a wife he could come home to and say: "Well, we're going to Chicago to-morrow to live, so pack up." I got so I never expected to live *anywhere*.' She laughed her little laugh again; Evylyn suspected that it was her society laugh.

'Your husband is a very able man, I imagine.'

'Oh, yes,' Mrs Ahearn assured her eagerly. 'He's brainy, Clarence is. Ideas and enthusiasm, you know. Finds out what he wants and then goes and gets it.'

Evylyn nodded. She was wondering if the men were still drinking punch back in the dining-room. Mrs Ahearn's history kept unfolding jerkily, but Evylyn had ceased to listen. The first odor of massed cigars began to drift in. It wasn't really a large house, she reflected; on an evening like this the library sometimes grew blue with smoke, and next day one had to leave the windows open for hours to air the heavy staleness out of the curtains. Perhaps this partnership might . . . she began to speculate on a new house . . .

Mrs Ahearn's voice drifted in on her:

'I really would like the recipe if you have it written down somewhere—'

Then there was a sound of chairs in the dining-room and the men strolled in. Evylyn saw at once that her worst fears were realized. Harold's face was flushed and his words ran together at the ends of sentences, while Tom Lowrie lurched when he walked and narrowly missed Irene's lap when he tried to sink onto the couch beside her. He sat there blinking dazedly at the company. Evylyn found herself blinking back at him, but she saw no humor in it. Joe Ambler was smiling contentedly and purring on his cigar. Only Ahearn and Milton Piper seemed unaffected.

'It's a pretty fine town, Ahearn,' said Ambler, 'you'll find that.'

'I've found it so,' said Ahearn pleasantly.

'You find it more, Ahearn,' said Harold, nodding emphatically, ''f I've an'thin' do 'th it.'

He soared into a eulogy of the city, and Evylyn wondered uncomfortably if it bored every one as it bored her. Apparently not. They were all listening attentively. Evylyn broke in at the first gap.

'Where've you been living, Mr Ahearn?' she asked interestedly. Then she remembered that Mrs Ahearn had told her, but it didn't matter. Harold mustn't talk so much. He was such an *ass* when he'd been drinking. But he plopped directly back in.

'Tell you, Ahearn. Firs' you wanna get a house up here on the hill. Get Stearne house or Ridgeway house. Wanna have it so people say: "There's Ahearn house." Solid, you know, tha's effec' it gives.'

Evylyn flushed. This didn't sound right at all. Still Ahearn didn't seem to notice anything amiss, only nodded gravely.

'Have you been looking—' But her words trailed off unheard as Harold's voice boomed on.

'Get house – tha's start. Then you get know people. Snobbish town first toward outsider, but not long – not after know you. People like you' – he indicated Ahearn and his wife with a sweeping gesture – 'all right. Cordial as an'thin' once get by first barrer-bar-barrer—' He swallowed, and then said 'barrier,' repeated it masterfully.

Evylyn looked appealingly at her brother-in-law, but before he could intercede a thick mumble had come crowding out of Tom Lowrie, hindered by the dead cigar, which he gripped firmly with his teeth.

'Huma uma ho huma ahdy um—'

'What?' demanded Harold earnestly.

Resignedly and with difficulty Tom removed the cigar – that is, he removed part of it, and then blew the remainder with a *whut* sound across the room, where it landed liquidly and limply in Mrs Ahearn's lap.

'Beg pardon,' he mumbled, and rose with the vague intention of going after it. Milton's hand on his coat collapsed him in time, and Mrs Ahearn not ungracefully flounced the tobacco from her skirt to the floor, never once looking at it.

'I was sayin',' continued Tom thickly, "fore 'at happened' – he waved his hand apologetically toward Mrs Ahearn – 'I was sayin' I heard all truth that Country Club matter.'

Milton leaned and whispered something to him.

'Lemme 'lone,' he said petulantly; 'know what I'm doin'. 'At's what they came for.'

Evylyn sat there in a panic, trying to make her mouth form words. She saw her sister's sardonic expression and Mrs Ahearn's face turning a vivid red. Ahearn was looking down at his watch-chain, fingering it.

'I heard who's been keepin' y' out, an' he's not a bit better'n you. I can fix whole damn thing up. Would've before, but I didn't know you. Harol' tol' me you felt bad about the thing—'

Milton Piper rose suddenly and awkwardly to his feet. In a second every one was standing tensely and Milton was saying something very hurriedly about having to go early, and the Ahearns were listening with eager intentness. Then Mrs Ahearn swallowed and turned with a forced smile toward Jessie. Evylyn saw Tom lurch forward and put his hand on Ahearn's shoulder – and suddenly she was listening to a new, anxious voice at her elbow, and, turning, found Hilda, the second maid.

'Please, Mis' Piper, I tank Yulie got her hand poisoned. It's all swole up and her cheeks is hot and she's moanin' an' groanin'—'

'Julie is?' Evylyn asked sharply. The party suddenly receded. She turned quickly, sought with her eyes for Mrs Ahearn, slipped toward her.

'If you'll excuse me, Mrs—' She had momentarily forgotten the name, but she went right on: 'My little girl's been taken sick. I'll be down when I can.' She turned and ran quickly up the stairs, retaining a confused picture of rays of cigar smoke and a loud discussion in the center of the room that seemed to be developing into an argument.

Switching on the light in the nursery, she found Julie tossing feverishly and giving out odd little cries. She put her hand against the cheeks. They were burning. With an exclamation she followed the arm down under the cover until she found the hand. Hilda was right. The whole thumb was swollen to the wrist and in the centre was a little inflamed sore. Blood-poisoning! her mind cried in terror. The bandage had come off the cut and she'd gotten something in it. She'd cut it at three o'clock – it was now nearly eleven. Eight hours. Blood-poisoning couldn't possibly develop so soon. She rushed to the 'phone.

Doctor Martin across the street was out. Doctor Foulke, their family physician, didn't answer. She racked her brains and in desperation called her throat specialist, and bit her lip furiously while he looked up the numbers of two physicians. During that interminable moment she thought she heard loud voices down-stairs – but she seemed to be in another world now. After fifteen minutes she located a physician who sounded angry and sulky at being called out of bed. She ran back to the nursery and, looking at the hand, found it was somewhat more swollen.

'Oh, God!' she cried, and kneeling beside the bed began smoothing back Julie's hair over and over. With a vague idea of getting some hot water, she rose and started toward the door, but the lace of her dress caught in the bed-rail and she fell forward on her hands and knees. She struggled up and jerked frantically at the lace. The bed moved and Julie groaned. Then more quietly but with suddenly fumbling fingers she found the pleat in front, tore the whole pannier completely off, and rushed from the room.

Out in the hall she heard a single loud, insistent voice, but as she reached the head of the stairs it ceased and an outer door banged.

The music-room came into view. Only Harold and Milton were there, the former leaning against a chair, his face very pale, his collar open, and his mouth moving loosely.

'What's the matter?'

Milton looked at her anxiously.

'There was a little trouble—'

Then Harold saw her and, straightening up with an effort, began to speak.

''Sult m'own cousin m'own house. God damn common nouveau rish. 'Sult m'own cousin—'

'Tom had trouble with Ahearn and Harold interfered,' said Milton.

'My Lord, Milton,' cried Evylyn, 'couldn't you have done something?'

'I tried; I—'

'Julie's sick,' she interrupted; 'she's poisoned herself. Get him to bed if you can.'

Harold looked up.

'Julie sick?'

Paying no attention, Evylyn brushed by through the dining-room, catching sight, with a burst of horror, of the big punch-bowl still on the table, the liquid from melted ice in its bottom. She heard steps on the front stairs – it was Milton helping Harold up – and then a mumble: 'Why, Julie's a'righ'.'

'Don't let him go into the nursery!' she shouted.

The hours blurred into a nightmare. The doctor arrived just before midnight and within a half-hour had lanced the wound. He left at two after giving her the addresses of two nurses to call up and promising to return at half past six. It was blood-poisoning.

At four, leaving Hilda by the bedside, she went to her room, and slipping with a shudder out of her evening dress, kicked it into a corner. She put on a house dress and returned to the nursery while Hilda went to make coffee.

Not until noon could she bring herself to look into Harold's room, but when she did it was to find him awake and staring very miserably at the ceiling. He turned blood-shot hollow eyes upon her. For a minute she hated him, couldn't speak. A husky voice came from the bed.

'What time is it?'

'Noon.'

'I made a damn fool—'

'It doesn't matter,' she said sharply. 'Julie's got blood-poisoning. They may' – she choked over the words – 'they think she'll have to lose her hand.'

'What?'

'She cut herself on that – that bowl.'

'Last night?'

'Oh, what does it matter?' she cried; 'she's got blood-poisoning. Can't you hear?'

He looked at her bewildered – sat half-way up in bed.

'I'll get dressed,' he said.

Her anger subsided and a great wave of weariness and pity for him rolled over her. After all, it was his trouble, too.

'Yes,' she answered listlessly, 'I suppose you'd better.'

IV

If Evylyn's beauty had hesitated in her early thirties it came to an abrupt decision just afterward and completely left her. A tentative outlay of wrinkles on her face suddenly deepened and flesh collected rapidly on her legs and hips and arms. Her mannerism of drawing her brows together had become an expression – it was habitual when she was reading or speaking and even while she slept. She was forty-six.

As in most families whose fortunes have gone down rather than up, she and Harold had drifted into a colorless antagonism. In repose they looked at each other with the toleration they might have felt for broken old chairs; Evylyn worried a little when he was sick and did her best to be cheerful under the wearying depression of living with a disappointed man.

Family bridge was over for the evening and she sighed with relief. She had made more mistakes than usual this evening and she didn't care. Irene shouldn't have made that remark about the infantry being particularly dangerous. There had been no letter for three weeks now, and, while this was nothing out of the ordinary, it never failed to make her nervous; naturally she hadn't known how many clubs were out.

Harold had gone up-stairs, so she stepped out on the porch for a breath of fresh air. There was a bright glamour of moonlight diffusing on the sidewalks and lawns, and with a little half yawn, half laugh, she remembered one long moonlight affair of her youth.

It was astonishing to think that life had once been the sum of her current love-affairs. It was now the sum of her current problems.

There was the problem of Julie – Julie was thirteen, and lately she was growing more and more sensitive about her deformity and preferred to stay always in her room reading. A few years before she had been frightened at the idea of going to school, and Evylyn could not bring herself to send her, so she grew up in her mother's shadow, a pitiful little figure with the artificial hand that she made no attempt to use but kept forlornly in her pocket. Lately she had been taking lessons in using it because Evylyn had feared she would cease to lift the arm altogether, but after the lessons, unless she made a move with it in listless obedience to her mother, the little hand would creep back to the pocket of her dress. For a while her dresses were made without pockets, but Julie had moped around the house so miserably at a loss all one month that Evylyn weakened and never tried the experiment again.

The problem of Donald had been different from the start. She had attempted vainly to keep him near her as she had tried to teach Julie to lean less on her – lately the problem of Donald had been snatched out of her hands; his division had been abroad for three months.

She yawned again – life was a thing for youth. What a happy youth she must have had! She remembered her pony, Bijou, and the trip to Europe with her mother when she was eighteen—

'Very, very complicated,' she said aloud and severely to the moon, and, stepping inside, was about to close the door when she heard a noise in the library and started.

It was Martha, the middle-aged servant: they kept only one now.

'Why, Martha!' she said in surprise.

Martha turned quickly.

'Oh, I thought you was up-stairs. I was jist—'

'Is anything the matter?'

Martha hesitated.

'No; I—' She stood there fidgeting. 'It was a letter, Mrs Piper, that I put somewhere.'

'A letter? Your own letter?' asked Evylyn, switching on the light.

'No, it was to you. 'Twas this afternoon, Mrs Piper, in the last mail. The postman give it to me and then the back door-bell rang. I had it in my hand, so I must have stuck it somewhere. I thought I'd just slip in now and find it.'

'What sort of a letter? From Mr Donald?'

'No, it was an advertisement, maybe, or a business letter. It was a long, narrow one, I remember.'

They began a search through the music-room, looking on trays and mantelpieces, and then through the library, feeling on the tops of rows of books. Martha paused in despair.

'I can't think where. I went straight to the kitchen. The dining-room, maybe.' She started hopefully for the dining-room, but turned suddenly at the sound of a gasp behind her. Evylyn had sat down heavily in a Morris chair, her brows drawn very close together, eyes blinking furiously.

'Are you sick?'

For a minute there was no answer. Evylyn sat there very still and Martha could see the very quick rise and fall of her bosom.

'Are you sick?' she repeated.

'No,' said Evylyn slowly, 'but I know where the letter is. Go 'way, Martha. I know.'

Wonderingly, Martha withdrew, and still Evylyn sat there, only the muscles around her eyes moving – contracting and relaxing and contracting again. She knew now where the letter was – she knew as well as if she had put it there herself. And she felt instinctively and unquestionably what the letter was. It was long and narrow like an advertisement, but up in the corner in large letters it said 'War Department' and, in smaller letters below, 'Official Business.' She knew it lay there in the big bowl with her name in ink on the outside and her soul's death within.

Rising uncertainly, she walked toward the dining-room, feeling her way along the bookcases and through the doorway. After a moment she found the light and switched it on.

There was the bowl, reflecting the electric light in crimson squares edged with black and yellow squares edged with blue, ponderous and glittering, grotesquely and triumphantly ominous. She took a step forward and paused again; another step and she would see over the top and into the inside – another step and she would see an edge of white – another step – her hands fell on the rough, cold surface—

In a moment she was tearing it open, fumbling with an obstinate fold, holding it before her while the typewritten page glared out and struck at her. Then it fluttered like a bird to the floor. The house that had seemed whirring, buzzing a moment since, was suddenly very quiet; a breath of air crept in through the open front door carrying the noise of a passing motor; she heard faint sounds from upstairs and then a grinding racket in the pipe behind the bookcases – her husband turning off a watertap—

And in that instant it was as if this were not, after all, Donald's hour except in so far as he was a market in the insidious contest that had gone on in sudden surges and long, listless interludes between Evylyn and this cold, malignant thing of beauty, a gift of enmity from a man whose face she had long since forgotten. With its massive, brooding passivity it lay there in the centre of her house as it had lain for years, throwing out the ice-like beams of a thousand eyes, perverse glitterings merging each into each, never aging, never changing.

Evylyn sat down on the edge of the table and stared at it, fascin ated. It seemed to be smiling now, a very cruel smile, as if to say:

'You see, this time I didn't have to hurt you directly. I didn't bother. You know it was I who took your son away. You known how cold I am and how hard and how beautiful, because once you were just as cold and hard and beautiful.'

The bowl seemed suddenly to turn itself over and then to distend and swell until it became a great canopy that glittered and trembled over the room, over the house, and, as the walls melted slowly into mist, Evylyn saw that it was still moving out, out and far away from her, shutting off far horizons and suns and moons and stars except as inky blots seen faintly through it. And under it walked all the people, and the light that came through to them was refracted and twisted until shadow seemed light and light seemed shadow – until the whole panoply of the world became changed and distorted under the twinkling heaven of the bowl.

Then there came a far-away, booming voice like a low, clear bell. It came from the center of the bowl and down the great sides to the ground and then bounced toward her eagerly.

'You see, I am fate,' it shouted, 'and stronger than your puny plans; and I am how-things-turn-out and I am different from your little dreams, and I am the flight of time and the end of beauty and unfulfilled desire; all the accidents and imperceptions and the little minutes that shape the crucial hours are mine. I am the exception that proves no rules, the limits of your control, the condiment in the dish of life.'

The booming sound stopped; the echoes rolled away over the wide land to the edge of the bowl that bounded the world and up the great sides and back to the center where they hummed for a moment and died. Then the great walls began slowly to bear down upon her, growing smaller and smaller, coming closer and closer as if to crush her; and as she clinched her hands and waited for the swift bruise of the cold glass, the bowl gave a sudden wrench and turned over – and lay there on the sideboard, shining and inscrutable, reflecting in a hundred prisms, myriad, many-colored glints and gleams and crossings and interlacings of light.

The cold wind blew in again through the front door, and with a desperate, frantic energy Evylyn stretched both her arms around the bowl. She must be quick – she must be strong. She tightened her arms until they ached, tautened the thin strips of muscle under her soft flesh, and with a mighty effort raised it and held it. She felt the wind blow cold on her back where her dress had come apart from the strain of her effort, and as she felt it she turned toward it and staggered under the great weight out through the library and on toward the front door. She must be quick – she must be strong. The blood in her arms throbbed dully and her knees kept giving way under her, but the feel of the cool glass was good.

Out the front door she tottered and over to the stone steps, and there, summoning every fibre of her soul and body for a last effort, swung herself half around – for a second, as she tried to loose her hold, her numb fingers clung to the rough surface, and in that second she slipped and, losing balance, toppled forward with a despairing cry, her arms still around the bowl . . . down . . .

Over the way lights went on; far down the block the crash was heard, and pedestrians rushed up wonderingly; up-stairs a tired man awoke from the edge of sleep and a little girl whimpered in a haunted doze. And all over the moonlit sidewalk around the still, black form, hundreds of prisms and cubes and splinters of glass reflected the light in little gleams of blue, and black edged with yellow, and yellow, and crimson edged with black.

The Four Fists

I

At the present time no one I know has the slightest desire to hit Samuel Meredith; possibly this is because a man over fifty is liable to be rather severely cracked at the impact of a hostile fist, but, for my part, I am inclined to think that all his hitable qualities have quite vanished. But it is certain that at various times in his life hitable qualities were in his face, as surely as kissable qualities have ever lurked in a girl's lips.

I'm sure every one has met a man like that, been casually introduced, even made a friend of him, yet felt he was the sort who aroused passionate dislike – expressed by some in the involuntary clinching of fists, and in others by mutterings about 'takin' a poke' and 'landin' a swift smash in ee eye.' In the juxtaposition of Samuel Meredith's features this quality was so strong that it influenced his entire life.

What was it? Not the shape, certainly, for he was a pleasant-looking man from earliest youth: broad-browed, with gray eyes that were frank and friendly. Yet I've heard him tell a room full of reporters angling for a 'success' story that he'd be ashamed to tell them the truth, that they wouldn't believe it, that it wasn't one story but four, that the public would not want to read about a man who had been walloped into prominence.

It all started at Phillips Andover Academy when he was fourteen. He had been brought up on a diet of caviar and bell-boys' legs in half the capitals of Europe, and it was pure luck that his mother had nervous prostration and had to delegate his education to less tender, less biassed hands.

At Andover he was given a roommate named Gilly Hood. Gilly was thirteen, undersized, and rather the school pet. From the September day when Mr Meredith's valet stowed Samuel's clothing in the best bureau and asked, on departing, 'hif there was hanything helse, Master Samuel?' Gilly cried out that the faculty had played him false. He felt like an irate frog in whose bowl has been put a goldfish.

'Good gosh!' he complained to his sympathetic contemporaries, 'he's a damn stuck-up Willie. He said, "Are the crowd here gentlemen?" and I said, "No, they're boys," and he said age didn't matter, and I said, "Who said it did?" Let him get fresh with me, the ole pieface!'

For three weeks Gilly endured in silence young Samuel's comments on the clothes and habits of Gilly's personal friends, endured French phrases in conversation, endured a hundred half-feminine meannesses that show what a nervous mother can do to a boy, if she keeps close enough to him – then a storm broke in the aquarium.

Samuel was out. A crowd had gathered to hear Gilly be wrathful about his roommate's latest sins.

'He said, "Oh, I don't like the windows open at night," he said, "except only a little bit,"' complained Gilly.

'Don't let him boss you.'

'Boss me? You bet he won't. I open those windows, I guess, but the darn fool won't take turns shuttin' 'em in the morning.'

'Make him, Gilly, why don't you?'

'I'm going to.' Gilly nodded his head in fierce agreement. 'Don't you worry. He needn't think I'm any ole butler.'

'Le's see you make him.'

At this point the darn fool entered in person and included the crowd in one of his irritating smiles. Two boys said, "Lo, Mer'dith'; the others gave him a chilly glance and went on talking to Gilly. But Samuel seemed unsatisfied.

'Would you mind not sitting on my bed?' he suggested politely to two of Gilly's particulars who were perched very much at ease.

'Huh?'

'My bed. Can't you understand English?'

This was adding insult to injury. There were several comments on the bed's sanitary condition and the evidence within it of animal life.

'S'matter with your old bed?' demanded Gilly truculently.

'The bed's all right, but—'

Gilly interrupted this sentence by rising and walking up to Samuel. He paused several inches away and eyed him fiercely.

'You an' your crazy ole bed,' he began. 'You an' your crazy—'

'Go to it, Gilly,' murmured some one.

'Show the darn fool—'

Samuel returned the gaze coolly.

'Well,' he said finally, 'it's my bed—'

He got no further, for Gilly hauled off and hit him succinctly in the nose.

'Yea! Gilly!'

'Show the big bully!'

'Just let him touch you – he'll see!'

The group closed in on them and for the first time in his life Samuel realized the insuperable inconvenience of being passionately detested. He gazed around helplessly at the glowering, violently hostile faces. He towered a head taller than his roommate, so if he hit back he'd be called a bully and have half a dozen more fights on his hands within five minutes; yet if he didn't he was a coward. For a moment he stood there facing Gilly's blazing eyes, and then, with a sudden choking sound, he forced his way through the ring and rushed from the room.

The month following bracketed the thirty most miserable days of his life. Every waking moment he was under the lashing tongues of his contemporaries; his habits and mannerisms became butts for intolerable witticisms and, of course, the sensitiveness of adolescence was a further thorn. He considered that he was a natural pariah; that the unpopularity at school would follow him through life. When he went home for the Christmas holidays he was so despondent that his father sent him to a nerve specialist. When he returned to Andover he arranged to arrive late so that he could be alone in the bus during the drive from station to school.

Of course when he had learned to keep his mouth shut every one promptly forgot all about him. The next autumn, with his realization that consideration for others was the discreet attitude, he made good use of the clean start given him by the shortness of boyhood memory. By the beginning of his senior year Samuel Meredith was one of the best-liked boys of his class – and no one was any stronger for him than his first friend and constant companion, Gilly Hood.

II

Samuel became the sort of college student who in the early nineties drove tandems and coaches and tallyhos between Princeton and Yale and New York City to show that they appreciated the social importance of football games. He believed passionately in good form – his choosing of gloves, his tying of ties, his holding of reins were imitated by impressionable freshmen. Outside of his own set he was considered rather a snob, but as his set was *the* set, it never worried him. He played football in the autumn, drank high-balls in the winter, and rowed in the spring. Samuel despised all those who were merely sportsmen without being gentlemen, or merely gentlemen without being sportsmen.

He lived in New York and often brought home several of his friends for the week-end. Those were the days of the horse-car and in case of a crush it was, of course, the proper thing for any one of Samuel's set to rise and deliver his seat to a standing lady with a formal bow. One night in Samuel's junior year he boarded a car with two of his intimates. There were three vacant seats. When Samuel sat down he noticed a heavy-eyed laboring man sitting next to him who smelt objectionably of garlic, sagged slightly against Samuel and, spreading a little as a tired man will, took up quite too much room.

The car had gone several blocks when it stopped for a quartet of young girls, and, of course, the three men of the world sprang to their feet and proffered their seats with due observance of form. Unfortunately, the laborer, being unacquainted with the code of neckties and tallyhos, failed to follow their example, and one young lady was left at an embarrassed stance. Fourteen eyes glared reproachfully at the barbarian; seven lips curled slightly; but the object of scorn stared stolidly into the foreground in sturdy unconsciousness of his despicable conduct. Samuel was the most violently affected. He was humiliated that any male should so conduct himself. He spoke aloud.

'There's a lady standing,' he said sternly.

That should have been quite enough, but the object of scorn only looked up blankly. The standing girl tittered and exchanged nervous glances with her companions. But Samuel was aroused.

'There's a lady standing,' he repeated, rather raspingly. The man seemed to comprehend.

'I pay my fare,' he said quietly.

Samuel turned red and his hands clinched, but the conductor was looking their way, so at a warning nod from his friends he subsided into sullen gloom.

They reached their destination and left the car, but so did the laborer, who followed them, swinging his little pail. Seeing his chance, Samuel no longer resisted his aristocratic inclination. He turned around and, launching a full-featured, dime-novel sneer, made a loud remark about the right of the lower animals to ride with human beings.

In a half-second the workman had dropped his pail and let fly at him. Unprepared, Samuel took the blow neatly on the jaw and sprawled full length into the cobblestone gutter.

'Don't laugh at me!' cried his assailant. 'I been workin' all day. I'm tired as hell!'

As he spoke the sudden anger died out of his eyes and the mask of weariness dropped again over his face. He turned and picked up his pail. Samuel's friends took a quick step in his direction.

'Wait!' Samuel had risen slowly and was motioning them back. Some time, somewhere, he had been struck like that before. Then he remembered – Gilly Hood. In the silence, as he dusted himself off, the whole scene in the room at Andover was before his eyes – and he knew intuitively that he had been wrong again. This man's strength, his rest, was the protection of his family. He had more use for his seat in the street-car than any young girl.

'It's all right,' said Samuel gruffly. 'Don't touch him. I've been a damn fool.'

Of course it took more than an hour, or a week, for Samuel to rearrange his ideas on the essential importance of good form. At first he simply admitted that his wrongness had made him powerless – as it had made him powerless against Gilly – but eventually his mistake about the workman influenced his entire attitude. Snobbishness is, after all, merely good breeding grown dictatorial; so Samuel's code remained, but the necessity of imposing it upon others had faded out in a certain gutter. Within that year his class had somehow stopped referring to him as a snob.

III

After a few years Samuel's university decided that it had shone long enough in the reflected glory of his neckties, so they declaimed to him in Latin, charged him ten dollars for the paper which proved him irretrievably educated, and sent him into the turmoil with much self-confidence, a few friends, and the proper assortment of harmless bad habits.

His family had by that time started back to shirt-sleeves, through a sudden decline in the sugar-market, and it had already unbuttoned its vest, so to speak, when Samuel went to work. His mind was that exquisite *tabula rasa* that a university education sometimes leaves, but he had both energy and influence, so he used his former ability as a dodging half-back in twisting through Wall Street crowds as runner for a bank.

His diversion was – women. There were half a dozen: two or three débutantes, an actress (in a minor way), a grass-widow, and one sentimental little brunette who was married and lived in a little house in Jersey City.

They had met on a ferry-boat. Samuel was crossing from New York on business (he had been working several years by this time) and he helped her look for a package that she had dropped in the crush.

'Do you come over often?' he inquired casually.

'Just to shop,' she said shyly. She had great brown eyes and the pathetic kind of little mouth. 'I've only been married three months, and we find it cheaper to live over here.'

'Does he – does your husband like your being alone like this?'

She laughed, a cheery young laugh.

'Oh, dear me, no. We were to meet for dinner but I must have misunderstood the place. He'll be awfully worried.'

'Well,' said Samuel disapprovingly, 'he ought to be. If you'll allow me I'll see you home.'

She accepted his offer thankfully, so they took the cable-car together. When they walked up the path to her little house they saw a light there; her husband had arrived before her.

'He's frightfully jealous,' she announced, laughingly apologetic.

'Very well,' answered Samuel, rather stiffly. 'I'd better leave you here.'

She thanked him and, waving a good night, he left her.

That would have been quite all if they hadn't met on Fifth Avenue one morning a week later. She started and blushed and seemed so glad to see him that they chatted like old friends. She was going to her dressmaker's, eat lunch alone at Taine's, shop all afternoon, and meet her husband on the ferry at five. Samuel told her that her husband was a very lucky man. She blushed again and scurried off.

Samuel whistled all the way back to his office, but about twelve o'clock he began to see that pathetic, appealing little mouth everywhere – and those brown eyes. He fidgeted when he looked at the clock; he thought of the grill down-stairs where he lunched and the heavy male conversation thereof, and opposed to that picture appeared another: a little table at Taine's with the brown eyes and the mouth a few feet away. A few minutes before twelve-thirty he dashed on his hat and rushed for the cable-car.

She was quite surprised to see him.

'Why – hello,' she said. Samuel could tell that she was just pleasantly frightened.

'I thought we might lunch together. It's so dull eating with a lot of men.'

She hesitated.

'Why, I suppose there's no harm in it. How could there be!'

It occurred to her that her husband should have taken lunch with her – but he was generally so hurried at noon. She told Samuel all about him; he was a little smaller than Samuel, but, oh, *much* better-looking. He was a bookkeeper and not making a lot of money, but they were very happy and expected to be rich within three or four years.

Samuel's grass-widow had been in a quarrelsome mood for three or four weeks, and, through contrast, he took an accentuated pleasure in this meeting; so fresh was she, and earnest, and faintly adventurous. Her name was Marjorie.

They made another engagement; in fact, for a month they lunched together two or three times a week. When she was sure that her husband would work late Samuel took her over to New Jersey on the ferry, leaving her always on the tiny front porch, after she had gone in and lit the gas to use the security of his masculine presence outside. This grew to be a ceremony – and it annoyed him. Whenever the comfortable glow fell out through the front windows, that was his *congé*; yet he never suggested coming in and Marjorie didn't invite him.

Then, when Samuel and Marjorie had reached a stage in which they sometimes touched each other's arms gently, just to show that they were very good friends, Marjorie and her husband had one of those ultrasensitive, supercritical quarrels that couples never indulge in unless they care a great deal about each other. It started with a cold mutton-chop or a leak in the gas-jet – and one day Samuel found her in Taine's, with dark shadows under her brown eyes and a terrifying pout.

By this time Samuel thought he was in love with Marjorie – so he played up the quarrel for all it was worth. He was her best friend and patted her hand – and leaned down close to her brown curls while she whispered in little sobs what her husband had said that morning; and he was a little more than her best friend when he took her over to the ferry in a hansom.

'Marjorie,' he said gently, when he left her, as usual, on the porch, 'if at any time you want to call on me, remember that I am always waiting, always waiting.'

She nodded gravely and put both her hands in his.

'I know,' she said. 'I know you're my friend, my best friend.'

Then she ran into the house and he watched there until the gas went on.

For the next week Samuel was in a nervous turmoil. Some persistently rational strain warned him that at bottom he and Marjorie had little in common, but in such cases there is usually so much mud in the water that one can seldom see to the bottom. Every dream and desire told him that he loved Marjorie, wanted her, had to have her.

The quarrel developed. Marjorie's husband took to staying in New York until late at night, came home several times disagreeably over-stimulated, and made her generally miserable. They must have had too much pride to talk it out – for Marjorie's husband was, after all, pretty decent – so it drifted on from one misunderstanding to another. Marjorie kept coming more and more to Samuel; when a woman can accept masculine sympathy it is much more satisfactory to her than crying to another girl. But Marjorie didn't realize how much she had begun to rely on him, how much he was part of her little cosmos.

One night, instead of turning away when Marjorie went in and lit the gas, Samuel went in, too, and they sat together on the sofa in the little parlor. He was very happy. He envied their home, and he felt that the man who neglected such a possession out of stubborn pride was a fool and unworthy of his wife. But when he kissed Marjorie for the first time she cried softly and told him to go. He sailed home on the wings of desperate excitement, quite resolved to fan this spark of romance, no matter how big the blaze or who was burned. At the time he considered that his thoughts were unselfishly of her; in a later perspective he knew that she had meant no more than the white screen in a motion picture: it was just Samuel – blind, desirous.

Next day at Taine's, when they met for lunch, Samuel dropped all pretense and made frank love to her. He had no plans, no definite intentions, except to kiss her lips again, to hold her in his arms and feel that she was very little and pathetic and lovable . . . He took her home, and this time they kissed until both their hearts beat high – words and phrases formed on his lips.

And then suddenly there were steps on the porch – a hand tried the outside door. Marjorie turned dead-white.

'Wait! she whispered to Samuel, in a frightened voice, but in angry impatience at the interruption he walked to the front door and threw it open.

Every one has seen such scenes on the stage – seen them so often that when they actually happen people behave very much like actors. Samuel felt that he was playing a part and the lines came quite naturally: he announced that all had a right to lead their own lives and looked at Marjorie's husband menacingly, as if daring him to doubt it. Marjorie's husband spoke of the sanctity of the home, forgetting that it hadn't seemed very holy to him lately; Samuel continued along the line of 'the right to happiness'; Marjorie's husband mentioned firearms and the divorce court. Then suddenly he stopped and scrutinized both of them – Marjorie in pitiful collapse on the sofa, Samuel haranguing the furniture in a consciously heroic pose.

'Go up-stairs, Marjorie,' he said, in a different tone.

'Stay where you are!' Samuel countered quickly.

Marjorie rose, wavered, and sat down, rose again and moved hesitatingly toward the stairs.

'Come outside,' said her husband to Samuel. 'I want to talk to you.'

Samuel glanced at Marjorie, tried to get some message from her eyes; then he shut his lips and went out.

There was a bright moon and when Marjorie's husband came down the steps Samuel could see plainly that he was suffering – but he felt no pity for him.

They stood and looked at each other, a few feet apart, and the husband cleared his throat as though it were a bit husky.

'That's my wife,' he said quietly, and then a wild anger surged up inside him. 'Damn you!' he cried – and hit Samuel in the face with all his strength.

In that second, as Samuel slumped to the ground, it flashed to him that he had been hit like that twice before, and simultaneously the incident altered like a dream – he felt suddenly awake. Mechanically he sprang to his feet and squared off. The other man was waiting, fists up, a yard away, but Samuel knew that though physically he had him by several inches and many pounds, he wouldn't hit him. The situation had miraculously and entirely changed – a moment before Samuel had seemed to himself heroic; now he seemed the cad, the outsider, and Marjorie's husband, silhouetted against the lights of the little house, the eternal heroic figure, the defender of his home.

There was a pause and then Samuel turned quickly away and went down the path for the last time.

IV

Of course, after the third blow Samuel put in several weeks at conscientious introspection. The blow years before at Andover had landed on his personal unpleasantness; the workman of his college days had jarred the snobbishness out of his system, and Marjorie's husband had given a severe jolt to his greedy selfishness. It threw women out of his ken until a year later, when he met his future wife; for the only sort of woman worth while seemed to be the one who could be protected as Marjorie's husband had protected her. Samuel could not imagine his grass-widow, Mrs De Ferriac, causing any very righteous blows on her own account.

His early thirties found him well on his feet. He was associated with old Peter Carhart, who was in those days a national figure. Carhart's physique was like a rough model for a statue of Hercules, and his record was just as solid – a pile made for the pure joy of it, without cheap extortion or shady scandal. He had been a great friend of Samuel's father, but he watched the son for six years before taking him into his own office. Heaven knows how many things he controlled at that time – mines, railroads, banks, whole cities. Samuel was very close to him, knew his likes and dislikes, his prejudices, weaknesses and many strengths.

One day Carhart sent for Samuel and, closing the door of his inner office, offered him a chair and a cigar.

'Everything O. K., Samuel?' he asked.

'Why, yes.'

'I've been afraid you're getting a bit stale.'

'Stale?' Samuel was puzzled.

'You've done no work outside the office for nearly ten years.'

'But I've had vacations, in the Adiron—'

Carhart waved this aside.

'I mean outside work. Seeing the things move that we've always pulled the strings of here.'

'No,' admitted Samuel; 'I haven't.'

'So,' he said abruptly, 'I'm going to give you an outside job that'll take about a month.'

Samuel didn't argue. He rather liked the idea and he made up his mind that, whatever it was, he would put it through just as Carhart wanted it. That was his employer's greatest hobby, and the men around him were as dumb under direct orders as infantry subalterns.

'You'll go to San Antonio and see Hamil,' continued Carhart. 'He's got a job on hand and he wants a man to take charge.'

Hamil was in charge of the Carhart interests in the Southwest, a man who had grown up in the shadow of his employer, and with whom, though they had never met, Samuel had had much official correspondence.

'When do I leave?'

'You'd better go to-morrow,' answered Carhart, glancing at the calendar. 'That's the 1st of May. I'll expect your report here on the 1st of June.'

Next morning Samuel left for Chicago, and two days later he was facing Hamil across a table in the office of the Merchants' Trust in San Antonio. It didn't take long to get the gist of the thing. It was a big deal in oil which concerned the buying up of seventeen huge adjoining ranches. This buying up had to be done in one week, and it was a pure squeeze. Forces had been set in motion that put the seventeen owners between the devil and the deep sea, and Samuel's part was simply to 'handle' the matter from a little village near Pueblo. With tact and efficiency the right man could bring it off without any friction, for it was merely a question of sitting at the wheel and keeping a firm hold. Hamil, with an astuteness many times valuable to his chief, had arranged a situation that would give a much greater clear gain than any dealing in the open market. Samuel shook hands with Hamil, arranged to return in two weeks, and left for San Felipe, New Mexico.

It occurred to him, of course, that Carhart was trying him out. Hamil's report on his handling of this might be a factor in something big for him, but even without that he would have done his best to put the thing through. Ten years in New York hadn't made him sentimental, and he was quite accustomed to finish everything he began – and a little bit more.

All went well at first. There was no enthusiasm, but each one of the seventeen ranchers concerned knew Samuel's business, knew what he had behind him, and that they had as little chance of holding out as flies on a window-pane. Some of them were resigned – some of them cared like the devil, but they'd talked it over, argued it with lawyers and couldn't see any possible loophole. Five of the ranches had oil, the other twelve were part of the chance, but quite as necessary to Hamil's purpose, in any event.

Samuel soon saw that the real leader was an early settler named

McIntyre, a man of perhaps fifty, gray-haired, clean-shaven, bronzed by forty New Mexico summers, and with those clear, steady eyes that Texas and New Mexico weather are apt to give. His ranch had not as yet shown oil, but it was in the pool, and if any man hated to lose his land McIntyre did. Every one had rather looked to him at first to avert the big calamity, and he had hunted all over the territory for the legal means with which to do it, but he had failed, and he knew it. He avoided Samuel assiduously, but Samuel was sure that when the day came for the signatures he would appear.

It came – a baking May day, with hot waves rising off the parched land as far as eyes could see – and as Samuel sat stewing in his little improvised office – a few chairs, a bench, and a wooden table – he was glad the thing was almost over. He wanted to get back East the worst way, and join his wife and children for a week at the seashore.

The meeting was set for four o'clock, and he was rather surprised at three-thirty when the door opened and McIntyre came in. Samuel could not help respecting the man's attitude, and feeling a bit sorry for him. McIntyre seemed closely related to the prairies, and Samuel had the little flicker of envy that city people feel toward men who live in the open.

'Afternoon,' said McIntyre, standing in the open doorway, with his feet apart and his hands on his hips.

'Hello, Mr McIntyre.' Samuel rose, but omitted the formality of offering his hand. He imagined the rancher cordially loathed him, and he hardly blamed him. McIntyre came in and sat down leisurely.

'You got us,' he said suddenly.

This didn't seem to require any answer.

'When I heard Carhart was back of this,' he continued, 'I gave up.'

'Mr Carhart is—' began Samuel, but McIntyre waved him silent.

'Don't talk about the dirty sneak-thief!'

'Mr McIntyre,' said Samuel briskly, 'if this half-hour is to be devoted to that sort of talk—'

'Oh, dry up, young man,' McIntyre interrupted, 'you can't abuse a man who'd do a thing like this.'

Samuel made no answer.

'It's simply a dirty filch. There just *are* skunks like him too big to handle.'

'You're being paid liberally,' offered Samuel.

'Shut up!' roared McIntyre suddenly. 'I want the privilege of talking.' He walked to the door and looked out across the land, the sunny, steaming pasturage that began almost at his feet and ended with the gray-green of the distant mountains. When he turned around his mouth was trembling.

'Do you fellows love Wall Street?' he said hoarsely, 'or wherever you do your dirty scheming—' He paused. 'I suppose you do. No critter gets so low that he doesn't sort of love the place he's worked, where he's sweated out the best he's had in him.'

Samuel watched him awkwardly. McIntyre wiped his forehead with a huge blue handkerchief, and continued:

'I reckon this rotten old devil had to have another million. I reckon we're just a few of the poor beggars he's blotted out to buy a couple more carriages or something.' He waved his hand toward the door. 'I built a house out there when I was seventeen, with these two hands. I took a wife there at twenty-one, added two wings, and with four mangy steers I started out. Forty summers I've saw the sun come up over those mountains and drop down red as blood in the evening, before the heat drifted off and the stars came out. I been happy in that house. My boy was born there and he died there, late one spring, in the hottest part of an afternoon like this. Then the wife and I lived there alone like we'd lived before, and sort of tried to have a home, after all, not a real home but nigh it – cause the boy always seemed around close, somehow, and we expected a lot of nights to see him runnin' up the path to supper.' His voice was shaking so he could hardly speak and he turned again to the door, his gray eyes contracted.

'That's my land out there,' he said, stretching out his arm, 'my land, by God— It's all I got in the world – and ever wanted.' He dashed his sleeve across his face, and his tone changed as he turned slowly and faced Samuel. 'But I suppose it's got to go when they want it – it's got to go.'

Samuel had to talk. He felt that in a minute more he would lose his head. So he began, as level-voiced as he could – in the sort of tone he saved for disagreeable duties.

'It's business, Mr McIntyre,' he said, 'it's inside the law. Perhaps we couldn't have bought out two or three of you at any price, but most of you did have a price. Progress demands some things—'

Never had he felt so inadequate, and it was with the greatest relief that he heard hoof-beats a few hundred yards away.

But at his words the grief in McIntyre's eyes had changed to fury.

'You and your dirty gang of crooks!' he cried. 'Not one of you has got an honest love for anything on God's earth! You're a herd of money-swine!'

Samuel rose and McIntyre took a step toward him.

'You long winded dude. You got our land – take that for Peter Carhart!'

He swung from the shoulder quick as lightning and down went Samuel in a heap. Dimly he heard steps in the doorway and knew that some one was holding McIntyre, but there was no need. The rancher had sunk down in his chair, and dropped his head in his hands.

Samuel's brain was whirring. He realized that the fourth fist had hit him, and a great flood of emotion cried out that the law that had inexorably ruled his life was in motion again. In a half-daze he got up and strode from the room.

The next ten minutes were perhaps the hardest of his life. People talk of the courage of convictions, but in actual life a man's duty to his family may make a rigid course seem a selfish indulgence of his own righteousness. Samuel thought mostly of his family, yet he never really wavered. That jolt had brought him to.

When he came back in the room there were a lot of worried faces waiting for him, but he didn't waste any time explaining.

'Gentlemen,' he said, 'Mr McIntyre has been kind enough to convince me that in this matter you are absolutely right, and the

Peter Carhart interests absolutely wrong. As far as I am concerned you can keep your ranches to the rest of your days.'

He pushed his way through an astounded gathering, and within a half-hour he had sent two telegrams that staggered the operator into complete unfitness for business; one was to Hamil in San Antonio; one was to Peter Carhart in New York.

Samuel didn't sleep much that night. He knew that for the first time in his business career he had made a dismal, miserable failure. But some instinct in him, stronger than will, deeper than training, had forced him to do what would probably end his ambitions and his happiness. But it was done and it never occurred to him that he could have acted otherwise.

Next morning two telegrams were waiting for him. The first was from Hamil. It contained three words:

'You blamed idiot!'

The second was from New York:

'Deal off come to New York immediately Carhart.'

Within a week things had happened. Hamil quarrelled furiously and violently defended his scheme. He was summoned to New York, and spent a bad half-hour on the carpet in Peter Carhart's office. He broke with the Carhart interests in July, and in August Samuel Meredith, at thirty-five years old, was, to all intents, made Carhart's partner. The fourth fist had done its work.

I suppose that there's a caddish streak in every man that runs crosswise across his character and disposition and general outlook. With some men it's secret and we never know it's there until they strike us in the dark one night. But Samuel's showed when it was in action, and the sight of it made people see red. He was rather lucky in that, because every time his little devil came up it met a reception that sent it scurrying down below in a sickly, feeble condition. It was the same devil, the same streak that made him order Gilly's friends off the bed, that made him go inside Marjorie's house.

If you could run your hand along Samuel Meredith's jaw you'd feel a lump. He admits he's never been sure which fist left it there, but he wouldn't lose it for anything. He says there's no cad like an old cad, and that sometimes just before making a decision, it's a great help to stroke his chin. The reporters call it a nervous characteristic, but it's not that. It's so he can feel again the gorgeous clarity, the lightning sanity of those four fists.

May Day

There had been a war fought and won and the great city of the conquering people was crossed with triumphal arches and vivid with thrown flowers of white, red, and rose. All through the long spring days the returning soldiers marched up the chief highway behind the strump of drums and the joyous, resonant wind of the brasses, while merchants and clerks left their bickerings and figurings and, crowding to the windows, turned their white-bunched faces gravely upon the passing battalions.

Never had there been such splendor in the great city, for the victorious war had brought plenty in its train, and the merchants had flocked thither from the South and West with their households to taste of all the luscious feasts and witness the lavish entertainments prepared – and to buy for their women furs against the next winter and bags of golden mesh and varicolored slippers of silk and silver and rose satin and cloth of gold.

So gaily and noisily were the peace and prosperity impending hymned by the scribes and poets of the conquering people that more and more spenders had gathered from the provinces to drink the wine of excitement, and faster and faster did the merchants dispose of their trinkets and slippers until they sent up a mighty cry for more trinkets and more slippers in order that they might give in barter what was demanded of them. Some even of them flung up their hands helplessly, shouting:

'Alas! I have no more slippers! and alas! I have no no more trinkets! May Heaven help me, for I know not what I shall do!'

But no one listened to their great outcry, for the throngs were far too busy – day by day, the foot soldiers trod jauntily the highway, and all exulted because the young men returning were pure and brave, sound of tooth and pink of cheek, and the young women of the land were virgins and comely both of face and of figure.

So during all this time there were many adventures that happened in the great city, and, of these, several – or perhaps one – are here set down.

I

At nine o'clock on the morning of the first of May, 1919, a young man spoke to the room clerk at the Biltmore Hotel, asking if Mr Philip Dean were registered there, and if so, could he be connected with Mr Dean's rooms. The inquirer was dressed in a well-cut, shabby suit. He was small, slender, and darkly handsome; his eyes were framed above with unusually long eyelashes and below with the blue semicircle of ill health, this latter effect heightened by an unnatural glow which coloured his face like a low, incessant fever.

Mr Dean was staying there. The young man was directed to a telephone at the side.

After a second his connection was made; a sleepy voice hallo'd from somewhere above.

'Mr Dean?' – this very eagerly – 'it's Gordon, Phil. It's Gordon Sterrett. I'm downstairs. I heard you were in New York and I had a hunch you'd be here.'

The sleepy voice became gradually enthusiastic. Well, how was Gordy, old boy! Well, he certainly was surprised and tickled! Would Gordy come right up, for Pete's sake!

A few minutes later Philip Dean, dressed in blue silk pyjamas, opened his door and the two young men greeted each other with a half-embarrassed exuberance. They were both about twenty-four, Yale graduates of the year before the war; but there the resemblance stopped abruptly. Dean was blond, ruddy, and rugged under his thin pyjamas. Everything about him radiated fitness and bodily comfort. He smiled frequently, showing large and prominent teeth.

'I was going to look you up,' he cried enthusiastically. 'I'm taking a couple of weeks off. If you'll sit down a sec. I'll be right with you. Going to take a shower.'

As he vanished into the bathroom his visitor's dark eyes roved nervously around the room, resting for a moment on a great English travelling bag in the corner and on a family of thick silk shirts littered on the chairs amid impressive neckties and soft woollen socks.

Gordon rose and, picking up one of the shirts, gave it a minute examination. It was of very heavy silk, yellow, with a pale blue stripe – and there were nearly a dozen of them. He stared involuntarily at his own shirt-cuffs – they were ragged and linty at the edges and soiled to a faint gray. Dropping the silk shirt, he held his coat-sleeves down and worked the frayed shirt-cuffs up till they were out of sight. Then he went to the mirror and looked at himself with listless, unhappy interest. His tie, of former glory, was faded and thumb-creased – it served no longer to hide the jagged buttonholes of his collar. He thought, quite without amusement, that only three years before he had received a scattering vote in the senior elections at college for being the best-dressed man in his class.

Dean emerged from the bathroom polishing his body.

'Saw an old friend of yours last night,' he remarked. 'Passed her in the lobby and couldn't think of her name to save my neck. That girl you brought up to New Haven senior year.'

Gordon started.

'Edith Bradin? That whom you mean?'

''At's the one. Damn good looking. She's still sort of a pretty doll – you know what I mean: as if you touched her she'd smear.'

He surveyed his shining self complacently in the mirror, smiled faintly, exposing a section of teeth.

'She must be twenty-three anyway,' he continued.

'Twenty-two last month,' said Gordon absently.

'What? Oh, last month. Well, I imagine she's down for the Gamma Psi dance. Did you know we're having a Yale Gamma Psi dance to-night at Delmonico's? You better come up, Gordy. Half of New Haven'll probably be there. I can get you an invitation.'

Draping himself reluctantly in fresh underwear, Dean lit a cigarette and sat down by the open window, inspecting his calves and knees under the morning sunshine which poured into the room.

'Sit down, Gordy,' he suggested, 'and tell me all about what you've been doing and what you're doing now and everything.'

Gordon collapsed unexpectedly upon the bed; lay there inert and spiritless. His mouth, which habitually dropped a little open when his face was in repose, became suddenly helpless and pathetic.

'What's the matter?' asked Dean quickly.

'Oh, God!'

'What's the matter?'

'Every God damn thing in the world,' he said miserably. 'I've absolutely gone to pieces, Phil. I'm all in.'

'Huh?'

'I'm all in.' His voice was shaking.

Dean scrutinized him more closely with appraising blue eyes.

'You certainly look all shot.'

'I am. I've made a hell of a mess of everything.' He paused. 'I'd better start at the beginning – or will it bore you?'

'Not at all; go on.' There was, however, a hesitant note in Dean's voice. This trip East had been planned for a holiday – to find Gordon Sterrett in trouble exasperated him a little.

'Go on,' he repeated, and then added half under his breath, 'Get it over with.'

'Well,' began Gordon unsteadily, 'I got back from France in February, went home to Harrisburg for a month, and then came down to New York to get a job. I got one – with an export company. They fired me yesterday.'

'Fired you?'

'I'm coming to that, Phil. I want to tell you frankly. You're about the only man I can turn to in a matter like this. You won't mind if I just tell you frankly, will you, Phil?'

Dean stiffened a bit more. The pats he was bestowing on his knees grew perfunctory. He felt vaguely that he was being unfairly saddled with responsibility; he was not even sure he wanted to be told. Though never surprised at finding Gordon Sterrett in mild difficulty, there was something in this present misery that repelled him and hardened him, even though it excited his curiosity.

'Go on.'

'It's a girl.'

'Hm.' Dean resolved that nothing was going to spoil his trip. If Gordon was going to be depressing, then he'd have to see less of Gordon.

'Her name is Jewel Hudson,' went on the distressed voice from the bed. 'She used to be "pure," I guess, up to about a year ago. Lived here in New York – poor family. Her people are dead now and she lives with an old aunt. You see it was just about the time I met her that everybody began to come back from France in droves – and all I did was to welcome the newly arrived and go on parties with 'em. That's the way it started, Phil, just from being glad to see everybody and having them glad to see me.'

'You ought to've had more sense.'

'I know,' Gordon paused, and then continued listlessly. 'I'm on my own now, you know, and Phil, I can't stand being poor. Then came this darn girl. She sort of fell in love with me for a while and, though I never intended to get so involved, I'd always seem to run into her somewhere. You can imagine the sort of work I was doing for those exporting people – of course, I always intended to draw; do illustrating for magazines; there's a pile of money in it.'

'Why didn't you? You've got to buckle down if you want to make good,' suggested Dean with cold formalism.

'I tried, a little, but my stuff's crude. I've got talent, Phil; I can draw – but I just don't know how. I ought to go to art school and I can't afford it. Well, things came to a crisis about a week ago. Just as I was down to about my last dollar this girl began bothering me. She wants some money; claims she can make trouble for me if she doesn't get it.'

'Can she?'

'I'm afraid she can. That's one reason I lost my job – she kept calling up the office all the time, and that was sort of the last straw down there. She's got a letter all written to send to my family. Oh, she's got me, all right. I've got to have some money for her.'

There was an awkward pause. Gordon lay very still, his hands clenched by his side.

'I'm all in,' he continued, his voice trembling. 'I'm half crazy, Phil. If I hadn't known you were coming East, I think I'd have killed myself. I want you to lend me three hundred dollars.'

Dean's hands, which had been patting his bare ankles, were suddenly quiet – and the curious uncertainty playing between the two became taut and strained.

After a second Gordon continued:

'I've bled the family until I'm ashamed to ask for another nickel.'

Still Dean made no answer.

'Jewel says she's got to have two hundred dollars.'

'Tell her where she can go.'

'Yes, that sounds easy, but she's got a couple of drunken letters I wrote her. Unfortunately she's not at all the flabby sort of person you'd expect.'

Dean made an expression of distaste.

'I can't stand that sort of woman. You ought to have kept away.'

'I know,' admitted Gordon wearily.

'You've got to look at things as they are. If you haven't got money you've got to work and stay away from women.'

'That's easy for you to say,' began Gordon, his eyes narrowing. 'You've got all the money in the world.'

'I most certainly have not. My family keep darn close tab on what I spend. Just because I have a little leeway I have to be extra careful not to abuse it.'

He raised the blind and let in a further flood of sunshine.

'I'm no prig, Lord knows,' he went on deliberately. 'I like pleasure – and I like a lot of it on a vacation like this, but you're – you're in awful shape. I never heard you talk just this way before. You seem to be sort of bankrupt – morally as well as financially.'

'Don't they usually go together?'

Dean shook his head impatiently.

'There's a regular aura about you that I don't understand. It's a sort of evil.'

'It's an air of worry and poverty and sleepless nights,' said Gordon, rather defiantly.

'I don't know.'

'Oh, I admit I'm depressing. I depress myself. But, my God, Phil, a week's rest and a new suit and some ready money and I'd be like – like I was. Phil, I can draw like a streak, and you know it. But half the time I haven't had the money to buy decent drawing materials – and I can't draw when I'm tired and discouraged and all in. With a little ready money I can take a few weeks off and get started.'

'How do I know you wouldn't use it on some other woman?'

'Why rub it in?' said Gordon quietly.

'I'm not rubbing it in. I hate to see you this way.'

'Will you lend me the money, Phil?'

'I can't decide right off. That's a lot of money and it'll be darn inconvenient for me.'

'It'll be hell for me if you can't – I know I'm whining, and it's all my own fault but – that doesn't change it.'

'When could you pay it back?'

This was encouraging. Gordon considered. It was probably wisest to be frank.

'Of course, I could promise to send it back next month, but – I'd better say three months. Just as soon as I start to sell drawings.'

'How do I know you'll sell any drawings?'

A new hardness in Dean's voice sent a faint chill of doubt over Gordon. Was it possible that he wouldn't get the money?

'I supposed you had a little confidence in me.'

'I did have – but when I see you like this I begin to wonder.'

'Do you suppose if I wasn't at the end of my rope I'd come to you like this? Do you think I'm enjoying it?' He broke off and bit his lip, feeling that he had better subdue the rising anger in his voice. After all, he was the suppliant.

'You seem to manage it pretty easily,' said Dean angrily. 'You put me in the position where, if I don't lend it to you, I'm a sucker – oh, yes, you do. And let me tell you it's no easy thing for me to get hold of three hundred dollars. My income isn't so big but that a slice like that won't play the deuce with it.'

He left his chair and began to dress, choosing his clothes carefully. Gordon stretched out his arms and clenched the edges of the bed, fighting back a desire to cry out. His head was splitting and whirring, his mouth was dry and bitter and he could feel the fever in his blood resolving itself into innumerable regular counts like a slow dripping from a roof.

Dean tied his tie precisely, brushed his eyebrows, and removed a piece of tobacco from his teeth with solemnity. Next he filled his cigarette case, tossed the empty box thoughtfully into the waste basket, and settled the case in his vest pocket.

'Had breakfast?' he demanded.

'No; I don't eat it any more.'

'Well, we'll go out and have some. We'll decide about that money later. I'm sick of the subject. I came East to have a good time.

'Let's go over to the Yale Club,' he continued moodily, and then added with an implied reproof: 'You've given up your job. You've got nothing else to do.'

'I'd have a lot to do if I had a little money,' said Gordon pointedly.

'Oh, for Heaven's sake drop the subject for a while! No point in glooming on my whole trip. Here, here's some money.'

He took a five-dollar bill from his wallet and tossed it over to Gordon, who folded it carefully and put it in his pocket. There was an added spot of color in his cheeks, an added glow that was not fever. For an instant before they turned to go out their eyes met and in that instant each found something that made him lower his own glance quickly. For in that instant they quite suddenly and definitely hated each other.

II

Fifth Avenue and Forty-fourth Street swarmed with the noon crowd. The wealthy, happy sun glittered in transient gold through the thick windows of the smart shops, lighting upon mesh bags and purses and strings of pearls in gray velvet cases; upon gaudy feather fans of many colors; upon the laces and silks of expensive dresses; upon the bad paintings and the fine period furniture in the elaborate show rooms of interior decorators.

Working-girls, in pairs and groups and swarms, loitered by these windows, choosing their future boudoirs from some resplendent display which included even a man's silk pajamas laid domestically across the bed. They stood in front of the jewelry stores and picked out their engagement rings, and their wedding rings and their platinum wrist watches, and then drifted on to inspect the feather fans and opera cloaks; meanwhile digesting the sandwiches and sundaes they had eaten for lunch.

All through the crowd were men in uniform, sailors from the great fleet anchored in the Hudson, soldiers with divisional insignia from Massachusetts to California, wanting fearfully to be noticed, and finding the great city thoroughly fed up with soldiers unless they were nicely massed into pretty formations and uncomfortable under the weight of a pack and rifle.

Through this medley Dean and Gordon wandered; the former interested, made alert by the display of humanity at its frothiest and gaudiest; the latter reminded of how often he had been one of the crowd, tired, casually fed, overworked, and dissipated. To Dean the struggle was significant, young, cheerful; to Gordon it was dismal, meaningless, endless.

In the Yale Club they met a group of their former classmates who greeted the visiting Dean vociferously. Sitting in a semicircle of lounges and great chairs, they had a highball all around.

Gordon found the conversation tiresome and interminable. They lunched together *en masse*, warmed with liquor as the afternoon began. They were all going to the Gamma Psi dance that night – it promised to be the best party since the war.

'Edith Bradin's coming,' said some one to Gordon. 'Didn't she used to be an old flame of yours? Aren't you both from Harrisburg?'

'Yes.' He tried to change the subject. 'I see her brother occasionally. He's sort of a socialistic nut. Runs a paper or something here in New York.'

'Not like his gay sister, eh?' continued his eager informant. 'Well, she's coming to-night with a junior named Peter Himmel.'

Gordon was to meet Jewel Hudson at eight o'clock – he had promised to have some money for her. Several times he glanced nervously at his wrist watch. At four, to his relief, Dean rose and announced that he was going over to Rivers Brothers to buy some collars and ties. But as they left the Club another of the party joined them, to Gordon's great dismay. Dean was in a jovial mood now, happy, expectant of the evening's party, faintly hilarious. Over in Rivers' he chose a dozen neckties, selecting each one after long consultations with the other man. Did he think narrow ties were coming back? And wasn't it a shame that Rivers couldn't get any more Welsh Margotson collars? There never was a collar like the 'Covington.'

Gordon was in something of a panic. He wanted the money immediately. And he was now inspired also with a vague idea of attending the Gamma Psi dance. He wanted to see Edith – Edith whom he hadn't met since one romantic night at the Harrisburg Country Club just before he went to France. The affair had died, drowned in the turmoil of the war and quite forgotten in the arabesque of these three months, but a picture of her, poignant, debonnaire, immersed in her own inconsequential chatter, recurred to him unexpectedly and brought a hundred memories with it. It was Edith's face that he had cherished through college with a sort of detached yet affectionate admiration. He had loved to draw her – around his room had been a dozen sketches of her – playing golf, swimming – he could draw her pert, arresting profile with his eyes shut.

They left Rivers' at five-thirty and paused for a moment on the sidewalk.

'Well,' said Dean genially, 'I'm all set now. Think I'll go back to the hotel and get a shave, haircut, and massage.'

'Good enough,' said the other man, 'I think I'll join you.'

Gordon wondered if he was to be beaten after all. With difficulty he restrained himself from turning to the man and snarling out, 'Go on away, damn you!' In despair he suspected that perhaps Dean had spoken to him, was keeping him along in order to avoid a dispute about the money.

They went into the Biltmore – a Biltmore alive with girls – mostly from the West and South, the stellar débutantes of many cities gathered for the dance of a famous fraternity of a famous university. But to Gordon they were faces in a dream. He gathered together his forces for a last appeal, was about to come out with he knew not what, when Dean suddenly excused himself to the other man and taking Gordon's arm led him aside.

'Gordy,' he said quickly, 'I've thought the whole thing over carefully and I've decided that I can't lend you that money. I'd like to oblige you, but I don't feel I ought to – it'd put a crimp in me for a month.'

Gordon, watching him dully, wondered why he had never before noticed how much those upper teeth projected.

'—I'm mighty sorry, Gordon,' continued Dean, 'but that's the way it is.'

He took out his wallet and deliberately counted out seventy-five dollars in bills.

'Here,' he said, holding them out, 'here's seventy-five; that makes eighty all together. That's all the actual cash I have with me, besides what I'll actually spend on the trip.'

Gordon raised his clenched hand automatically, opened it as though it were a tongs he was holding, and clenched it again on the money.

'I'll see you at the dance,' continued Dean. 'I've got to get along to the barber shop.'

'So-long,' said Gordon in a strained and husky voice.

'So-long.'

Dean began to smile, but seemed to change his mind. He nodded briskly and disappeared.

But Gordon stood there, his handsome face awry with distress, the roll of bills clenched tightly in his hand. Then, blinded by sudden tears, he stumbled clumsily down the Biltmore steps.

III

About nine o'clock of the same night two human beings came out of a cheap restaurant in Sixth Avenue. They were ugly, ill-nourished, devoid of all except the very lowest form of intelligence, and without even that animal exuberance that in itself brings color into life; they were lately vermin-ridden, cold, and hungry in a dirty town of a strange land; they were poor, friendless; tossed as driftwood from their births, they would be tossed as driftwood to their deaths. They were dressed in the uniform of the United States Army, and on the shoulder of each was the insignia of a drafted division from New Jersey, landed three days before.

The taller of the two was named Carrol Key, a name hinting that in his veins, however thinly diluted by generations of degeneration, ran blood of some potentiality. But one could stare endlessly at the long, chinless face, the dull, watery eyes, and high check-bones, without finding a suggestion of either ancestral worth or native resourcefulness.

His companion was swart and bandy-legged, with rat-eyes and a much-broken hooked nose. His defiant air was obviously a pretense, a weapon of protection borrowed from that world of snarl and snap, of physical bluff and physical menace, in which he had always lived. His name was Gus Rose.

Leaving the café they sauntered down Sixth Avenue, wielding toothpicks with great gusto and complete detachment.

'Where to?' asked Rose, in a tone which implied that he would not be surprised if Key suggested the South Sea Islands.

'What you say we see if we can getta holda some liquor?' Prohibition was not yet. The ginger in the suggestion was caused by the law forbidding the selling of liquor to soldiers.

Rose agreed enthusiastically.

'I got an idea,' continued Key, after a moment's thought, 'I got a brother somewhere.'

'In New York?'

'Yeah. He's an old fella.' He meant that he was an elder brother. 'He's a waiter in a hash joint.'

'Maybe he can get us some.'

'I'll say he can!'

'B'lieve me, I'm goin' to get this darn uniform off me to-morra.'

Never get me in it again, neither. I'm goin' to get me some regular clothes.'

'Say, maybe I'm not.'

As their combined finances were something less than five dollars, this intention can be taken largely as a pleasant game of words, harmless and consoling. It seemed to please both of them, however, for they reinforced it with chuckling and mention of personages high in biblical circles, adding such further emphasis as 'Oh, boy!' 'You know!' and 'I'll say so!' repeated many times over.

The entire mental pabulum of these two men consisted of an offended nasal comment extended through the years upon the institution – army, business, or poor-house – which kept them alive, and toward their immediate superior in that institution. Until that very morning the institution had been the 'government' and the immediate superior had been the 'Cap'n' – from these two they had glided out and were now in the vaguely uncomfortable state before they should adopt their next bondage. They were uncertain, resentful, and somewhat ill at ease. This they hid by pretending an elaborate relief at being out of the army, and by assuring each other that military discipline should never again rule their stubborn, liberty-loving wills. Yet, as a matter of fact, they would have felt more at home in a prison than in this new-found and unquestionable freedom.

Suddenly Key increased his gait. Rose, looking up and following his glance, discovered a crowd that was collecting fifty yards down the street. Key chuckled and began to run in the direction of the crowd; Rose thereupon also chuckled and his short bandy legs twinkled beside the long, awkward strides of his companion.

Reaching the outskirts of the crowd they immediately became an indistinguishable part of it. It was composed of ragged civilians somewhat the worse for liquor, and of soldiers representing many divisions and many stages of sobriety, all clustered around a gesticulating little Jew with long black whiskers, who was waving his arms and delivering an excited but succinct harangue. Key and Rose, having wedged themselves into the approximate parquet, scrutinized him with acute suspicion, as his words penetrated their common consciousness.

'—What have you got outa the war?' he was crying fiercely. 'Look arounja, look arounja! Are you rich? Have you got a lot of money offered you? – no; you're lucky if you're alive and got both your legs; you're lucky if you came back an' find your wife ain't gone off with some other fella that had the money to buy himself out of the war! That's when you're lucky! Who got anything out of it except J. P. Morgan an' John D. Rockerfeller?'

At this point the little Jew's oration was interrupted by the hostile impact of a fist upon the point of his bearded chin and he toppled backward to a sprawl on the pavement.

'God damn Bolsheviki!' cried the big soldier-blacksmith who had delivered the blow. There was a rumble of approval, the crowd closed in nearer.

The Jew staggered to his feet, and immediately went down again before a half-dozen reaching-in fists. This time he stayed down, breathing heavily, blood oozing from his lip where it was cut within and without.

There was a riot of voices, and in a minute Rose and Key found themselves flowing with the jumbled crowd down Sixth Avenue under the leadership of a thin civilian in a slouch hat and the brawny soldier who had summarily ended the oration. The crowd had marvellously swollen to formidable proportions and a stream of more non-committal citizens followed it along the sidewalks lending their moral support by intermittent huzzas.

'Where we goin'?' yelled Key to the man nearest him.

His neighbor pointed up to the leader in the slouch hat.

'That guy knows where there's a lot of 'em! We're goin' to show 'em!'

'We're goin' to show 'em!' whispered Key delightedly to Rose, who repeated the phrase rapturously to a man on the other side.

Down Sixth Avenue swept the procession, joined here and there by soldiers and marines, and now and then by civilians, who came up with the inevitable cry that they were just out of the army themselves, as if presenting it as a card of admission to a newly formed Sporting and Amusement Club.

Then the procession swerved down a cross street and headed for Fifth Avenue and the word filtered here and there that they were bound for a Red meeting at Tolliver Hall.

'Where is it?'

The question went up the line and a moment later the answer floated back. Tolliver Hall was down on Tenth Street. There was a bunch of other sojers who was goin' to break it up and was down there now!

But Tenth Street had a faraway sound and at the word a general groan went up and a score of the procession dropped out. Among these were Rose and Key, who slowed down to a saunter and let the more enthusiastic sweep on by.

'I'd rather get some liquor,' said Key as they halted and made their way to the sidewalk amid cries of 'Shell hole!' and 'Quitters!'

'Does your brother work around here?' asked Rose, assuming the air of one passing from the superficial to the eternal.

'He oughta,' replied Key. 'I ain't seen him for a coupla years. I been out to Pennsylvania since. Maybe he don't work at night anyhow. It's right along here. He can get us some o'right if he ain't gone.'

They found the place after a few minutes' patrol of the street – a shoddy tablecloth restaurant between Fifth Avenue and Broadway. Here Key went inside to inquire for his brother George, while Rose waited on the sidewalk.

'He ain't here no more,' said Key emerging. 'He's a waiter up to Delmonico's.'

Rose nodded wisely, as if he'd expected as much. One should not be surprised at a capable man changing jobs occasionally. He knew a waiter once – there ensued a long conversation as they walked as to whether waiters made more in actual wages than in tips – it was decided that it depended on the social tone of the joint wherein the waiter labored. After having given each other vivid pictures of millionaires dining at Delmonico's and throwing away fifty-dollar bills after their first quart of champagne, both men thought privately of becoming waiters. In fact, Key's narrow brow was secreting a resolution to ask his brother to get him a job.

'A waiter can drink up all the champagne those fellas leave in bottles,' suggested Rose with some relish, and then added as an afterthought, 'Oh, boy!'

By the time they reached Delmonico's it was half past ten, and they were surprised to see a stream of taxis driving up to the door one after the other and emitting marvelous, hatless young ladies, each one attended by a stiff young gentleman in evening clothes.

'It's a party,' said Rose with some awe. 'Maybe we better not go in. He'll be busy.'

'No, he won't. He'll be o'right.'

After some hesitation they entered what appeared to them to be the least elaborate door and, indecision falling upon them immediately, stationed themselves nervously in an inconspicuous corner of the small dining-room in which they found themselves. They took off their caps and held them in their hands. A cloud of gloom fell upon them and both started when a door at one end of the room crashed open, emitting a comet-like waiter who streaked across the floor and vanished through another door on the other side.

There had been three of these lightning passages before the seekers mustered the acumen to hail a waiter. He turned, looked at them suspiciously, and then approached with soft, catlike steps, as if prepared at any moment to turn and flee.

'Say,' began Key, 'say, do you know my brother? He's a waiter here.'

'His name is Key,' annotated Rose.

Yes, the waiter knew Key. He was up-stairs, he thought. There was a big dance going on in the main ballroom. He'd tell him.

Ten minutes later George Key appeared and greeted his brother with the utmost suspicion; his first and most natural thought being that he was going to be asked for money.

George was tall and weak chinned, but there his resemblance to his brother ceased. The waiter's eyes were not dull, they were alert and twinkling, and his manner was suave, in-door, and faintly superior. They exchanged formalities. George was married and had three children. He seemed fairly interested, but not impressed by the news that Carrol had been abroad in the army. This disappointed Carrol.

'George,' said the younger brother, these amenities having been disposed of, 'we want to get some booze, and they won't sell us none. Can you get us some?'

George considered.

'Sure. Maybe I can. It may be half an hour, though.'

'All right,' agreed Carrol, 'we'll wait.'

At this Rose started to sit down in a convenient chair, but was hailed to his feet by the indignant George.

'Hey! Watch out, you! Can't sit down here! This room's all set for a twelve o'clock banquet.'

'I ain't goin' to hurt it,' said Rose resentfully. 'I been through the delouser.'

'Never mind,' said George sternly, 'if the head waiter seen me here talkin' he'd romp all over me.'

'Oh.'

The mention of the head waiter was full explanation to the other two; they fingered their overseas caps nervously and waited for a suggestion.

'I tell you,' said George, after a pause, 'I got a place you can wait; you just come here with me.'

They followed him out the far door, through a deserted pantry and up a pair of dark winding stairs, emerging finally into a small room chiefly furnished by piles of pails and stacks of scrubbing brushes, and illuminated by a single dim electric light. There he left them, after soliciting two dollars and agreeing to return in half an hour with a quart of whiskey.

'George is makin' money, I bet,' said Key gloomily as he seated himself on an inverted pail. 'I bet he's making fifty dollars a week.'

Rose nodded his head and spat.

'I bet he is, too.'

'What'd he say the dance was of?'

'A lot of college fellas. Yale College.'

They both nodded solemnly at each other.

'Wonder where that crowda sojers is now?'

'I don't know. I know that's too damn long to walk for me.'

'Me too. You don't catch me walkin' that far.'

Ten minutes later restlessness seized them.

'I'm goin' to see what's out here,' said Rose, stepping cautiously toward the other door.

It was a swinging door of green baize and he pushed it open a cautious inch.

'See anything?'

For answer Rose drew in his breath sharply.

'Doggone! Here's some liquor I'll say!'

'Liquor?'

Key joined Rose at the door, and looked eagerly.

'I'll tell the world that's liquor,' he said, after a moment of concentrated gazing.

It was a room about twice as large as the one they were in – and in it was prepared a radiant feast of spirits. There were long walls of alternating bottles set along two white covered tables; whiskey, gin, brandy, French and Italian vermouths, and orange juice, not to mention an array of syphons and two great empty punch bowls. The room was as yet uninhabited.

'It's for this dance they're just starting,' whispered Key; 'hear the violins playin'? Say, boy, I wouldn't mind havin' a dance.'

They closed the door softly and exchanged a glance of mutual comprehension. There was no need of feeling each other out.

'I'd like to get my hands on a coupla those bottles,' said Rose emphatically.

'Me too.'

'Do you suppose we'd get seen?'

Key considered.

'Maybe we better wait till they start drinkin' 'em. They got 'em all laid out now, and they know how many of them there are.'

They debated this point for several minutes. Rose was all for getting his hands on a bottle now and tucking it under his coat before any one came into the room. Key, however, advocated caution. He was afraid he might get his brother in trouble. If they waited till some of the bottles were opened it'd be all right to take one, and everybody'd think it was one of the college fellas.

While they were still engaged in argument George Key hurried through the room and, barely grunting at them, disappeared by way of the green baize door. A minute later they heard several corks pop, and then the sound of cracking ice and splashing liquid. George was mixing the punch.

The soldiers exchanged delighted grins.

'Oh, boy!' whispered Rose.

George reappeared.

'Just keep low, boys,' he said quickly. 'I'll have your stuff for you in five minutes.'

He disappeared through the door by which he had come.

As soon as his footsteps receded down the stairs, Rose, after a cautious look, darted into the room of delights and reappeared with a bottle in his hand.

'Here's what I say,' he said, as they sat radiantly digesting their first drink. 'We'll wait till he comes up, and we'll ask him if we can't just stay here and drink what he brings us – see. We'll tell him we haven't got any place to drink it – see. Then we can sneak in there whenever there ain't nobody in that there room and tuck a bottle under our coats. We'll have enough to last us a coupla days – see?'

'Sure,' agreed Rose enthusiastically. 'Oh, boy! And if we want to we can sell it to sojers any time we want to.'

They were silent for a moment thinking rosily of this idea. Then Key reached up and unhooked the collar of his O. D. coat.

'It's hot in here, ain't it?'

Rose agreed earnestly.

'Hot as hell.'

IV

She was still quite angry when she came out of the dressing-room and crossed the intervening parlor of politeness that opened onto the hall – angry not so much at the actual happening which was, after all, the merest commonplace of her social existence, but because it had occurred on this particular night. She had no quarrel with herself. She had acted with that correct mixture of dignity and reticent pity which she always employed. She had succinctly and deftly snubbed him.

It had happened when their taxi was leaving the Biltmore – hadn't gone half a block. He had lifted his right arm awkwardly – she was on his right side – and attempted to settle it snugly around the crimson fur-trimmed opera cloak she wore. This in itself had been a mistake. It was inevitably more graceful for a young man attempting to embrace a young lady of whose acquiescence he was not certain, to first put his far arm around her. It avoided that awkward movement of raising the near arm.

His second *faux pas* was unconscious. She had spent the afternoon at the hairdresser's; the idea of any calamity overtaking her hair was extremely repugnant – yet as Peter made his unfortunate attempt the point of his elbow had just faintly brushed it. That was his second *faux pas*. Two were quite enough.

He had begun to murmur. At the first murmur she had decided that he was nothing but a college boy – Edith was twenty-two, and anyhow, this dance, first of its kind since the war, was reminding her, with the accelerating rhythm of its associations, of something else – of another dance and another man, a man for whom her feelings had been little more than a sad-eyed, adolescent mooniness. Edith Bradin was falling in love with her recollection of Gordon Sterrett.

So she came out of the dressing-room at Delmonico's and stood for a second in the doorway looking over the shoulders of a black dress in front of her at the groups of Yale men who flitted like dignified black moths around the head of the stairs. From the room she had left drifted out the heavy fragrance left by the passage to and fro of many scented young beauties – rich perfumes and the fragile memory-laden dust of fragrant powders. This odor drifting out acquired the tang of cigarette smoke in the hall, and then settled sensuously down the stairs and permeated the ballroom where the Gamma Psi dance was to be held. It was an odor she knew well, exciting, stimulating, restlessly sweet – the odor of a fashionable dance.

She thought of her own appearance. Her bare arms and shoulders were powdered to a creamy white. She knew they looked very soft and would gleam like milk against the black backs that were to silhouette them tonight. The hairdressing had been a success; her reddish mass of hair was piled and crushed and creased to an arrogant marvel of mobile curves. Her lips were finely made of deep carmine; the irises of her eyes were delicate, breakable blue, like china eyes. She was a complete, infinitely delicate, quite perfect thing of beauty, flowing in an even line from a complex coiffure to two small slim feet.

She thought of what she would say to-night at this revel, faintly prestiged already by the sounds of high and low laughter and slippered footsteps, and movements of couples up and down the stairs. She would talk the language she had talked for many years – her line – made up of the current expressions, bits of journalese and college slang strung together into an intrinsic whole, careless, faintly provocative, delicately sentimental. She smiled faintly as she heard a girl sitting on the stairs near her say: 'You don't know the half of it, dearie!'

And as she smiled her anger melted for a moment, and closing her eyes she drew in a deep breath of pleasure. She dropped her arms to her side until they were faintly touching the sleek sheath that covered and suggested her figure. She had never felt her own softness so much nor so enjoyed the whiteness of her own arms.

'I smell sweet,' she said to herself simply, and then came another thought – 'I'm made for love.'

She liked the sound of this and thought it again; then in inevitable succession came her new-born riot of dreams about Gordon. The twist of her imagination which, two months before, had disclosed to her her unguessed desire to see him again, seemed now to have been leading up to this dance, this hour.

For all her sleek beauty, Edith was a grave, slow-thinking girl. There was a streak in her of that same desire to ponder, of that adolescent idealism that had turned her brother socialist and pacifist. Henry Bradin had left Cornell, where he had been an instructor in economics, and had come to New York to pour the latest cures for incurable evils into the columns of a radical weekly newspaper.

Edith, less fatuously, would have been content to cure Gordon Sterrett. There was a quality of weakness in Gordon that she wanted to take care of; there was a helplessness in him that she wanted to protect. And she wanted someone she had known a long while, someone who had loved her a long while. She was a little tired; she wanted to get married. Out of a pile of letters, half a dozen pictures and as many memories, and this weariness, she had decided that next time she saw Gordon their relations were going to be changed. She would say something that would change them. There was this evening. This was her evening. All evenings were her evenings.

Then her thoughts were interrupted by a solemn undergraduate with a hurt look and an air of strained formality who presented himself before her and bowed unusually low. It was the man she had come with, Peter Himmel. He was tall and humorous, with horned-rimmed glasses and an air of attractive whimsicality. She suddenly rather disliked him – probably because he had not succeeded in kissing her.

'Well,' she began, 'are you still furious at me?'

'Not at all.'

She stepped forward and took his arm.

'I'm sorry,' she said softly. 'I don't know why I snapped out that way. I'm in a bum humor to-night for some strange reason. I'm sorry.'

'S'all right,' he mumbled, 'don't mention it.'

He felt disagreeably embarrassed. Was she rubbing in the fact of his late failure?

'It was a mistake,' she continued, on the same consciously gentle key. 'We'll both forget it.' For this he hated her.

A few minutes later they drifted out on the floor while the dozen swaying, sighing members of the specially hired jazz orchestra informed the crowded ballroom that 'if a saxophone and me are left alone why then two is com-pan-ee!'

A man with a mustache cut in.

'Hello,' he began reprovingly. 'You don't remember me.'

'I can't just think of your name,' she said lightly – 'and I know you so well.'

'I met you up at —' His voice trailed disconsolately off as a man with very fair hair cut in. Edith murmured a conventional 'Thanks, loads – cut in later,' to the *inconnu*.

The very fair man insisted on shaking hands enthusiastically. She placed him as one of the numerous Jims of her acquaintance – last name a mystery. She remembered even that he had a peculiar rhythm in dancing and found as they started that she was right.

'Going to be here long?' he breathed confidentially.

She leaned back and looked up at him.

'Couple of weeks.'

'Where are you?'

'Biltmore. Call me up some day.'

'I mean it,' he assured her. 'I will. We'll go to tea.'

'So do I – Do.'

A dark man cut in with intense formality.

'You don't remember me, do you?' he said gravely.

'I should say I do. Your name's Harlan.'

'No-ope. Barlow.'

'Well, I knew there were two syllables anyway. You're the boy that played the ukulele so well up at Howard Marshall's house party.'

'I played – but not—'

A man with prominent teeth cut in. Edith inhaled a slight cloud of whiskey. She liked men to have had something to drink; they were so much more cheerful, and appreciative and complimentary – much easier to talk to.

'My name's Dean, Philip Dean,' he said cheerfully. 'You don't remember me, I know, but you used to come up to New Haven with a fellow I roomed with senior year, Gordon Sterrett.'

Edith looked up quickly.

'Yes, I went up with him twice – to the Pump and Slipper and the Junior prom.'

'You've seen him, of course,' said Dean carelessly. 'He's here tonight. I saw him just a minute ago.'

Edith started. Yet she had felt quite sure he would be here.

'Why, no, I haven't—'

A fat man with red hair cut in.

'Hello, Edith,' he began.

'Why – hello there—'

She slipped, stumbled lightly.

'I'm sorry, dear,' she murmured mechanically.

She had seen Gordon – Gordon very white and listless, leaning against the side of a doorway, smoking and looking into the ball-room. Edith could see that his face was thin and wan – that the hand he raised to his lips with a cigarette was trembling. They were dancing quite close to him now.

'—They invite so darn many extra fellas that you—' the short man was saying.

'Hello, Gordon,' called Edith over her partner's shoulder. Her heart was pounding wildly.

His large dark eyes were fixed on her. He took a step in her direction. Her partner turned her away – she heard his voice bleating—

'—but half the stags get lit and leave before long, so—'

Then a low tone at her side.

'May I, please?'

She was dancing suddenly with Gordon; one of his arms was around her; she felt it tighten spasmodically; felt his hand on her back with the fingers spread. Her hand holding the little lace hand-kerchief was crushed in his.

'Why Gordon,' she began breathlessly.

'Hello, Edith.'

She slipped again – was tossed forward by her recovery until her face touched the black cloth of his dinner coat. She loved him – she knew she loved him – then for a minute there was silence while a strange feeling of uneasiness crept over her. Something was wrong.

Of a sudden her heart wrenched, and turned over as she realized what it was. He was pitiful and wretched, a little drunk, and miserably tired.

'Oh—' she cried involuntarily.

His eyes looked down at her. She saw suddenly that they were blood-streaked and rolling uncontrollably.

'Gordon,' she murmured, 'we'll sit down; I want to sit down.'

They were nearly in mid-floor, but she had seen two men start toward her from opposite sides of the room, so she halted, seized Gordon's limp hand and led him bumping through the crowd, her mouth tight shut, her face a little pale under her rouge, her eyes trembling with tears.

She found a place high up on the soft-carpeted stairs, and he sat down heavily beside her.

'Well,' he began, staring at her unsteadily, 'I certainly am glad to see you, Edith.'

She looked at him without answering. The effect of this on her was immeasurable. For years she had seen men in various stages of intoxication, from uncles all the way down to chauffeurs, and her feelings had varied from amusement to disgust, but here for the first time she was seized with a new feeling – an unutterable horror.

'Gordon,' she said accusingly and almost crying, 'you look like the devil.'

He nodded. 'I've had trouble, Edith.'

'Trouble?'

'All sorts of trouble. Don't you say anything to the family, but I'm all gone to pieces. I'm a mess, Edith.'

His lower lip was sagging. He seemed scarcely to see her.

'Can't you – can't you,' she hesitated, 'can't you tell me about it, Gordon? You know I'm always interested in you.'

She bit her lip – she had intended to say something stronger, but found at the end that she couldn't bring it out.

Gordon shook his head dully. 'I can't tell you. You're a good woman. I can't tell a good woman the story.'

'Rot,' she said, defiantly. 'I think it's a perfect insult to call any one a good woman in that way. It's a slam. You've been drinking, Gordon.'

'Thanks.' He inclined his head gravely. 'Thanks for the information.'

'Why do you drink?'

'Because I'm so damn miserable.'

'Do you think drinking's going to make it any better?'

'What you doing – trying to reform me?'

'No; I'm trying to help you, Gordon. Can't you tell me about it?'

'I'm in an awful mess. Best thing you can do is to pretend not to know me.'

'Why, Gordon?'

'I'm sorry I cut in on you – its unfair to you. You're pure woman – and all that sort of thing. Here, I'll get some one else to dance with you.'

He rose clumsily to his feet, but she reached up and pulled him down beside her on the stairs.

'Here, Gordon. You're ridiculous. You're hurting me. You're acting like a – like a crazy man.'

'I admit it. I'm a little crazy. Something's wrong with me, Edith. There's something left me. It doesn't matter.'

'It does, tell me.'

'Just that. I was always queer – little bit different from other boys. All right in college, but now it's all wrong. Things have been snapping inside me for four months like little hooks on a dress, and it's about to come off when a few more hooks go. I'm very gradually going loony.'

He turned his eyes full on her and began to laugh, and she shrank away from him.

'What *is* the matter?'

'Just me,' he repeated. 'I'm going loony. This whole place is like a dream to me – this Delmonico's—'

As he talked she saw he had changed utterly. He wasn't at all light and gay and careless – a great lethargy and discouragement had come over him. Revulsion seized her, followed by a faint, surprising boredom. His voice seemed to come out of a great void.

'Edith,' he said, 'I used to think I was clever, talented, an artist. Now I know I'm nothing. Can't draw, Edith. Don't know why I'm telling you this.'

She nodded absently.

'I can't draw, I can't do anything. I'm poor as a church mouse.' He laughed, bitterly and rather too loud. 'I've become a damn beggar, a leech on my friends. I'm a failure. I'm poor as hell.'

Her distaste was growing. She barely nodded this time, waiting for her first possible cue to rise.

Suddenly Gordon's eyes filled with tears.

'Edith,' he said, turning to her with what was evidently a strong effort at self-control, 'I can't tell you what it means to me to know there's one person left who's interested in me.'

He reached out and patted her hand, and involuntarily she drew it away.

'It's mighty fine of you,' he repeated.

'Well,' she said slowly, looking him in the eye, 'any one's always glad to see an old friend – but I'm sorry to see you like this, Gordon.'

There was a pause while they looked at each other, and the momentary eagerness in his eyes wavered. She rose and stood looking at him, her face quite expressionless.

'Shall we dance?' she suggested, coolly.

Love is fragile – she was thinking – but perhaps the pieces are saved, the things that hovered on lips, that might have been said. The new love words, the tendernesses learned, are treasured up for the next lover.

V

Peter Himmel, escort to the lovely Edith, was unaccustomed to being snubbed; having been snubbed, he was hurt and embarrassed, and ashamed of himself. For a matter of two months he had been on special delivery terms with Edith Bradin, and knowing that the one excuse and explanation of the special delivery letter is its value in sentimental correspondence, he had believed himself quite sure of his ground. He searched in vain for any reason why she should have taken this attitude in the matter of a simple kiss.

Therefore when he was cut in on by the man with the mustache he went out into the hall and, making up a sentence, said it over to himself several times. Considerably deleted, this was it:

'Well, if any girl ever led a man on and then jolted him, she did – and she has no kick coming if I go out and get beautifully boiled.'

So he walked through the supper room into a small room adjoining it, which he had located earlier in the evening. It was a room in which there were several large bowls of punch flanked by many bottles. He took a seat beside the table which held the bottles.

At the second highball, boredom, disgust, the monotony of time, the turbidity of events, sank into a vague background before which glittering cobwebs formed. Things became reconciled to themselves, things lay quietly on their shelves; the troubles of the day arranged themselves in trim formation and at his curt wish of dismissal, marched off and disappeared. And with the departure of worry came brilliant, permeating symbolism. Edith became a flighty, negligible girl, not to be worried over; rather to be laughed at. She fitted like a figure of his own dream into the surface world forming about him. He himself became in a measure symbolic, a type of the continent bacchanal, the brilliant dreamer at play.

Then the symbolic mood faded and as he sipped his third highball his imagination yielded to the warm glow and he lapsed into a state similar to floating on his back in pleasant water. It was at this point that he noticed that a green baize door near him was open about two inches, and that through the aperture a pair of eyes were watching him intently.

'Hm,' murmured Peter calmly.

The green door closed – and then opened again – a bare half inch this time.

'Peek-a-boo,' murmured Peter.

The door remained stationary and then he became aware of a series of tense intermittent whispers.

'One guy.'

'What's he doin'?'

'He's sittin' lookin'.'

'He better beat it off. We gotta get another li'l' bottle.'

Peter listened while the words filtered into his consciousness.

'Now this,' he thought, 'is most remarkable.'

He was excited. He was jubilant. He felt that he had stumbled upon a mystery. Affecting an elaborate carelessness he arose and walked around the table – then, turning quickly, pulled open the green door, precipitating Private Rose into the room.

Peter bowed.

'How do you do?' he said.

Private Rose set one foot slightly in front of the other, poised for fight, flight, or compromise.

'How do you do?' repeated Peter politely.

'I'm o'right.'

'Can I offer you a drink?'

Private Rose looked at him searchingly, suspecting possible sarcasm.

'O'right,' he said finally.

Peter indicated a chair.

'Sit down.'

'I got a friend,' said Rose, 'I got a friend in there.' He pointed to the green door.

'By all means let's have him in.'

Peter crossed over, opened the door and welcomed in Private Key, very suspicious and uncertain and guilty. Chairs were found and the three took their seats around the punch bowl. Peter gave them each a highball and offered them a cigarette from his case. They accepted both with some diffidence.

'Now,' continued Peter easily, 'may I ask why you gentlemen prefer to lounge away your leisure hours in a room which is chiefly furnished, as far as I can see, with scrubbing brushes. And when the human race has progressed to the stage where seventeen thousand chairs are manufactured on every day except Sunday—' He paused. Rose and Key regarded him vacantly. 'Will you tell me,' went on Peter, 'why you choose to rest yourselves on articles intended for the transportation of water from one place to another?'

At this point Rose contributed a grunt to the conversation.

'And lastly,' finished Peter, 'will you tell me why, when you are in a building beautifully hung with enormous candelabra, you prefer to spend these evening hours under one anemic electric light?'

Rose looked at Key; Key looked at Rose. They laughed; they laughed uproariously; they found it was impossible to look at each other without laughing. But they were not laughing with this man – they were laughing at him. To them a man who talked after this fashion was either raving drunk or raving crazy.

'You are Yale men, I presume,' said Peter, finishing his highball and preparing another.

They laughed again.

'Na-ah.'

'So? I thought perhaps you might be members of that lowly section of the university known as the Sheffield Scientific School.'

'Na-ah.'

'Hm. Well, that's too bad. No doubt you are Harvard men, anxious to preserve your incognito in this this paradise of violet blue, as the newspapers say.'

'Na-ah,' said Key scornfully, 'we was just waitin' for somebody.'

'Ah,' exclaimed Peter, rising and filling their glasses, 'very interestin'. Had a date with a scrublady, eh?'

They both denied this indignantly.

'It's all right,' Peter reassured them, 'don't apologize. A scrublady's as good as any lady in the world. Kipling says "Any lady and Judy O'Grady under the skin."'

'Sure,' said Key, winking broadly at Rose.

'My case, for instance,' continued Peter, finishing his glass. 'I got a girl up here that's spoiled. Spoildest darn girl I ever saw. Refused to kiss me; no reason whatsoever. Led me on deliberately to think sure I want to kiss you and then plunk! Threw me over! What's the younger generation comin' to?'

'Say tha's hard luck,' said Key – 'that's awful hard luck.'

'Oh, boy!' said Rose.

'Have another?' said Peter.

'We got in a sort of fight for a while,' said Key after a pause, 'but it was too far away.'

'A fight? – tha's stuff!' said Peter, seating himself unsteadily. 'Fight 'em all! I was in the army.'

'This was with a Bolshevik fella.'

'Tha's stuff!' exclaimed Peter, enthusiastic. 'That's what I say! Kill the Bolshevik! Exterminate 'em!'

'We're Americuns,' said Rose, implying a sturdy, defiant patriotism.

'Sure,' said Peter. 'Greatest race in the world! We're all Americuns! Have another.'

They had another.

VI

At one o'clock a special orchestra, special even in a day of special orchestras, arrived at Delmonico's, and its members, seating themselves arrogantly around the piano, took up the burden of providing music for the Gamma Psi Fraternity. They were headed by a famous flute-player, distinguished throughout New York for his feat of standing on his head and shimmying with his shoulders while he played the latest jazz on his flute. During his performance the lights were extinguished except for the spotlight on the flute-player and another roving beam that threw flickering shadows and changing kaleidoscopic colors over the massed dancers.

Edith had danced herself into that tired, dreamy state habitual only with débutantes, a state equivalent to the glow of a noble soul after several long highballs. Her mind floated vaguely on the bosom of her music; her partners changed with the unreality of phantoms under the colorful shifting dusk, and to her present coma it seemed as if days had passed since the dance began. She had talked on many fragmentary subjects with many men. She had been kissed once and made love to six times. Earlier in the evening different under-graduates had danced with her, but now, like all the more popular girls there, she had her own entourage – that is, half a dozen gallants had singled her out or were alternating her charms with those of some other chosen beauty; they cut in on her in regular, inevitable succession.

Several times she had seen Gordon – he had been sitting a long time on the stairway with his palm to his head, his dull eyes fixed at an infinite speck on the floor before him, very depressed, he looked, and quite drunk – but Edith each time had averted her glance hurriedly. All that seemed long ago; her mind was passive now, her senses were lulled to trance-like sleep; only her feet danced and her voice talked on in hazy sentimental banter.

But Edith was not nearly so tired as to be incapable of moral indignation when Peter Himmel cut in on her, sublimely and happily drunk. She gasped and looked up at him.

'Why, *Peter!*'

'I'm a li'l' stewed, Edith.'

'Why, Peter, you're a *peach*, you are! Don't you think it's a bum way of doing – when you're with me?'

Then she smiled unwillingly, for he was looking at her with owlish sentimentality varied with a silly spasmodic smile.

'Darlin' Edith,' he began earnestly, 'you know I love you, don't you?'

'You tell it well.'

'I love you – and I merely wanted you to kiss me,' he added sadly.

His embarrassment, his shame, were both gone. She was a mos' beautiful girl in whole worl'. Mos' beautiful eyes, like stars above. He wanted to 'pologize – firs', for presuming try to kiss her; second, for drinking – but he'd been so discouraged 'cause he had thought she was mad at him—

The red-fat man cut in, and looking up at Edith smiled radiantly.

'Did you bring any one?' she asked.

No. The red-fat man was a stag.

'Well, would you mind – would it be an awful bother for you to – to take me home to-night?' (this extreme diffidence was a charming affectation on Edith's part – she knew that the red-fat man would immediately dissolve into a paroxysm of delight).

'Bother? Why, good Lord, I'd be darn glad to! You know I'd be darn glad to.'

'Thanks *loads!* You're awfully sweet.'

She glanced at her wrist-watch. It was half-past one. And, as she said 'half-past one' to herself, it floated vaguely into her mind that her brother had told her at luncheon that he worked in the office of his newspaper until after one-thirty every evening.

Edith turned suddenly to her current partner.

'What street is Delmonico's on, anyway?'

'Street? Oh, why Fifth Avenue, of course.'

'I mean, what cross street?'

'Why – let's see – it's on Forty-fourth Street.'

This verified what she had thought. Henry's office must be across the street and just around the corner, and it occurred to her immediately that she might slip over for a moment and surprise him, float in on him, a shimmering marvel in her new crimson opera cloak and 'cheer him up.' It was exactly the sort of thing Edith revelled in doing – an unconventional, jaunty thing. The idea reached out and gripped at her imagination – after an instant's hesitation she had decided.

'My hair is just about to tumble entirely down,' she said pleasantly to her partner; 'would you mind if I go and fix it?'

'Not at all.'

'You're a peach.'

A few minutes later, wrapped in her crimson opera cloak, she flitted down a side-stairs, her cheeks glowing with excitement at her little adventure. She ran by a couple who stood at the door – a weak-chinned waiter and an over-rouged young lady, in hot dispute – and opening the outer door stepped into the warm May night.

VII

The over-rouged young lady followed her with a brief, bitter glance – then turned again to the weak-chinned waiter and took up her argument.

'You better go up and tell him I'm here,' she said defiantly, 'or I'll go up myself.'

'No, you don't!' said George sternly.

The girl smiled sardonically.

'Oh, I don't, don't I? Well, let me tell you I know more college fellas and more of 'em know me, and are glad to take me out on a party, than you ever saw in your whole life.'

'Maybe so—'

'Maybe so,' she interrupted. 'Oh, it's all right for any of 'em like that one that just ran out – God knows where *she* went – it's all right for them that are asked here to come or go as they like – but when I want to see a friend they have some cheap, ham-slinging, bring-me-a-doughnut waiter to stand here and keep me out.'

'See here,' said the elder Key indignantly, 'I can't lose my job. Maybe this fella you're talkin' about doesn't want to see you.'

'Oh, he wants to see me all right.'

'Anyways, how could I find him in all that crowd?'

'Oh, he'll be there,' she asserted confidently. 'You just ask anybody for Gordon Sterrett and they'll point him out to you. They all know each other, those fellas.'

She produced a mesh bag, and taking out a dollar bill handed it to George.

'Here,' she said, 'here's a bribe. You find him and give him my message. You tell him if he isn't here in five minutes I'm coming up.'

George shook his head pessimistically, considered the question for a moment, wavered violently, and then withdrew.

In less than the allotted time Gordon came down-stairs. He was drunker than he had been earlier in the evening and in a different way. The liquor seemed to have hardened on him like a crust. He was heavy and lurching – almost incoherent when he talked.

''Lo, Jewel,' he said thickly. 'Came right away. Jewel, I couldn't get that money. Tried my best.'

'Money nothing!' she snapped. 'You haven't been near me for ten days. What's the matter?'

He shook his head slowly.

'Been very low, Jewel. Been sick.'

'Why didn't you tell me if you were sick. I don't care about the money that bad. I didn't start bothering you about it at all until you began neglecting me.'

Again he shook his head.

'Haven't been neglecting you. Not at all.'

'Haven't! You haven't been near me for three weeks, unless you been so drunk you didn't know what you were doing.'

'Been sick, Jewel,' he repeated, turning his eyes upon her wearily.

'You're well enough to come and play with your society friends here all right. You told me you'd meet me for dinner, and you said you'd have some money for me. You didn't even bother to ring me up.'

'I couldn't get any money.'

'Haven't I just been saying that doesn't matter? I wanted to see *you*, Gordon, but you seem to prefer your somebody else.'

He denied this bitterly.

'Then get your hat and come along,' she suggested.

Gordon hesitated – and she came suddenly close to him and slipped her arms around his neck.

'Come on with me, Gordon,' she said in a half whisper. 'We'll go over to Devineries' and have a drink, and then we can go up to my apartment.'

'I can't, Jewel,—'

'You can,' she said intensely.

'I'm sick as a dog!'

'Well, then, you oughtn't to stay here and dance.'

With a glance around him in which relief and despair were mingled, Gordon hesitated; then she suddenly pulled him to her and kissed him with soft, pulpy lips.

'All right,' he said heavily. 'I'll get my hat.'

VIII

When Edith came out into the clear blue of the May night she found the Avenue deserted. The windows of the big shops were dark; over their doors were drawn great iron masks until they were only shadowy tombs of the late day's splendor. Glancing down toward Forty-second Street she saw a commingled blur of lights from the all-night restaurants. Over on Sixth Avenue the elevated, a flare of fire, roared across the street between the glimmering parallels of light at the station and streaked along into the crisp dark. But at Forty-fourth Street it was very quiet.

Pulling her cloak close about her Edith darted across the Avenue. She started nervously as a solitary man passed her and said in a hoarse whisper – 'Where bound, kiddo?' She was reminded of a night in her childhood when she had walked around the block in her pajamas and a dog had howled at her from a mystery-big backyard.

In a minute she had reached her destination, a two-story, comparatively old building on Forty-fourth, in the upper window of which she thankfully detected a wisp of light. It was bright enough outside for her to make out the sign beside the window – the *New York Trumpet*. She stepped inside a dark hall and after a second saw the stairs in the corner.

Then she was in a long, low room furnished with many desks and hung on all sides with file copies of newspapers. There were only two occupants. They were sitting at different ends of the room, each wearing a green eye-shade and writing by a solitary desk light.

For a moment she stood uncertainly in the doorway, and then

both men turned around simultaneously and she recognized her brother.

'Why, Edith!' He rose quickly and approached her in surprise, removing his eye-shade. He was tall, lean, and dark, with black, piercing eyes under very thick glasses. They were far-away eyes that seemed always fixed just over the head of the person to whom he was talking.

He put his hands on her arms and kissed her cheek.

'What is it?' he repeated in some alarm.

'I was at a dance across at Delmonico's, Henry,' she said excitedly, 'and I couldn't resist tearing over to see you.'

'I'm glad you did.' His alertness gave way quickly to a habitual vagueness. 'You oughtn't to be out alone at night though, ought you?'

The man at the other end of the room had been looking at them curiously, but at Henry's beckoning gesture he approached. He was loosely fat with little twinkling eyes, and, having removed his collar and tie, he gave the impression of a Middle-Western farmer on a Sunday afternoon.

'This is my sister,' said Henry. 'She dropped in to see me.'

'How do you do?' said the fat man, smiling. 'My name's Bartholomew, Miss Bradin. I know your brother has forgotten it long ago.'

Edith laughed politely.

'Well,' he continued, 'not exactly gorgeous quarters we have here, are they?'

Edith looked around the room.

'They seem very nice,' she replied. 'Where do you keep the bombs?'

'The bombs?' repeated Bartholomew, laughing. 'That's pretty good – the bombs. Did you hear her, Henry? She wants to know where we keep the bombs. Say, that's pretty good.'

Edith swung herself onto a vacant desk and sat dangling her feet over the edge. Her brother took a seat beside her.

'Well,' he asked, absent-mindedly, 'how do you like New York this trip?'

'Not bad. I'll be over at the Biltmore with the Hoyts until Sunday. Can't you come to luncheon to-morrow?'

He thought a moment.

'I'm especially busy,' he objected, 'and I hate women in groups.'

'All right,' she agreed, unruffled. 'Let's you and me have luncheon together.'

'Very well.'

'I'll call for you at twelve.'

Bartholomew was obviously anxious to return to his desk, but apparently considered that it would be rude to leave without some parting pleasantry.

'Well' – he began awkwardly.

They both turned to him.

'Well, we – we had an exciting time earlier in the evening.'

The two men exchanged glances.

'You should have come earlier,' continued Bartholomew, somewhat encouraged. 'We had a regular vaudeville.'

'Did you really?'

'A serenade,' said Henry. 'A lot of soldiers gathered down there in the street and began to yell at the sign.'

'Why?' she demanded.

'Just a crowd,' said Henry, abstractedly. 'All crowds have to howl. They didn't have anybody with much initiative in the lead, or they'd probably have forced their way in here and smashed things up.'

'Yes,' said Bartholomew, turning again to Edith, 'you should have been here.'

He seemed to consider this a sufficient cue for withdrawal, for he turned abruptly and went back to his desk.

'Are the soldiers all set against the Socialists?' demanded Edith of her brother. 'I mean do they attack you violently and all that?'

Henry replaced his eye-shade and yawned.

'The human race has come a long way,' he said casually, 'but most of us are throw-backs; the soldiers don't know what they want, or what they hate, or what they like. They're used to acting in large bodies, and they seem to have to make demonstrations. So it happens to be against us. There've been riots all over the city to-night. It's May Day, you see.'

'Was the disturbance here pretty serious?'

'Not a bit,' he said scornfully. 'About twenty-five of them stopped in the street about nine o'clock, and began to bellow at the moon.'

'Oh' – She changed the subject. 'You're glad to see me, Henry?'

'Why, sure.'

'You don't seem to be.'

'I am.'

'I suppose you think I'm a – a waster. Sort of the World's Worst Butterfly.'

Henry laughed.

'Not at all. Have a good time while you're young. Why? Do I seem like the priggish and earnest youth?'

'No—' She paused, '—but somehow I began thinking how absolutely different the party I'm on is from – from all your purposes. It seems sort of – of incongruous, doesn't it? – me being at a party like that, and you over here working for a thing that'll make that sort of party impossible ever any more, if your ideas work.'

'I don't think of it that way. You're young, and you're acting just as you were brought up to act. Go ahead – have a good time.'

Her feet, which had been idly swinging, stopped and her voice dropped a note.

'I wish you'd – you'd come back to Harrisburg and have a good time. Do you feel sure that you're on the right track—'

'You're wearing beautiful stockings,' he interrupted. 'What on earth are they?'

'They're embroidered,' she replied, glancing down. 'Aren't they cunning?' She raised her skirts and uncovered slim, silk-sheathed calves. 'Or do you disapprove of silk stockings?'

He seemed slightly exasperated, bent his dark eyes on her piercingly.

'Are you trying to make me out as criticizing you in any way, Edith?'

'Not at all—'

She paused. Bartholomew had uttered a grunt. She turned and saw that he had left his desk and was standing at the window.

'What is it?' demanded Henry.

'People,' said Bartholomew, and then after an instant: 'Whole jam of them. They're coming from Sixth Avenue.'

'People?'

The fat man pressed his nose to the pane.

'Soldiers, by God!' he said emphatically. 'I had an idea they'd come back.'

Edith jumped to her feet, and running over joined Bartholomew at the window.

'There's a lot of them!' she cried excitedly. 'Come here, Henry!'

Henry readjusted his shade, but kept his seat.

'Hadn't we better turn out the lights?' suggested Bartholomew.

'No. They'll go away in a minute.'

'They're not,' said Edith, peering from the window. 'They're not even thinking of going away. There's more of them coming. Look – there's a whole crowd turning the corner of Sixth Avenue.'

By the yellow glow and blue shadows of the street lamp she could see that the sidewalk was crowded with men. They were mostly in uniform, some sober, some enthusiastically drunk, and over the whole swept an incoherent clamor and shouting.

Henry rose, and going to the window exposed himself as a long silhouette against the office lights. Immediately the shouting became a steady yell, and a rattling fusillade of small missiles, corners of tobacco plugs, cigarette-boxes, and even pennies beat against the window. The sounds of the racket now began floating up the stairs as the folding doors revolved.

'They're coming up!' cried Bartholomew.

Edith turned anxiously to Henry.

'They're coming up, Henry.'

From down-stairs in the lower hall their cries were now quite audible.

'—God damn Socialists!'

'Pro-Germans! Boche-lovers!'

'Second floor, front! Come on!'

'We'll get the sons—'

The next five-minutes passed in a dream. Edith was conscious that the clamor burst suddenly upon the three of them like a cloud of rain, that there was a thunder of many feet on the stairs, that Henry had seized her arm and drawn her back toward the rear of the office. Then the door opened and an overflow of men were forced into the room – not the leaders, but simply those who happened to be in front.

'Hello, Bo!'

'Up late, ain't you?'

'You an' your girl. Damn *you!*'

She noticed that two very drunken soldiers had been forced to the front, where they wobbled fatuously – one of them was short and dark, the other was tall and weak of chin.

Henry stepped forward and raised his hand.

'Friends!' he said.

The clamor faded into a momentary stillness, punctuated with mutterings.

'Friends!' he repeated, his far-away eyes fixed over the heads of the crowd, 'you're injuring no one but yourselves by breaking in here to-night. Do we look like rich men? Do we look like Germans? I ask you in all fairness—'

'Pipe down!'

'I'll say you do!'

'Say, who's your lady friend, buddy?'

A man in civilian clothes, who had been pawing over a table, suddenly held up a newspaper.

'Here it is!' he shouted. 'They wanted the Germans to win the war!'

A new overflow from the stairs was shouldered in and of a sudden the room was full of men all closing around the pale little group at the back. Edith saw that the tall soldier with the weak chin was still in front. The short dark one had disappeared.

She edged slightly backward, stood close to the open window, through which came a clear breath of cool night air.

Then the room was a riot. She realized that the soldiers were surging forward, glimpsed the fat man swinging a chair over his head – instantly the lights went out, and she felt the push of warm bodies under rough cloth, and her ears were full of shouting and trampling and hard breathing.

A figure flashed by her out of nowhere, tottered, was edged sideways, and of a sudden disappeared helplessly out through the open window with a frightened, fragmentary cry that died staccato on the bosom of the clamor. By the faint light streaming from the building backing on the area Edith had a quick impression that it had been the tall soldier with the weak chin.

Anger rose astonishingly in her. She swung her arms wildly, edged blindly toward the thickest of the scuffling. She heard grunts, curses, the muffled impact of fists.

'Henry!' she called frantically, 'Henry!'

Then, it was minutes later, she felt suddenly that there were other figures in the room. She heard a voice, deep, bullying, authoritative; she saw yellow rays of light sweeping here and there in the fracas. The cries became more scattered. The scuffling increased and then stopped.

Suddenly the lights were on and the room was full of policemen, clubbing left and right. The deep voice boomed out:

'Here now! Here now! Here now!'

And then.

'Quiet down and get out! Here now!'

The room seemed to empty like a wash-bowl. A policeman fast-grappled in the corner released his hold on his soldier antagonist and started him with a shove toward the door. The deep voice continued. Edith perceived now that it came from a bull-necked police captain standing near the door.

'Here now! This is no way! One of your own sojers got shoved out of the back window an' killed hisself!'

'Henry!' called Edith, 'Henry!'

She beat wildly with her fists on the back of the man in front of her; she brushed between two others; fought, shrieked, and beat her way to a very pale figure sitting on the floor close to a desk.

'Henry,' she cried passionately, 'what's the matter? What's the matter? Did they hurt you?'

His eyes were shut. He groaned and then looking up said disgustedly—

'They broke my leg. My God, the fools!'

'Here now!' called the police captain. 'Here now! Here now!'

IX

'Childs', Fifty-ninth Street,' at eight o'clock of any morning differs from its sisters by less than the width of their marble tables or the degree of polish on the frying-pans. You will see there a crowd of poor people with sleep in the corners of their eyes, trying to look straight before them at their food so as not to see the other poor people. But Childs', Fifty-ninth, four hours earlier is quite unlike any Childs' restaurant from Portland, Maine. Within its pale but sanitary walls one finds a noisy medley of chorus girls, college boys, débutantes, rakes, *filles de joie* – a not unrepresentative mixture of the gayest of Broadway, and even of Fifth Avenue.

In the early morning of May the second it was unusually full. Over the marble-topped tables were bent the excited faces of flappers whose fathers owned individual villages. They were eating buckwheat cakes and scrambled eggs with relish and gusto, an accomplishment that it would have been utterly impossible for them to repeat in the same place four hours later.

Almost the entire crowd were from the Gamma Psi dance at Delmonico's except for several chorus girls from a midnight revue who sat at a side table and wished they'd taken off a little more make-up after the show. Here and there a drab, mouse-like figure, desperately out of place, watched the butterflies with a weary, puzzled curiosity. But the drab figure was the exception. This was the morning after May Day, and celebration was still in the air.

Gus Rose, sober but a little dazed, must be classed as one of the drab figures. How he had got himself from Forty-fourth Street to Fifty-ninth Street after the riot was only a hazy half-memory. He had seen the body of Carrol Key put in an ambulance and driven off, and then he had started up town with two or three soldiers. Somewhere between Forty-fourth Street and Fifty-ninth Street the other soldiers had met some women and disappeared. Rose had wandered to Columbus Circle and chosen the gleaming lights of Childs' to minister to his craving for coffee and doughnuts. He walked in and sat down.

All around him floated airy, inconsequential chatter and high-pitched laughter. At first he failed to understand, but after a puzzled five minutes he realized that this was the aftermath of some gay party. Here and there a restless, hilarious young man wandered fraternally and familiarly between the tables, shaking hands indiscriminately and pausing occasionally for a facetious chat, while excited waiters, bearing cakes and eggs aloft, swore at him silently, and bumped him out of the way. To Rose, seated at the most inconspicuous and least crowded table, the whole scene was a colorful circus of beauty and riotous pleasure.

He became gradually aware, after a few moments, that the couple seated diagonally across from him, with their backs to the crowd, were not the least interesting pair in the room. The man was drunk. He wore a dinner coat with a dishevelled tie and shirt swollen by spillings of water and wine. His eyes, dim and bloodshot, roved unnaturally from side to side. His breath came short between his lips.

'He's been on a spree!' thought Rose.

The woman was almost if not quite sober. She was pretty, with dark eyes and feverish high color, and she kept her active eyes fixed on her companion with the alertness of a hawk. From time to time she would lean and whisper intently to him, and he would answer by inclining his head heavily or by a particularly ghoulish and repellent wink.

Rose scrutinized them dumbly for some minutes, until the woman gave him a quick, resentful look; then he shifted his gaze to two of the most conspicuously hilarious of the promenaders who were on a protracted circuit of the tables. To his surprise he recognized in one of them the young man by whom he had been so ludicrously entertained at Delmonico's. This started him thinking of Key with a vague sentimentality, not unmixed with awe. Key was dead. He had fallen thirty-five feet and split his skull like a cracked cocoanut.

'He was a darn good guy,' thought Rose mournfully. 'He was a darn good guy, o'right. That was awful hard luck about him.'

The two promenaders approached and started down between Rose's table and the next, addressing friends and strangers alike with jovial familiarity. Suddenly Rose saw the fair-haired one with the prominent teeth stop, look unsteadily at the man and girl opposite, and then begin to move his head disapprovingly from side to side.

The man with the blood-shot eyes looked up.

'Gordy,' said the promenader with the prominent teeth, 'Gordy.'

'Hello,' said the man with the stained shirt thickly.

Prominent Teeth shook his finger pessimistically at the pair, giving the woman a glance of aloof condemnation.

'What'd I tell you Gordy?'

Gordon stirred in his seat.

'Go to hell!' he said.

Dean continued to stand there shaking his finger. The woman began to get angry.

'You go way!' she cried fiercely. 'You're drunk, that's what you are!'

'So's he,' suggested Dean, staying the motion of his finger and pointing it at Gordon.

Peter Himmel ambled up, owlish now and oratorically inclined.

'Here now,' he began as if called upon to deal with some petty dispute between children. 'Wha's all trouble?'

'You take your friend away,' said Jewel tartly. 'He's bothering us.'

'What's at?'

'You heard me!' she said shrilly. 'I said to take your drunken friend away.'

Her rising voice rang out above the clatter of the restaurant and a waiter came hurrying up.

'You gotta be more quiet!'

'That fella's drunk,' she cried. 'He's insulting us.'

'Ah-ha, Gordy,' persisted the accused. 'What'd I tell you.' He turned to the waiter. 'Gordy an' I friends. Been tryin' help him, haven't I, Gordy?'

Gordy looked up.

'Help me? Hell, no!'

Jewel rose suddenly, and seizing Gordon's arm assisted him to his feet.

'Come on, Gordy!' she said, leaning toward him and speaking in a half whisper. 'Let's us get out of here. This fella's got a mean drunk on.'

Gordon allowed himself to be urged to his feet and started toward the door. Jewel turned for a second and addressed the provoker of their flight.

'I know all about *you*!' she said fiercely. 'Nice friend, you are, I'll say. He told me about you.'

Then she seized Gordon's arm, and together they made their way through the curious crowd, paid their check, and went out.

'You'll have to sit down,' said the waiter to Peter after they had gone.

'What's 'at? Sit down?'

'Yes – or get out.'

Peter turned to Dean.

'Come on,' he suggested. 'Let's beat up this waiter.'

'All right.'

They advanced toward him, their faces grown stern. The waiter retreated.

Peter suddenly reached over to a plate on the table beside him and picking up a handful of hash tossed it into the air. It descended as a languid parabola in snowflake effect on the heads of those near by.

'Hey! Ease up!'

'Put him out!'

'Sit down, Peter!'

'Cut out that stuff!'

Peter laughed and bowed.

'Thank you for your kind applause, ladies and gents. If some one will lend me some more hash and a tall hat we will go on with the act.'

The bouncer bustled up.

'You've gotta get out!' he said to Peter.

'Hell, no!'

'He's my friend!' put in Dean indignantly.

A crowd of waiters were gathering. 'Put him out!'

'Better go, Peter.'

There was a short struggle and the two were edged and pushed toward the door.

'I got a hat and a coat here!' cried Peter.

'Well, go get 'em and be spry about it!'

The bouncer released his hold on Peter, who, adopting a ludicrous air of extreme cunning, rushed immediately around to the other side of the table, where he burst into derisive laughter and thumbed his nose at the exasperated waiters.

'Think I just better wait a l'il longer,' he announced.

The chase began. Four waiters were sent around one way and four another. Dean caught hold of two of them by the coat, and another struggle took place before the pursuit of Peter could be resumed; he was finally pinioned after overturning a sugar-bowl and several cups of coffee. A fresh argument ensued at the cashier's desk, where Peter attempted to buy another dish of hash to take with him and throw at policemen.

But the commotion upon his exit proper was dwarfed by another phenomenon which drew admiring glances and a prolonged involuntary 'Oh-h-h!' from every person in the restaurant.

The great plate-glass front had turned to a deep creamy blue, the color of a Maxfield Parrish moonlight – a blue that seemed to press close upon the pane as if to crowd its way into the restaurant. Dawn had come up in Columbus Circle, magical, breathless dawn, silhouetting the great statue of the immortal Christopher, and mingling in a curious and uncanny manner with the fading yellow electric light inside.

X

Mr In and Mr Out are not listed by the census-taker. You will search for them in vain through the social register or the births, marriages, and deaths, or the grocer's credit list. Oblivion has swallowed them and the testimony that they ever existed at all is vague and shadowy, and inadmissible in a court of law. Yet I have it upon the best authority that for a brief space Mr In and Mr Out lived, breathed, answered to their names and radiated vivid personalities of their own.

During the brief span of their lives they walked in their native garments down the great highway of a great nation; were laughed at, sworn at, chased, and fled from. Then they passed and were heard of no more.

They were already taking form dimly, when a taxicab with the top open breezed down Broadway in the faintest glimmer of May dawn. In this car sat the souls of Mr In and Mr Out discussing with amazement the blue light that had so precipitately colored the sky behind the statue of Christopher Columbus, discussing with bewilderment the old, gray faces of the early risers which skimmed palely along the street like blown bits of paper on a gray lake. They were agreed on all things, from the absurdity of the bouncer in Childs' to the absurdity of the business of life. They were dizzy with the extreme maudlin happiness that the morning had awakened in their glowing souls. Indeed, so fresh and vigorous was their pleasure in living that they felt it should be expressed by loud cries.

'Ye-ow-ow!' hooted Peter, making a megaphone with his hands – and Dean joined in with a call that, though equally significant and symbolic, derived its resonance from its very inarticulateness.

'Yo-ho! Yea! Yoho! Yo-buba!'

Fifty-third Street was a bus with a dark, bobbed-hair beauty atop; Fifty-second was a street cleaner who dodged, escaped, and sent up a yell of, 'Look where you're aimin'!' in a pained and grieved voice. At Fiftieth Street a group of men on a very white sidewalk in front of a very white building turned to stare after them, and shouted:

'Some party, boys!'

At Forty-ninth Street Peter turned to Dean. 'Beautiful morning,' he said gravely, squinting up his owlish eyes.

'Probably is.'

'Go get some breakfast, hey?'

Dean agreed – with additions.

'Breakfast and liquor.'

'Breakfast and liquor,' repeated Peter, and they looked at each other, nodding. 'That's logical.'

Then they both burst into loud laughter.

'Breakfast and liquor! Oh, gosh!'

'No such thing,' announced Peter.

'Don't serve it? Ne'mind. We force 'em serve it. Bring pressure bear.'

'Bring logic bear.'

The taxi cut suddenly off Broadway, sailed along a cross street, and stopped in front of a heavy tomb-like building in Fifth Avenue.

'What's idea?'

The taxi-driver informed them that this was Delmonico's.

This was somewhat puzzling. They were forced to devote several minutes to intense concentration, for if such an order had been given there must have been a reason for it.

'Somep'm 'bouta coat,' suggested the taxi-man.

That was it. Peter's overcoat and hat. He had left them at Delmonico's. Having decided this, they disembarked from the taxi and strolled toward the entrance arm in arm.

'Hey!' said the taxi-driver.

'Huh?'

'You better pay me.'

They shook their heads in shocked negation.

'Later, not now – we give orders, you wait.'

The taxi-driver objected; he wanted his money now. With the

scornful condescension of men exercising tremendous self-control they paid him.

Inside Peter groped in vain through a dim, deserted check-room in search of his coat and derby.

'Gone, I guess. Somebody stole it.'

'Some Sheff student.'

'All probability.'

'Never mind,' said Dean, nobly. 'I'll leave mine here too – then we'll both be dressed the same.'

He removed his overcoat and hat and was hanging them up when his roving glance was caught and held magnetically by two large squares of cardboard tacked to the two coat-room doors. The one on the left-hand door bore the word 'In' in big black letters, and the one on the right-hand door flaunted the equally emphatic word 'Out.'

'Look!' he exclaimed happily—

Peter's eyes followed his pointing finger.

'What?'

'Look at the signs. Let's take 'em.'

'Good idea.'

'Probably pair very rare an' valuable signs. Probably come in handy.'

Peter removed the left-hand sign from the door and endeavoured to conceal it about his person. The sign being of considerable proportions, this was a matter of some difficulty. An idea flung itself at him, and with an air of dignified mystery he turned his back. After an instant he wheeled dramatically around, and stretching out his arms displayed himself to the admiring Dean. He had inserted the sign in his vest, completely covering his shirt front. In effect, the word 'In' had been painted upon his shirt in large black letters.

'Yoho!' cheered Dean. 'Mister In.'

He inserted his own sign in like manner.

'Mister Out!' he announced triumphantly. 'Mr In meet Mr Out.'

They advanced and shook hands. Again laughter overcame them and they rocked in a shaken spasm of mirth.

'Yoho!'

'We probably get a flock of breakfast.'

'We'll go – go to the Commodore.'

Arm in arm they sallied out the door, and turning east in Forty-fourth Street set out for the Commodore.

As they came out a short dark soldier, very pale and tired, who had been wandering listlessly along the sidewalk, turned to look at them.

He started over as though to address them, but as they immediately bent on him glances of withering unrecognition, he waited until they had started unsteadily down the street, and then followed at about forty paces, chuckling to himself and saying 'Oh, boy!' over and over under his breath, in delighted, anticipatory tones.

Mr In and Mr Out were meanwhile exchanging pleasantries concerning their future plans.

'We want liquor; we want breakfast. Neither without the other. One and indivisible.'

'We want both 'em!'

'Both 'em!'

It was quite light now, and passers-by began to bend curious eyes on the pair. Obviously they were engaged in a discussion, which afforded each of them intense amusement, for occasionally a fit of laughter would seize upon them so violently that, still with their arms interlocked, they would bend nearly double.

Reaching the Commodore, they exchanged a few spicy epigrams with the sleepy-eyed doorman, navigated the revolving door with some difficulty, and then made their way through a thinly populated but startled lobby to the dining-room, where a puzzled waiter showed them an obscure table in a corner. They studied the bill of fare helplessly, telling over the items to each other in puzzled mumbles.

'Don't see any liquor here,' said Peter reproachfully.

The waiter became audible but unintelligible.

'Repeat,' continued Peter, with patient tolerance, 'that there seems to be unexplained and quite distasteful lack of liquor upon bill of fare.'

'Here!' said Dean confidently, 'let me handle him.' He turned to the waiter – 'Bring us – bring us—' He scanned the bill of fare anxiously. 'Bring us a quart of champagne and a – a – probably ham sandwich.'

The waiter looked doubtful.

'Bring it!' roared Mr In and Mr Out in chorus.

The waiter coughed and disappeared. There was a short wait during which they were subjected without their knowledge to a careful scrutiny by the head-waiter. Then the champagne arrived, and at the sight of it Mr In and Mr Out became jubilant.

'Imagine their objecting to us having champagne for breakfast – jus' imagine.'

They both concentrated upon the vision of such an awesome possibility, but the feat was too much for them. It was impossible for their joint imaginations to conjure up a world where any one might object to any one else having champagne for breakfast. The waiter drew the cork with an enormous *pop* – and their glasses immediately foamed with pale yellow froth.

'Here's health, Mr In.'

'Here's same to you, Mr Out.'

The waiter withdrew; the minutes passed; the champagne became low in the bottle.

'It's – it's mortifying,' said Dean suddenly.

'Wha's mortifying?'

'The idea their objecting us having champagne breakfast.'

'Mortifying?' Peter considered. 'Yes, tha's word – mortifying.'

Again they collapsed into laughter, howled, swayed, rocked back and forth in their chairs, repeating the word 'mortifying' over and over to each other – each repetition seeming to make it only more brilliantly absurd.

After a few more gorgeous minutes they decided on another quart. Their anxious waiter consulted his immediate superior, and this discreet person gave implicit instructions that no more champagne should be served. Their check was brought.

Five minutes later, arm in arm, they left the Commodore and made their way through a curious, staring crowd along Forty-second

Street, and up Vanderbilt Avenue to the Biltmore. There, with sudden cunning, they rose to the occasion and traversed the lobby, walking fast and standing unnaturally erect.

Once in the dining-room they repeated their performance. They were torn between intermittent convulsive laughter and sudden spasmodic discussions of politics, college, and the sunny state of their dispositions. Their watches told them that it was now nine o'clock, and a dim idea was born in them that they were on a memorable party, something that they would remember always. They lingered over the second bottle. Either of them had only to mention the word 'mortifying' to send them both into riotous gasps. The dining-room was whirring and shifting now; a curious lightness permeated and rarefied the heavy air.

They paid their check and walked out into the lobby.

It was at this moment that the exterior doors revolved for the thousandth time that morning, and admitted into the lobby a very pale young beauty with dark circles under her eyes, attired in a much-rumpled evening dress. She was accompanied by a plain stout man, obviously not an appropriate escort.

At the top of the stairs this couple encountered Mr In and Mr Out.

'Edith,' began Mr In, stepping toward her hilariously and making a sweeping bow, 'darling, good morning.'

The stout man glanced questioningly at Edith, as if merely asking her permission to throw this man summarily out of the way.

''Scuse familiarity,' added Peter, as an afterthought. 'Edith, good-morning.'

He seized Dean's elbow and impelled him into the foreground.

'Meet Mr In, Edith, my bes' frien'. Inseparable. Mr In and Mr Out.'

Mr Out advanced and bowed; in fact, he advanced so far and bowed so low that he tipped slightly forward and only kept his balance by placing a hand lightly on Edith's shoulder.

'I'm Mr Out, Edith,' he mumbled pleasantly, 'S'misterin Misterout.'

''Smisterinanout,' said Peter proudly.

But Edith stared straight by them, her eyes fixed on some infinite speck in the gallery above her. She nodded slightly to the stout man, who advanced bull-like and with a sturdy brisk gesture pushed Mr In and Mr Out to either side. Through this alley he and Edith walked.

But ten paces farther on Edith stopped again – stopped and pointed to a short, dark soldier who was eying the crowd in general, and the tableau of Mr In and Mr Out in particular, with a sort of puzzled, spell-bound awe.

'There,' cried Edith. 'See there!'

Her voice rose, became somewhat shrill. Her pointing finger shook slightly.

'There's the soldier who broke my brother's leg.'

There were a dozen exclamations; a man in a cutaway coat left his place near the desk and advanced alertly; the stout person made a sort of lightning-like spring toward the short, dark soldier, and then the lobby closed around the little group and blotted them from the sight of Mr In and Mr Out.

But to Mr In and Mr Out this event was merely a particolored iridescent segment of a whirring, spinning world.

They heard loud voices; they saw the stout man spring; the picture suddenly blurred.

Then they were in an elevator bound skyward.

'What floor, please?' said the elevator man.

'Any floor,' said Mr In.

'Top floor,' said Mr Out.

'This is the top floor,' said the elevator man.

'Have another floor put on,' said Mr Out.

'Higher,' said Mr In.

'Heaven,' said Mr Out.

XI

In a bedroom of a small hotel just off Sixth Avenue Gordon Sterrett awoke with a pain in the back of his head and a sick throbbing in all his veins. He looked at the dusky gray shadows in the corners of the room and at a raw place on a large leather chair in the corner where it had long been in use. He saw clothes, dishevelled, rumpled clothes on the floor and he smelt stale cigarette smoke and stale liquor. The windows were tight shut. Outside the bright sunlight had thrown a dust-filled beam across the sill – a beam broken by the head of the wide wooden bed in which he had slept. He lay very quiet – comatose, drugged, his eyes wide, his mind clicking wildly like an unoiled machine.

It must have been thirty seconds after he perceived the sunbeam with the dust on it and the rip on the large leather chair that he had the sense of life close beside him, and it was another thirty seconds after that before he realized that he was irrevocably married to Jewel Hudson.

He went out half an hour later and bought a revolver at a sporting goods store. Then he took a taxi to the room where he had been living on East Twenty-seventh Street, and, leaning across the table that held his drawing materials, fired a cartridge into his head just behind the temple.

'O Russet Witch!'

I

Merlin Grainger was employed by the Moonlight Quill Bookshop, which you may have visited, just around the corner from the Ritz-Carlton on Forty-seventh Street. The Moonlight Quill is, or rather was, a very romantic little store, considered radical and admitted dark. It was spotted interiorly with red and orange posters of breathless exotic intent, and lit no less by the shiny reflecting bindings of special editions than by the great squat lamp of crimson satin that, lighted through all the day, swung overhead. It was truly a mellow bookshop. The words 'Moonlight Quill' were worked over the door in a sort of serpentine embroidery. The windows seemed always full of something that had passed the literary censors with little to spare; volumes with covers of deep orange which offered their titles on little white paper squares. And over all there was the smell of the musk, which the clever, inscrutable Mr Moonlight Quill ordered to be sprinkled about – the smell half of a curiosity shop in Dickens' London and half of a coffee-house on the warm shores of the Bosphorus.

From nine until five-thirty Merlin Grainger asked bored old ladies in black and young men with dark circles under their eyes if they 'cared for this fellow' or were interested in first editions. Did they buy novels with Arabs on the cover, or books which gave Shakespeare's newest sonnets as dictated psychically to Miss Sutton of South Dakota? he sniffed. As a matter of fact, his own taste ran to these latter, but as an employee at the Moonlight Quill he assumed for the working day the attitude of a disillusioned connoisseur.

After he had crawled over the window display to pull down the front shade at five-thirty every afternoon, and said good-bye to the mysterious Mr Moonlight Quill and the lady clerk, Miss McCracken, and the lady stenographer, Miss Masters, he went home to the girl, Caroline. He did not eat supper with Caroline. It is unbelievable that Caroline would have considered eating off his bureau with the collar buttons dangerously near the cottage cheese, and the ends of Merlin's necktie just missing his glass of milk – he had never asked her to eat with him. He ate alone. He went into Braegdort's delicatessen on Sixth Avenue and bought a box of crackers, a tube of anchovy paste, and some oranges, or else a little jar of sausages and some potato salad and a bottled soft drink, and with these in a brown package he went to his room at Fifty-something West Fifty-eighth Street and ate his supper and saw Caroline.

Caroline was a very young and gay person who lived with some older lady and was possibly nineteen. She was like a ghost in that she never existed until evening. She sprang into life when the lights went on in her apartment at about six, and she disappeared, at the latest, about midnight. Her apartment was a nice one, in a nice building with a white stone front, opposite the south side of Central Park. The back of her apartment faced the single window of the single room occupied by the single Mr Grainger.

He called her Caroline because there was a picture that looked like her on the jacket of a book of that name down at the Moonlight Quill.

Now, Merlin Grainger was a thin young man of twenty-five, with dark hair and no mustache or beard or anything like that, but Caroline was dazzling and light, with a shimmering morass of russet waves to take the place of hair, and the sort of features that remind you of kisses – the sort of features you thought belonged to your first love, but know, when you come across an old picture, didn't. She dressed in pink or blue usually, but of late she had sometimes put on a slender black gown that was evidently her especial pride, for whenever she wore it she would stand regarding a certain place on the wall, which Merlin thought must be a mirror. She sat usually in the profile chair near the window, but sometimes honored the *chaise longue* by the lamp, and often she leaned 'way back and smoked a cigarette with posturings of her arms and hands that Merlin considered very graceful.

At another time she had come to the window and stood in it magnificently, and looked out because the moon had lost its way and was dripping the strangest and most transforming brilliance into the areaway between, turning the motif of ash-cans and clothes-lines into a vivid impressionism of silver casks and gigantic gossamer cobwebs. Merlin was sitting in plain sight, eating cottage cheese with sugar and milk on it; and so quickly did he reach out for the window cord that he tipped the cottage cheese into his lap with his free hand – and the milk was cold and the sugar made spots on his trousers, and he was sure that she had seen him after all.

Sometimes there were callers – men in dinner coats, who stood and bowed, hat in hand and coat on arm, as they talked to Caroline; then bowed some more and followed her out of the light, obviously bound for a play or for a dance. Other young men came and sat and smoked cigarettes, and seemed trying to tell Caroline something – she sitting either in the profile chair and watching them with eager intentness or else in the *chaise longue* by the lamp, looking very lovely and youthfully inscrutable indeed.

Merlin enjoyed these calls. Of some of the men he approved. Others won only his grudging toleration, one or two he loathed – especially the most frequent caller, a man with black hair and a black goatee and a pitch-dark soul, who seemed to Merlin vaguely familiar, but whom he was never quite able to recognize.

Now, Merlin's whole life was not 'bound up with this romance he had constructed'; it was not 'the happiest hour of his day.' He never arrived in time to rescue Caroline from 'clutches'; nor did he even marry her. A much stranger thing happened than any of these, and it is this strange thing that will presently be set down here. It began one October afternoon when she walked briskly into the mellow interior of the Moonlight Quill.

It was a dark afternoon, threatening rain and the end of the world, and done in that particularly gloomy gray in which only

New York afternoons indulge. A breeze was crying down the streets, whisking along battered newspapers and pieces of things, and little lights were pricking out all the windows – it was so desolate that one was sorry for the tops of sky-scrapers lost up there in the dark green and gray heaven, and felt that now surely the farce was to close, and presently all the buildings would collapse like card houses, and pile up in a dusty, sardonic heap upon all the millions who presumed to wind in and out of them.

At least these were the sort of musings that lay heavily upon the soul of Merlin Grainger, as he stood by the window putting a dozen books back in a row, after a cyclonic visit by a lady with ermine trimmings. He looked out of the window full of the most distressing thoughts – of the early novels of H. G. Wells, of the book of Genesis, of how Thomas Edison had said that in thirty years there would be no dwelling-houses upon the island, but only a vast and turbulent bazaar; and then he set the last book right side up, turned – and Caroline walked coolly into the shop.

She was dressed in a jaunty but conventional walking costume – he remembered this when he thought about it later. Her skirt was plaid, pleated like a concertina; her jacket was a soft but brisk tan; her shoes and spats were brown and her hat, small and trim, completed her like the top of a very expensive and beautifully filled candy box.

Merlin, breathless and startled, advanced nervously toward her.

'Good-afternoon—' he said, and then stopped – why, he did not know, except that it came to him that something very portentous in his life was about to occur, and that it would need no furbishing but silence, and the proper amount of expectant attention. And in that minute before the thing began to happen he had the sense of a breathless second hanging suspended in time: he saw through the glass partition that bounded off the little office the malevolent conical head of his employer, Mr Moonlight Quill, bent over his correspondence. He saw Miss McCracken and Miss Masters as two patches of hair drooping over piles of paper; he saw the crimson lamp overhead, and noticed with a touch of pleasure how really pleasant and romantic it made the book-store seem.

Then the thing happened, or rather it began to happen. Caroline picked up a volume of poems lying loose upon a pile, fingered it absently with her slender white hand, and suddenly, with an easy gesture, tossed it upward toward the ceiling, where it disappeared in the crimson lamp and lodged there, seen through the illuminated silk as a dark, bulging rectangle. This pleased her – she broke into young, contagious laughter, in which Merlin found himself presently joining.

'It stayed up!' she cried merrily. 'It stayed up, didn't it?' To both of them this seemed the height of brilliant absurdity. Their laughter mingled, filled the bookshop, and Merlin was glad to find that her voice was rich and full of sorcery.

'Try another,' he found himself suggesting – 'try a red one.'

At this her laughter increased, and she had to rest her hands upon the stack to steady herself.

'Try another,' she managed to articulate between spasms of mirth. 'Oh, golly, try another!'

'Try two.'

'Yes, try two. Oh, I'll choke if I don't stop laughing. Here it goes.'

Suiting her action to the word, she picked up a red book and sent it in a gentle hyperbola toward the ceiling, where it sank into the lamp beside the first. It was a few minutes before either of them could do more than rock back and forth in helpless glee; but then by mutual agreement they took up the sport anew, this time in unison. Merlin seized a large, specially bound French classic and whirled it upward. Applauding his own accuracy, he took a best-seller in one hand and a book on barnacles in the other, and waited breathlessly while she made her shot. Then the business waxed fast and furious – sometimes they alternated, and, watching, he found how supple she was in every movement; sometimes one of them made shot after shot picking up the nearest book, sending it off, merely taking time to follow it with a glance before reaching for another. Within three minutes they had cleared a little place on the table, and the lamp of crimson satin was so bulging with books that it was near breaking.

'Silly game, basket-ball,' she cried scornfully as a book left her hand. 'High-school girls play it in hideous bloomers.'

'Idiotic,' he agreed.

She paused in the act of tossing a book, and replaced it suddenly in its position on the table.

'I think we've got room to sit down now,' she said gravely.

They had; they had cleared an ample space for two. With a faint touch of nervousness Merlin glanced toward Mr Moonlight Quill's glass partition, but the three heads were still bent earnestly over their work, and it was evident that they had not seen what had gone on in the shop. So when Caroline put her hands on the table and hoisted herself up Merlin calmly imitated her, and they sat side by side looking very earnestly at each other.

'I had to see you,' she began, with a rather pathetic expression in her brown eyes.

'I know.'

'It was that last time,' she continued, her voice trembling a little, though she tried to keep it steady. 'I was frightened. I don't like you to eat off the dresser. I'm so afraid you'll – you'll swallow a collar button.'

'I did once – almost,' he confessed reluctantly, 'but it's not so easy, you know. I mean you can swallow the flat part easy enough or else the other part – that is, separately – but for a whole collar button you'd have to have a specially made throat.' He was astonishing himself by the debonnaire appropriateness of his remarks. Words seemed for the first time in his life to run at him shrieking to be used, gathering themselves into carefully arranged squads and platoons, and being presented to him by punctilious adjutants of paragraphs.

'That's what scared me,' she said. 'I knew you had to have a specially made throat – and I knew, at least I felt sure, that you didn't have one.'

He nodded frankly.

'I haven't. It costs money to have one – more money unfortunately than I possess.'

He felt no shame in saying this – rather a delight in making the admission – he knew that nothing he could say or do would be beyond her comprehension; least of all his poverty, and the practical impossibility of ever extricating himself from it.

Caroline looked down at her wrist watch, and with a little cry slid from the table to her feet.

'It's after five,' she cried. 'I didn't realize. I have to be at the Ritz at five-thirty. Let's hurry and get this done. I've got a bet on it.'

With one accord they set to work. Caroline began the matter by seizing a book on insects and sending it whizzing, and finally crashing through the glass partition that housed Mr Moonlight Quill. The proprietor glanced up with a wild look, brushed a few pieces of glass from his desk, and went on with his letters. Miss McCracken gave no sign of having heard – only Miss Masters started and gave a little frightened scream before she bent to her task again.

But to Merlin and Caroline it didn't matter. In a perfect orgy of energy they were hurling book after book in all directions, until sometimes three or four were in the air at once, smashing against shelves, cracking the glass of pictures on the walls, falling in bruised and torn heaps upon the floor. It was fortunate that no customers happened to come in, for it is certain they would never have come in again – the noise was too tremendous, a noise of smashing and ripping and tearing, mixed now and then with the tinkling of glass, the quick breathing of the two throwers, and the intermittent outbursts of laughter to which both of them periodically surrendered.

At five-thirty Caroline tossed a last book at the lamp, and so gave the final impetus to the load it carried. The weakened silk tore and dropped its cargo in one vast splattering of white and color to the already littered floor. Then with a sigh of relief she turned to Merlin and held out her hand.

'Good-by,' she said simply.

'Are you going?' He knew she was. His question was simply a lingering wile to detain her and extract for another moment that dazzling essence of light he drew from her presence, to continue his enormous satisfaction in her features, which were like kisses and, he thought, like the features of a girl he had known back in 1910. For a minute he pressed the softness of her hand – then she smiled and withdrew it and, before he could spring to open the door, she had done it herself and was gone out into the turbid and ominous twilight that brooded narrowly over Forty-seventh Street.

I would like to tell you how Merlin, having seen how beauty regards the wisdom of the years, walked into the little partition of Mr Moonlight Quill and gave up his job then and there; thence issuing out into the street a much finer and nobler and increasingly ironic man. But the truth is much more commonplace. Merlin Grainger stood up and surveyed the wreck of the bookshop, the ruined volumes, the torn silk remnants of the once beautiful crimson lamp, the crystalline sprinkling of broken glass which lay in iridescent dust over the whole interior – and then he went to a corner where a broom was kept and began cleaning up and rearranging and, as far as he was able, restoring the shop to its former condition. He found that, though some few of the books were uninjured, most of them had suffered in varying extents. The backs were off some, the pages were torn from others, still others were just slightly cracked in the front, which, as all careless book returners know, makes a book unsalable, and therefore second-hand.

Nevertheless by six o'clock he had done much to repair the damage. He had returned the books to their original places, swept the floor, and put new lights in the sockets overhead. The red shade itself was ruined beyond redemption, and Merlin thought in some trepidation that the money to replace it might have to come out of his salary. At six, therefore, having done the best he could, he crawled over the front window display to pull down the blind. As he was treading delicately back, he saw Mr Moonlight Quill rise from his desk, put on his overcoat and hat, and emerge into the shop. He nodded mysteriously at Merlin and went toward the door. With his hand on the knob he paused, turned around, and in a voice curiously compounded of ferocity and uncertainty, he said:

'If that girl comes in here again, you tell her to behave.'

With that he opened the door, drowning Merlin's meek 'Yessir' in its creak, and went out.

Merlin stood there for a moment, deciding wisely not to worry about what was for the present only a possible futurity, and then he went into the back of the shop and invited Miss Masters to have supper with him at Pulpat's French Restaurant, where one could still obtain red wine at dinner, despite the Great Federal Government. Miss Masters accepted.

'Wine makes me feel all tingly,' she said.

Merlin laughed inwardly as he compared her to Caroline, or rather as he didn't compare her. There was no comparison.

II

Mr Moonlight Quill, mysterious, exotic, and oriental in temperament was, nevertheless, a man of decision. And it was with decision that he approached the problem of his wrecked shop. Unless he should make an outlay equal to the original cost of his entire stock – a step which for certain private reasons he did not wish to take – it would be impossible for him to continue in business with the Moonlight Quill as before. There was but one thing to do. He promptly turned his establishment from an up-to-the-minute bookstore into a second-hand bookshop. The damaged books were marked down from twenty five to fifty per cent, the name over the door whose serpentine embroidery had once shone so insolently bright, was allowed to grow dim and take on the indescribably vague color of old paint, and, having a strong penchant for ceremonial, the proprietor even went so far as to buy two skull-caps of shoddy red felt, one for himself and one for his clerk, Merlin Grainger. Moreover, he let his goatee grow until it resembled the tail-feathers of an ancient sparrow and substituted for a once dapper business suit a reverence-inspiring affair of shiny alpaca.

In fact, within a year after Caroline's catastrophic visit to the bookshop the only thing in it that preserved any semblance of being up to date was Miss Masters. Miss McCracken had followed in the footsteps of Mr Moonlight Quill and become an intolerable dowd.

For Merlin too, from a feeling compounded of loyalty and listlessness, had let his exterior take on the semblance of a deserted garden. He accepted the red felt skull-cap as a symbol of his decay. Always a young man known as a 'pusher,' he had been, since the day of his graduation from the manual training department of a New York High School, an inveterate brusher of clothes, hair, teeth, and even eyebrows, and had learned the value of laying all his clean socks toe upon toe and heel upon heel in a certain drawer of his bureau, which would be known as the sock drawer.

These things, he felt, had won him his place in the greatest splendor of the Moonlight Quill. It was due to them that he was not still making 'chests useful for keeping things,' as he was taught with breathless practicality in High School, and selling them to whoever had use of such chests – possibly undertakers. Nevertheless when the progressive Moonlight Quill became the retrogressive Moonlight Quill he preferred to sink with it, and so took to letting his suits gather undisturbed the wispy burdens of the air and to throwing his socks indiscriminately into the shirt drawer, the underwear drawer, and even into no drawer at all. It was not uncommon in his new carelessness to let many of his clean clothes go directly back to the laundry without having ever been worn, a common eccentricity of impoverished bachelors. And this in the face of his favorite magazines, which at that time were fairly staggering with articles by successful authors against the frightful impudence of the condemned poor, such as the buying of wearable shirts and nice cuts of meat, and the fact that they preferred good investments in personal jewelry to respectable ones in four per cent saving-banks.

It was indeed a strange state of affairs and a sorry one for many worthy and God-fearing men. For the first time in the history of the Republic almost any negro north of Georgia could change a one-dollar bill. But as at that time the cent was rapidly approaching the purchasing power of the Chinese ubu and was only a thing you got back occasionally after paying for a soft drink, and could use merely in getting your correct weight, this was perhaps not so strange a phenomenon as it at first seems. It was too curious a state of things, however, for Merlin Grainger to take the step that he did take – the hazardous, almost involuntary step of proposing to Miss Masters. Stranger still that she accepted him.

It was at Pulpat's on Saturday night and over a $1.75 bottle of water diluted with *vin ordinaire* that the proposal occurred.

'Wine makes me feel all tingly, doesn't it you?' chattered Miss Masters gaily.

'Yes,' answered Merlin absently; and then, after a long and pregnant pause: 'Miss Masters – Olive – I want to say something to you if you'll listen to me.'

The tingliness of Miss Masters (who knew what was coming) increased until it seemed that she would shortly be electrocuted by her own nervous reactions. But her 'Yes, Merlin,' came without a sign or flicker of interior disturbance. Merlin swallowed a stray bit of hair that he found in his mouth.

'I have no fortune,' he said with the manner of making an announcement. 'I have no fortune at all.'

Their eyes met, locked, became wistful, and dreamy and beautiful.

'Olive,' he told her, 'I love you.'

'I love you too, Merlin,' she answered simply. 'Shall we have another bottle of wine?'

'Yes,' he cried, his heart beating at a great rate. 'Do you mean—'

'To drink to our engagement,' she interrupted bravely. 'May it be a short one!'

'No!' he almost shouted, bringing his fist fiercely down upon the table. 'May it last forever!'

'What?'

'I mean – oh, I see what you mean. You're right. May it be a short one.' He laughed and added, 'My error.'

After the wine arrived they discussed the matter thoroughly.

'We'll have to take a small apartment at first,' he said, 'and I believe, yes, by golly, I know there's a small one in the house where I live, a big room and a sort of a dressing-room-kitchenette and the use of a bath on the same floor.'

She clapped her hands happily, and he thought how pretty she was really, that is, the upper part of her face – from the bridge of the nose down she was somewhat out of true. She continued enthusiastically:

'And as soon as we can afford it we'll take a real swell apartment, with an elevator and a telephone girl.'

'And after that a place in the country – and a car.'

'I can't imagine nothing more fun. Can you?'

Merlin fell silent a moment. He was thinking that he would have to give up his room, the fourth floor rear. Yet it mattered very little now. During the past year and a half – in fact, from the very date of Caroline's visit to the Moonlight Quill – he had never seen her. For a week after that visit her lights had failed to go on – darkness brooded out into the areaway, seemed to grope blindly in at his expectant, uncurtained window. Then the lights had appeared at last, and instead of Caroline and her callers they showed a stodgy family – a little man with a bristly mustache and a full-bosomed woman who spent her evenings patting her hips and rearranging bric-à-brac. After two days of them Merlin had callously pulled down his shade.

No, Merlin could think of nothing more fun than rising in the world with Olive. There would be a cottage in a suburb, a cottage painted blue, just one class below the sort of cottages that are of white stucco with a green roof. In the grass around the cottage would be rusty trowels and a broken green bench and a baby-carriage with a wicker body that sagged to the left. And around the grass and the baby-carriage and the cottage itself, around his whole world there would be the arms of Olive, a little stouter, the arms of her neo-Olivian period, when, as she walked, her cheeks would tremble up and down ever so slightly from too much face-massaging. He could hear her voice now, two spoons' length away:

'I knew you were going to say this to-night, Merlin. I could see—'

She could see. Ah – suddenly he wondered how much she could see. Could she see that the girl who had come in with a party of three men and sat down at the next table was Caroline? Ah, could she see that? Could she see that the men brought with them liquor far more potent than Pulpat's red ink condensed threefold . . . ?

Merlin stared breathlessly, half-hearing through an auditory ether Olive's low, soft monologue, as like a persistent honey-bee she sucked sweetness from her memorable hour. Merlin was listening to the clinking of ice and the fine laughter of all four at some pleasantry – and that laughter of Caroline's that he knew so well stirred him, lifted him, called his heart imperiously over to her table, whither it obediently went. He could see her quite plainly, and he fancied that in the last year and a half she had changed, if ever so slightly. Was it the light or were her cheeks a little thinner and her eyes less fresh, if more liquid, than of old? Yet the shadows were still purple in her russet hair; her mouth hinted yet of kisses, as did the profile that came sometimes between his eyes and a row of books, when it was twilight in the bookshop where the crimson lamp presided no more.

And she had been drinking. The threefold flush in her cheeks was compounded of youth and wine and fine cosmetic – that he could tell. She was making great amusement for the young man on her left and the portly person on her right, and even for the old fellow opposite her, for the latter from time to time uttered the shocked and mildly reproachful cackles of another generation. Merlin caught the words of a song she was intermittently singing—

'Just snap your fingers at care,
Don't cross the bridge 'til you're there—'

The portly person filled her glass with chill amber. A waiter after several trips about the table, and many helpless glances at Caroline, who was maintaining a cheerful, futile questionnaire as to the succulence of this dish or that, managed to obtain the semblance of an order and hurried away . . .

Olive was speaking to Merlin—

'When, then?' she asked, her voice faintly shaded with disappointment. He realized that he had just answered no to some question she had asked him.

'Oh, sometime.'

'Don't you – care?'

A rather pathetic poignancy in her question brought his eyes back to her.

'As soon as possible, dear,' he replied with surprising tenderness. 'In two months – in June.'

'So soon?' Her delightful excitement quite took her breath away.

'Oh, yes, I think we'd better say June. No use waiting.'

Olive began to pretend that two months was really too short a time for her to make preparations. Wasn't he a bad boy! Wasn't he impatient, though! Well, she'd show him he mustn't be too quick with *her*. Indeed he was so sudden she didn't exactly know whether she ought to marry him at all.

'June,' he repeated sternly.

Olive sighed and smiled and drank her coffee, her little finger lifted high above the others in true refined fashion. A stray thought came to Merlin that he would like to buy five rings and throw at it.

'By gosh!' he exclaimed aloud. Soon he *would* be putting rings on one of her fingers.

His eyes swung sharply to the right. The party of four had become so riotous that the head-waiter had approached and spoken to them. Caroline was arguing with this head-waiter in a raised voice, a voice so clear and young that it seemed as though the whole restaurant would listen – the whole restaurant except Olive Masters, self-absorbed in her new secret.

'How do you do?' Caroline was saying. 'Probably the handsomest head-waiter in captivity. Too much noise? Very unfortunate. Something'll have to be done about it. Gerald' – she addressed the man on her right – 'the head-waiter says there's too much noise. Appeals to us to have it stopped. What'll I say?'

'Sh!' remonstrated Gerald, with laughter. 'Sh!' and Merlin heard him add in an undertone: 'All the bourgeoisie will be aroused. This is where the floorwalkers learn French.'

Caroline sat up straight in sudden alertness.

'Where's a floorwalker?' she cried. 'Show me a floorwalker.' This seemed to amuse the party, for they all, including Caroline, burst into renewed laughter. The head-waiter, after a last conscientious but despairing admonition, became Gallic with his shoulders and retired into the background.

Pulpat's, as every one knows, has the unvarying respectability of the table d'hôte. It is not a gay place in the conventional sense. One comes, drinks the red wine, talks perhaps a little more and a little louder than usual under the low, smoky ceilings, and then goes home. It closes up at nine-thirty, tight as a drum; the policeman is paid off and given an extra bottle of wine for the missis, the coat-room girl hands her tips to the collector, and then darkness crushes the little round tables out of sight and life. But excitement was prepared for Pulpat's this evening – excitement of no mean variety. A girl with russet, purple-shadowed hair mounted to her table-top and began to dance thereon.

'*Sacré nom de Dieu!* Come down off there!' cried the head-waiter. 'Stop that music!'

But the musicians were already playing so loud that they could pretend not to hear his order; having once been young, they played louder and gayer than ever, and Caroline danced with grace and vivacity, her pink, filmy dress swirling about her, her agile arms playing in supple, tenuous gestures along the smoky air.

A group of Frenchmen at a table near by broke into cries of applause, in which other parties joined – in a moment the room was full of clapping and shouting; half the diners were on their feet, crowding up, and on the outskirts the hastily summoned proprietor was giving indistinct vocal evidences of his desire to put an end to this thing as quickly as possible.

'... Merlin!' cried Olive, awake, aroused at last; 'she's such a wicked girl! Let's get out – now!'

The fascinated Merlin protested feebly that the check was not paid.

'It's all right. Lay five dollars on the table. I despise that girl. I can't *bear* to look at her.' She was on her feet now, tugging at Merlin's arm.

Helplessly, listlessly, and then with what amounted to downright unwillingness, Merlin rose, followed Olive dumbly as she picked her way through the delirious clamor, now approaching its height and threatening to become a wild and memorable riot. Submissively he took his coat and stumbled up half a dozen steps into the moist April air outside, his ears still ringing with the sound of light feet on the table and of laughter all about and over the little world of the café. In silence they walked along toward Fifth Avenue and a bus.

It was not until next day that she told him about the wedding – how she had moved the date forward: it was much better that they should be married on the first of May.

III

And married they were, in a somewhat stuffy manner, under the chandelier of the flat where Olive lived with her mother. After marriage came elation, and then, gradually, the growth of weariness. Responsibility descended upon Merlin, the responsibility of making his thirty dollars a week and her twenty suffice to keep them respectably fat and to hide with decent garments the evidence that they were.

It was decided after several weeks of disastrous and well-nigh humiliating experiments with restaurants that they would join the great army of the delicatessen-fed, so he took up his old way of life again, in that he stopped every evening at Braegdort's delicatessen and bought potatoes in salad, ham in slices, and sometimes even stuffed tomatoes in bursts of extravagance.

Then he would trudge homeward, enter the dark hallway, and climb three rickety flights of stairs covered by an ancient carpet of long obliterated design. The hall had an ancient smell – of the vegetables of 1880, of the furniture polish in vogue when 'Adam-and-Eve' Bryan ran against William McKinley, of portières an ounce heavier with dust, from worn-out shoes and lint from dresses turned long since into patch-work quilts. This smell would pursue him up the stairs, revivified and made poignant at each landing by the aura of contemporary cooking, then, as he began the next flight, diminishing into the odor of the dead routine of dead generations.

Eventually would occur the door of his room, which slipped open with indecent willingness and closed with almost a sniff upon his 'Hello, dear! Got a treat for you to-night.'

Olive, who always rode home on the bus to 'get a morsel of air,' would be making the bed and hanging up things. At his call she would come up to him and give him a quick kiss with wide-open eyes, while he held her upright like a ladder, his hands on her two arms, as though she were a thing without equilibrium, and would, once he relinquished hold, fall stiffly backward to the floor. This is the kiss that comes in with the second year of marriage, succeeding the bridegroom kiss (which is rather stagey at best, say those who know about such things, and apt to be copied from passionate movies).

Then came supper, and after that they went out for a walk, up two blocks and through Central Park, or sometimes to a moving picture, which taught them patiently that they were the sort of people for whom life was ordered, and that something very grand and brave and beautiful would soon happen to them if they were docile and obedient to their rightful superiors and kept away from pleasure.

Such was their day for three years. Then change came into their lives: Olive had a baby, and as a result Merlin had a new influx of material resources. In the third week of Olive's confinement, after an hour of nervous rehearsing, he went into the office of Mr Moonlight Quill and demanded an enormous increase in salary.

'I've been here ten years,' he said; 'since I was nineteen. I've always tried to do my best in the interests of the business.'

Mr Moonlight Quill said that he would think it over. Next morning he announced, to Merlin's great delight, that he was going to put into effect a project long premeditated – he was going to retire from active work in the bookshop, confining himself to periodic visits and leaving Merlin as manager with a salary of fifty dollars a week and a one-tenth interest in the business. When the old man finished, Merlin's cheeks were glowing and his eyes full of tears. He seized his employer's hand and shook it violently, saying over and over again:

'It's very nice of you, sir. It's very white of you. It's very, very nice of you.'

So after ten years of faithful work in the store he had won out at last. Looking back, he saw his own progress toward this hill of elation no longer as a sometimes sordid and always gray decade of worry and failing enthusiasm and failing dreams, years when the moonlight had grown duller in the areaway and the youth had faded out of Olive's face, but as a glorious and triumphant climb over obstacles which he had determinedly surmounted by unconquerable will-power. The optimistic self-delusion that had kept him from misery was seen now in the golden garments of stern resolution. Half a dozen times he had taken steps to leave the Moonlight Quill and soar upward, but through sheer faint-heartedness he had stayed on. Strangely enough he now thought that those were times when he had exerted tremendous persistence and had 'determined' to fight it out where he was.

At any rate, let us not for this moment begrudge Merlin his new and magnificent view of himself. He had arrived. At thirty he had reached a post of importance. He left the shop that evening fairly radiant, invested every penny in his pocket in the most tremendous feast that Braegdort's delicatessen offered, and staggered homeward with the great news and four gigantic paper bags. The fact that Olive was too sick to eat, that he made himself faintly but unmistakably ill by a struggle with four stuffed tomatoes, and that most of the food deteriorated rapidly in an iceless ice-box all next day did not mar the occasion. For the first time since the week of his marriage Merlin Grainger lived under a sky of unclouded tranquility.

The baby boy was christened Arthur, and life became dignified, significant, and, at length, centered. Merlin and Olive resigned themselves to a somewhat secondary place in their own cosmos; but what they lost in personality they regained in a sort of primordial pride. The country house did not come, but a month in an Asbury Park boarding-house each summer filled the gap; and during Merlin's two weeks' holiday this excursion assumed the air of a really merry jaunt – especially when, with the baby asleep in a wide room opening technically on the sea, Merlin strolled with Olive along the thronged board-walk puffing at his cigar and trying to look like twenty thousand a year.

With some alarm at the slowing up of the days and the accelerating of the years, Merlin became thirty-one, thirty-two – then almost with a rush arrived at that age which, with all its washing and panning, can only muster a bare handful of the precious stuff of youth: he became thirty-five. And one day on Fifth Avenue he saw Caroline.

It was Sunday, a radiant, flowerful Easter morning and the avenue was a pageant of lilies and cutaways and happy April-colored bonnets. Twelve o'clock: the great churches were letting out their people – St Simon's, St Hilda's, the Church of the Epistles, opened their doors like wide mouths until the people pouring forth surely resembled happy laughter as they met and strolled and chattered, or else waved white bouquets at waiting chauffeurs.

In front of the Church of the Epistles stood its twelve vestrymen, carrying out the time-honored custom of giving away Easter eggs full of face-powder to the church-going débutantes of the year. Around them delightedly danced the two thousand miraculously groomed children of the very rich, correctly cute and curled, shining like sparkling little jewels upon their mothers' fingers. Speaks the sentimentalist for the children of the poor? Ah, but the children of the rich, laundered, sweet-smelling, complexioned of the country, and, above all, with soft, in door voices.

Little Arthur was five, child of the middle class. Undistinguished, unnoticed, with a nose that forever marred what Grecian yearnings his features might have had, he held tightly to his mother's warm, sticky hand, and, with Merlin on his other side, moved upon the home-coming throng. At Fifty-third Street, where there were two churches, the congestion was at its thickest, its richest. Their progress was of necessity retarded to such an extent that even little Arthur had not the slightest difficulty in keeping up. Then it was that Merlin perceived an open landaulet of deepest crimson, with handsome nickel trimmings, glide slowly up to the curb and come to a stop. In it sat Caroline.

She was dressed in black, a tight-fitting gown trimmed with lavender, flowered at the waist with a corsage of orchids. Merlin started and then gazed at her fearfully. For the first time in the eight years since his marriage he was encountering the girl again. But a girl no longer. Her figure was slim as ever – or perhaps not quite, for a certain boyish swagger, a sort of insolent adolescence, had gone the way of the first blooming of her cheeks. But she was beautiful; dignity was there now, and the charming lines of a fortuitous nine-and-twenty; and she sat in the car with such perfect appropriateness and self-possession that it made him breathless to watch her.

Suddenly she smiled – the smile of old, bright as that very Easter and its flowers, mellower than ever – yet somehow with not quite the radiance and infinite promise of that first smile back there in the bookshop nine years before. It was a steelier smile, disillusioned and sad.

But it was soft enough and smile enough to make a pair of young men in cutaway coats hurry over, to pull their high hats off their wetted, iridescent hair; to bring them, flustered and bowing, to the edge of her landaulet, where her lavender gloves gently touched their gray ones. And these two were presently joined by another, and then two more, until there was a rapidly swelling crowd around the landaulet. Merlin would hear a young man beside him say to his perhaps well-favored companion:

'If you'll just pardon me a moment, there's some one I *have* to speak to. Walk right ahead. I'll catch up.'

Within three minutes every inch of the landaulet, front, back, and side, was occupied by a man – a man trying to construct a sentence clever enough to find its way to Caroline through the stream of conversation. Luckily for Merlin a portion of little Arthur's clothing had chosen the opportunity to threaten a collapse, and Olive had hurriedly rushed him over against a building for some extemporaneous repair work, so Merlin was able to watch, unhindered, the salon in the street.

The crowd swelled. A row formed in back of the first, two more behind that. In the midst, an orchid rising from a black bouquet, sat Caroline enthroned in her obliterated car, nodding and crying salutations and smiling with such true happiness that, of a sudden, a new relay of gentlemen had left their wives and consorts and were striding toward her.

The crowd, now phalanx deep, began to be augmented by the merely curious; men of all ages who could not possibly have known Caroline jostled over and melted into the circle of ever-increasing diameter, until the lady in lavender was the center of a vast impromptu auditorium.

All about her were faces – clean-shaven, bewhiskered, old, young, ageless, and now, here and there, a woman. The mass was rapidly spreading to the opposite curb, and, as St Anthony's around the corner let out its box-holders, it overflowed to the sidewalk and crushed up against the iron picket-fence of a millionaire across the street. The motors speeding along the avenue were compelled to stop, and in a jiffy were piled three, five, and six deep at the edge of the crowd; auto-busses, top-heavy turtles of traffic, plunged into the jam, their passengers crowding to the edges of the roofs in wild excitement and peering down into the center of the mass, which presently could hardly be seen from the mass's edge.

The crush had become terrific. No fashionable audience at a Yale-Princeton football game, no damp mob at a world's series, could be compared with the panoply that talked, stared, laughed, and honked about the lady in black and lavender. It was stupendous; it was terrible. A quarter mile down the block a half-frantic policeman called his precinct; on the same corner a frightened civilian crashed in the glass of a fire-alarm and sent in a wild paen for all the fire-engines of the city; up in an apartment high in one of the tall buildings a hysterical old maid telephoned in turn for the prohibition enforcement agent, the special deputies on Bolshevism, and the maternity ward of Belle-vue Hospital.

The noise increased. The first fire-engine arrived, filling the

Sunday air with smoke, clanging and crying a brazen, metallic message down the high, resounding walls. In the notion that some terrible calamity had overtaken the city, two excited deacons ordered special services immediately and set tolling the great bells of St Hilda's and St Anthony's, presently joined by the jealous gongs of St Simon's and the Church of the Epistles. Even far off in the Hudson and the East River the sounds of the commotion were heard, and the ferry-boats and tugs and ocean liners set up sirens and whistles that sailed in melancholy cadence, now varied, now reiterated, across the whole diagonal width of the city from Riverside Drive to the gray water-fronts of the lower East Side . . .

In the center of her landaulet sat the lady in black and lavender, chatting pleasantly first with one, then with another of that fortunate few in cutaways who had found their way to speaking distance in the first rush. After a while she glanced around her and beside her with a look of growing annoyance.

She yawned and asked the man nearest her if he couldn't run in somewhere and get her a glass of water. The man apologized in some embarrassment. He could not have moved hand or foot. He could not have scratched his own ear . . .

As the first blast of the river sirens keened along the air, Olive fastened the last safety-pin in little Arthur's rompers and looked up. Merlin saw her start, stiffen slowly like hardening stucco, and then give a little gasp of surprise and disapproval.

'That woman,' she cried suddenly. 'Oh!'

She flashed a glance at Merlin that mingled reproach and pain, and without another word gathered up little Arthur with one hand, grasped her husband by the other, and darted amazingly in a winding, bumping canter through the crowd. Somehow people gave way before her; somehow she managed to retain her grasp on her son and husband; somehow she managed to emerge two blocks up, battered and dishevelled, into an open space, and, without slowing up her pace, darted down a side-street. Then at last, when uproar had died away into a dim and distant clamor, did she come to a walk and set little Arthur upon his feet.

'And on Sunday, too! Hasn't she disgraced herself enough?' This was her only comment. She said it to Arthur, as she seemed to address her remarks to Arthur throughout the remainder of the day. For some curious and esoteric reason she had never once looked at her husband during the entire retreat.

IV

The years between thirty-five and sixty-five revolve before the passive mind as one unexplained, confusing merry-go-round. True, they are a merry-go-round of ill-gaited and wind-broken horses, painted first in pastel colors, then in dull grays and browns, but perplexing and intolerably dizzy the thing is, as never were the merry-go-rounds of childhood or adolescence, as never, surely, were the certain-coursed, dynamic roller-coasters of youth. For most men and women these thirty years are taken up with a gradual withdrawal from life, a retreat first from a front with many shelters, those myriad amusements and curiosities of youth, to a line with less, when we peel down our ambitions to one ambition, our recreations to one recreation, our friends to a few to whom we are anæsthetic; ending up at last in a solitary, desolate strong point that is not strong, where the shells now whistle abominably, now are but half-heard as, by turns frightened and tired, we sit waiting for death.

At forty, then, Merlin was no different from himself at thirty-five; a larger paunch, a gray twinkling near his ears, a more certain lack of vivacity in his walk. His forty-five differed from his forty by a like margin, unless one mention a slight deafness in his left ear. But at fifty-five the process had become a chemical change of immense rapidity. Yearly he was more and more an 'old man' to his family – senile almost, so far as his wife was concerned. He was by this time complete owner of the bookshop. The mysterious Mr Moonlight Quill, dead some five years and not survived by his wife, had deeded the whole stock and store to him, and there he still spent his days, conversant now by name with almost all that man has recorded for three thousand years, a human catalogue, an authority upon tooling and binding, upon folios and first editions, an accurate inventory of a thousand authors whom he could never have understood and had certainly never read.

At sixty-five he distinctly doddered. He had assumed the melancholy habits of the aged so often portrayed by the second old man in standard Victorian comedies. He consumed vast warehouses of time searching for mislaid spectacles. He 'nagged' his wife and was nagged in turn. He told the same jokes three or four times a year at the family table, and gave his son weird, impossible directions as to his conduct in life. Mentally and materially he was so entirely different from the Merlin Grainger of twenty-five that it seemed incongruous that he should bear the same name.

He worked still in the bookshop with the assistance of a youth, whom, of course, he considered very idle, indeed, and a new young woman, Miss Gaffney. Miss McCracken, ancient and unvenerable as himself, still kept the accounts. Young Arthur was gone into Wall Street to sell bonds, as all the young men seemed to be doing in that day. This, of course, was as it should be. Let old Merlin get what magic he could from his books – the place of young King Arthur was in the counting-house.

One afternoon at four when he had slipped noiselessly up to the front of the store on his soft-soled slippers, led by a newly formed habit, of which, to be fair, he was rather ashamed, of spying upon the young man clerk, he looked casually out of the front window, straining his faded eyesight to reach the street. A limousine, large, portentous, impressive, had drawn to the curb, and the chauffeur, after dismounting and holding some sort of conversation with persons in the interior of the car, turned about and advanced in a bewildered fashion toward the entrance of the Moonlight Quill. He opened the door, shuffled in, and, glancing uncertainly at the old man in the skull-cap, addressed him in a thick, murky voice, as though his words came through a fog.

'Do you – do you sell additions?'

Merlin nodded.

'The arithmetic books are in the back of the store.'

The chauffeur took off his cap and scratched a close-cropped, fuzzy head.

'Oh, naw. This I want's a detecatif story.' He jerked a thumb back toward the limousine. 'She seen it in the paper. Firs' addition.'

Merlin's interest quickened. Here was possibly a big sale.

'Oh, editions. Yes, we've advertised some firsts, but – detective stories, I – don't – believe— What was the title?'

'I forget. About a crime.'

'About a crime. I have – well, I have "The Crimes of the Borgias" – full morocco, London 1769, beautifully—'

'Naw,' interrupted the chauffeur, 'this was one fella did this crime. She seen you had it for sale in the paper.' He rejected several possible titles with the air of a connoisseur.

'"Silver Bones,"' he announced suddenly out of a slight pause.

'What?' demanded Merlin, suspecting that the stiffness of his sinews were being commented on.

'Silver Bones. That was the guy that done the crime.'

'Silver Bones?'

'Silver Bones. Indian, maybe.'

Merlin stroked his grizzly cheeks.

'Gees, Mister,' went on the prospective purchaser, 'if you wanna save me an awful bawlin' out jes' try an' think. The old lady goes wile if everything don't run smooth.'

But Merlin's musings on the subject of Silver Bones were as futile as his obliging search through the shelves, and five minutes later a very dejected charioteer wound his way back to his mistress. Through the glass Merlin could see the visible symbols of a tremendous uproar going on in the interior of the limousine. The chauffeur made wild, appealing gestures of his innocence, evidently to no avail, for when he turned around and climbed back into the driver's seat his expression was not a little dejected.

Then the door of the limousine opened and gave forth a pale and slender young man of about twenty, dressed in the attenuation of fashion and carrying a wisp of a cane. He entered the shop, walked past Merlin, and proceeded to take out a cigarette and light it. Merlin approached him.

'Anything I can do for you, sir?'

'Old boy,' said the youth coolly, 'there are several things. You can first let me smoke my ciggy in here out of sight of that old lady in the limousine, who happens to be my grandmother. Her knowledge as to whether I smoke it or not before my majority happens to be a matter of five thousand dollars to me. The second thing is that you should look up your first edition of the "Crime of Sylvester Bonnard" that you advertised in last Sunday's *Times*. My grandmother there happens to want to take it off your hands.'

Detecatif story! Crime of somebody! Silver Bones! All was explained. With a faint deprecatory chuckle, as if to say that he would have enjoyed this had life put him in the habit of enjoying anything, Merlin doddered away to the back of his shop where his treasures were kept, to get this latest investment which he had picked up rather cheaply at the sale of a big collection.

When he returned with it the young man was drawing on his cigarette and blowing out quantities of smoke with immense satisfaction.

'My God!' he said. 'She keeps me so close to her the entire day running idiotic errands that this happens to be my first puff in six hours. What's the world coming to, I ask you, when a feeble old lady in the milk-toast era can dictate to a man as to his personal vices? I happen to be unwilling to be so dictated to. Let's see the book.'

Merlin passed it to him tenderly and the young man, after opening it with a carelessness that gave a momentary jump to the book-dealer's heart, ran through the pages with his thumb.

'No illustrations, eh?' he commented. 'Well, old boy, what's it worth? Speak up! We're willing to give you a fair price, though why I don't know.'

'One hundred dollars,' said Merlin with a frown.

The young man gave a startled whistle.

'Whew! Come on. You're not dealing with somebody from the cornbelt. I happen to be a city-bred man and my grandmother happens to be a city-bred woman, though I'll admit it'd take a special tax appropriation to keep her in repair. We'll give you twenty-five dollars, and let me tell you that's liberal. We've got books in our attic, up in our attic with my old play-things, that were written before the old boy that wrote this was born.'

Merlin stiffened, expressing a rigid and meticulous horror.

'Did your grandmother give you twenty-five dollars to buy this with?'

'She did not. She gave me fifty, but she expects change. I know that old lady.'

'You tell her,' said Merlin with dignity, 'that she has missed a very great bargain.'

'Give you forty,' urged the young man. 'Come on now – be reasonable and don't try to hold us up—'

Merlin had wheeled around with the precious volume under his arm and was about to return it to its special drawer in his office when there was a sudden interruption. With unheard-of magnificence the front door burst rather than swung open, and admitted into the dark interior a regal apparition in black silk and fur which bore rapidly down upon him. The cigarette leaped from the fingers of the urban young man and he gave breath to an inadvertent 'Damn!' – but it was upon Merlin that the entrance seemed to have the most remarkable and incongruous effect – so strong an effect that the greatest treasure of his shop slipped from his hand and joined the cigarette on the floor. Before him stood Caroline.

She was an old woman, an old woman remarkably preserved, unusually handsome, unusually erect, but still an old woman. Her hair was a soft, beautiful white, elaborately dressed and jewelled; her face, faintly rouged à la grande dame, showed webs of wrinkles at the edges of her eyes and two deeper lines in the form of stanchions connected her nose with the corners of her mouth. Her eyes were dim, ill natured, and querulous.

But it was Caroline without a doubt: Caroline's features though in decay; Caroline's figure, if brittle and stiff in movement; Caroline's manner, unmistakably compounded of a delightful insolence and an enviable self assurance; and, most of all, Caroline's voice, broken and shaky, yet with a ring in it that still could and did make chauffeurs want to drive laundry wagons and cause cigarettes to fall from the fingers of urban grandsons.

She stood and sniffed. Her eyes found the cigarette upon the floor.

'What's that?' she cried. The words were not a question – they were an entire litany of suspicion, accusation, confirmation, and decision. She tarried over them scarcely an instant. 'Stand up!' she said to her grandson, 'stand up and blow that nicotine out of your lungs!'

The young man looked at her in trepidation.

'Blow!' she commanded.

He pursed his lips feebly and blew into the air.

'Blow!' she repeated, more peremptorily than before.

He blew again, helplessly, ridiculously.

'Do you realize,' she went on briskly, 'that you've forfeited five thousand dollars in five minutes?'

Merlin momentarily expected the young man to fall pleading upon his knees, but such is the nobility of human nature that he remained standing – even blew again into the air, partly from nervousness, partly, no doubt, with some vague hope of reingratiating himself.

'Young ass!' cried Caroline. 'Once more, just once more and you leave college and go to work.'

This threat had such an overwhelming effect upon the young man that he took on an even paler pallor than was natural to him. But Caroline was not through.

'Do you think I don't know what you and your brothers, yes, and your asinine father too, think of me? Well, I do. You think I'm senile. You think I'm soft. I'm not!' She struck herself with her fist as though to prove that she was a mass of muscle and sinew. 'And I'll have more brains left when you've got me laid out in the drawing-room some sunny day than you and the rest of them were born with.'

'But Grandmother—'

'Be quiet. You, a thin little stick of a boy, who if it weren't for my money might have risen to be a journey-man barber out in the Bronx – Let me see your hands. Ugh! The hands of a barber – *you* presume to be smart with *me*, who once had three counts and a bonafide duke, not to mention half a dozen papal titles pursue me from the city of Rome to the city of New York.' She paused, took breath. 'Stand up! Blow!'

The young man obediently blew. Simultaneously the door opened and an excited gentleman of middle age who wore a coat and hat trimmed with fur, and seemed, moreover, to be trimmed with the same sort of fur himself on upper lip and chin, rushed into the store and up to Caroline.

'Found you at last,' he cried. 'Been looking for you all over town. Tried your house on the 'phone and your secretary told me he thought you'd gone to a bookshop called the Moonlight—'

Caroline turned to him irritably.

'Do I employ you for your reminiscences?' she snapped. 'Are you my tutor or my broker?'

'Your broker,' confessed the fur-trimmed man, taken somewhat aback. 'I beg your pardon. I came about that phonograph stock. I can sell for a hundred and five.'

'Then do it.'

'Very well. I thought I'd better—'

'Go sell it. I'm talking to my grandson.'

'Very well. I—'

'Good-by.'

'Good by, Madame.' The fur-trimmed man made a slight bow and hurried in some confusion from the shop.

'As for you,' said Caroline, turning to her grandson, 'you stay just where you are and be quiet.'

She turned to Merlin and included his entire length in a not unfriendly survey. Then she smiled and he found himself smiling too. In an instant they had both broken into a cracked but none the less spontaneous chuckle. She seized his arm and hurried him to the other side of the store. There they stopped, faced each other, and gave vent to another long fit of senile glee.

'It's the only way,' she gasped in a sort of triumphant malignity. 'The only thing that keeps old folks like me happy is the sense that they can make other people step around. To be old and rich and have poor descendants is almost as much fun as to be young and beautiful and have ugly sisters.'

'Oh, yes,' chuckled Merlin. 'I know. I envy you.'

She nodded, blinking.

'The last time I was in here, forty years ago,' she said, 'you were a young man very anxious to kick up your heels.'

'I was,' he confessed.

'My visit must have meant a good deal to you.'

'You have all along,' he exclaimed. 'I thought – I used to think at first that you were a real person – human, I mean.'

She laughed.

'Many men have thought me inhuman.'

'But now,' continued Merlin excitedly, 'I understand. Understanding is allowed to us old people – after nothing much matters. I see now that on a certain night when you danced upon a table-top you were nothing but my romantic yearning for a beautiful and perverse woman.'

Her old eyes were far away, her voice no more than the echo of a forgotten dream.

'How I danced that night! I remember.'

'You were making an attempt at me. Olive's arms were closing about me and you warned me to be free and keep my measure of youth and irresponsibility. But it seemed like an effect gotten up at the last moment. It came too late.'

'You are very old,' she said inscrutably. 'I did not realize.'

'Also I have not forgotten what you did to me when I was thirty-five. You shook me with that traffic tie-up. It was a magnificent effort. The beauty and power you radiated! You became personified even to my wife, and she feared you. For weeks I wanted to slip out of the house at dark and forget the stuffiness of life with music and cocktails and a girl to make me young. But then – I no longer knew how.'

'And now you are so very old.'

With a sort of awe she moved back and away from him.

'Yes, leave me!' he cried. 'You are old also; the spirit withers with the skin. Have you come here only to tell me something I had best forget: that to be old and poor is perhaps more wretched than to be old and rich; to remind me that *my* son hurls my gray failure in my face?'

'Give me my book,' she commanded harshly. 'Be quick, old man!'

Merlin looked at her once more and then patiently obeyed. He picked up the book and handed it to her, shaking his head when she offered him a bill.

'Why go through the farce of paying me? Once you made me wreck these very premises.'

'I did,' she said in anger, 'and I'm glad. Perhaps there had been enough done to ruin *me*.'

She gave him a glance, half disdain, half ill-concealed uneasiness, and with a brisk word to her urban grandson moved toward the door.

Then she was gone – out of his shop – out of his life. The door clicked. With a sigh he turned and walked brokenly back toward the glass partition that enclosed the yellowed accounts of many years as well as the mellowed, wrinkled Miss McCracken.

Merlin regarded her parched, cobwebbed face with an odd sort of pity. She, at any rate, had had less from life than he. No rebellious, romantic spirit cropping out unbidden had, in its memorable moments, given her life a zest and a glory.

Then Miss McCracken looked up and spoke to him:

'Still spunky old piece, isn't she?'

Merlin started.

'Who?'

'Old Alicia Dare. Mrs Thomas Allerdyce she is now, of course; has been these thirty years.'

'What? I don't understand you.' Merlin sat down suddenly in his swivel chair; his eyes were wide.

'Why, surely, Mr Grainger, you can't tell me that you've forgotten her, when for ten years she was the most notorious character in New York. Why, one time when she was the corespondent in the Throckmorton divorce case she attracted so much attention on Fifth Avenue that there was a traffic tie-up. Didn't you read about it in the papers.'

'I never used to read the papers.' His ancient brain was whirring.

'Well, you can't have forgotten the time she came in here and ruined the business. Let me tell you I came near asking Mr Moonlight Quill for my salary, and clearing out.'

'Do you mean that – that you *saw* her?'

'Saw her! How could I help it with the racket that went on. Heaven knows Mr Moonlight Quill didn't like it either, but of course *he* didn't say anything. He was daffy about her and she could twist him around her little finger. The second he opposed one of her whims she'd threaten to tell his wife on him. Served him right. The idea of that man falling for a pretty adventuress! Of course he was never rich enough for *her*, even though the shop paid well in those days.'

'But when I saw her,' stammered Merlin, 'that is, when I *thought* I saw her, she lived with her mother.'

'Mother, trash!' said Miss McCracken indignantly. 'She had a woman there she called "Aunty" who was no more related to her than I am. Oh, she was a bad one – but clever. Right after the Throckmorton divorce case she married Thomas Allerdyce, and made herself secure for life.'

'Who was she?' cried Merlin. 'For God's sake what was she – a witch?'

'Why, she was Alicia Dare, the dancer, of course. In those days you couldn't pick up a paper without finding her picture.'

Merlin sat very quiet, his brain suddenly fatigued and stilled. He was an old man now indeed, so old that it was impossible for him to dream of ever having been young, so old that the glamour was gone out of the world, passing not into the faces of children and into the persistent comforts of warmth and life, but passing out of the range of sight and feeling. He was never to smile again or to sit in a long reverie when spring evenings wafted the cries of children in at his window until gradually they became the friends of his boyhood out there, urging him to come and play before the last dark came down. He was too old now even for memories.

That night he sat at supper with his wife and son, who had used him for their blind purposes. Olive said:

'Don't sit there like a death's-head. Say something.'

'Let him sit quiet,' growled Arthur. 'If you encourage him he'll tell us a story we've heard a hundred times before.'

Merlin went up-stairs very quietly at nine o'clock. When he was in his room and had closed the door tight he stood by it for a moment, his thin limbs trembling. He knew now that he had always been a fool.

'O Russet Witch!'

But it was too late. He had angered Providence by resisting too many temptations. There was nothing left but heaven, where he would meet only those who, like him, had wasted earth.

Crazy Sunday

I

It was Sunday – not a day, but rather a gap between two other days. Behind, for all of them, lay sets and sequences, the long waits under the crane that swung the microphone, the hundreds miles a day by automobiles to and fro across a county, the struggles of rival ingenuities in the conference rooms, the ceaseless compromise, the clash and strain of many personalities fighting for their lives. And now Sunday, with individual life starting up again, with a glow kindling in eyes that had been glazed with monotony the afternoon before. Slowly as the hours waned they came awake like *Puppenfeen* in a toy shop: an intense colloquy in a corner, lovers disappearing to neck in a hall. And the feeling of 'Hurry, it's not too late, but for God's sake hurry before the blessed forty hours of leisure are over.'

Joel Coles was writing continuity. He was twenty-eight and not yet broken by Hollywood. He had had what were considered nice assignments since his arrival six months before and he submitted his scenes and sequences with enthusiasm. He referred to himself modestly as a hack but really did not think of it that way. His mother had been a successful actress; Joel had spent his childhood between London and New York trying to separate the real from the unreal, or at least to keep one guess ahead. He was a handsome man with the pleasant cow-brown eyes that in 1913 had gazed out at Broadway audiences from his mother's face.

When the invitation came it made him sure that he was getting somewhere. Ordinarily he did not go out on Sundays but stayed sober and took work home with him. Recently they had given him a Eugene O'Neill play destined for a very important lady indeed. Everything he had done so far had pleased Miles Calman, and Miles Calman was the only director on the lot who did not work under a supervisor and was responsible to the money men alone. Everything was clicking into place in Joel's career. ('This is Mr Calman's secretary. Will you come to tea from four to six Sunday – he lives in Beverly Hills, number—.')

Joel was flattered. It would be a party out of the top-drawer. It was a tribute to himself as a young man of promise. The Marion Davies crowd, the high-hats, the big currency numbers, perhaps even Dietrich and Garbo and the Marquis, people who were not seen everywhere, would probably be at Calman's.

'I won't take anything to drink,' he assured himself. Calman was audibly tired of rummies, and thought it was a pity the industry could not get along without them.

Joel agreed that writers drank too much – he did himself, but he wouldn't this afternoon. He wished Miles would be within hearing when the cocktails were passed to hear his succinct, unobtrusive, 'No, thank you.'

Miles Calman's house was built for great emotional moments – there was an air of listening, as if the far silences of its vistas hid an audience, but this afternoon it was thronged, as though people had been bidden rather than asked. Joel noted with pride that only two other writers from the studio were in the crowd, an ennobled limey and, somewhat to his surprise, Nat Keogh, who had evoked Calman's impatient comment on drunks.

Stella Calman (Stella Walker, of course) did not move on to her other guests after she spoke to Joel. She lingered – she looked at him with the sort of beautiful look that demands some sort of acknowledgement and Joel drew quickly on the dramatic adequacy inherited from his mother:

'Well, you look about sixteen! Where's your kiddy car?'

She was visibly pleased; she lingered. He felt that he should say something more, something confident and easy – he had first met her when she was struggling for bits in New York. At the moment a tray slid up and Stella put a cocktail glass into his hand.

'Everybody's afraid, aren't they?' he said, looking at it absently. 'Everybody watches for everybody else's blunders, or tries to make sure they're with people that'll do them credit. Of course that's not true in your house,' he covered himself hastily. 'I just meant generally in Hollywood.'

Stella agreed. She presented several people to Joel as if he were very important. Reassuring himself that Miles was at the other side of the room, Joel drank the cocktail.

'So you have a baby?' he said. 'That's the time to look out. After a pretty woman has had her first child, she's very vulnerable, because she wants to be reassured about her own charm. She's got to have some new man's unqualified devotion to prove to herself she hasn't lost anything.'

'I never get anybody's unqualified devotion,' Stella said rather resentfully.

'They're afraid of your husband.'

'You think that's it?' She wrinkled her brow over the idea; then the conversation was interrupted at the exact moment Joel would have chosen.

Her attentions had given him confidence. Not for him to join safe groups, to slink to refuge under the wings of such acquaintances as he saw about the room. He walked to the window and looked out towards the Pacific, colourless under its sluggish sunset. It was good here – the American Riviera and all that, if there were ever time to enjoy it. The handsome, well-dressed people in the room, the lovely girls, and the – well, the lovely girls. You couldn't have everything.

He saw Stella's fresh boyish face, with the tired eyelid that always drooped a little over one eye, moving about among her guests and he wanted to sit with her and talk a long time as if she were a girl instead of a name; he followed her to see if she paid anyone as much attention as she had paid him. He took another cocktail – not because he needed confidence but because she had given him so much of it. Then he sat down beside the director's mother.

'Your son's gotten to be a legend, Mrs Calman – Oracle and a Man of Destiny and all that. Personally, I'm against him but I'm in a minority. What do you think of him? Are you impressed? Are you surprised how far he's gone?'

'No, I'm not surprised,' she said calmly. 'We always expected a lot from Miles.'

'Well now, that's unusual,' remarked Joel. 'I always think all mothers are like Napoleon's mother. My mother didn't want me to have anything to do with the entertainment business. She wanted me to go to West Point and be safe.'

'We always had every confidence in Miles.'

He stood by the built-in bar of the dining-room with the good-humoured, heavy-drinking, highly paid Nat Keogh.

'—I made a hundred grand during the year and lost forty grand gambling, so now I've hired a manager.'

'You mean an agent,' suggested Joel.

'No, I've got that too. I mean a manager. I make over everything to my wife and then he and my wife get together and hand me out the money. I pay him five thousand a year to hand me out my money.'

'You mean your agent.'

'No, I mean my manager, and I'm not the only one – a lot of other irresponsible people have him.'

'Well, if you're irresponsible why are you responsible enough to hire a manager?'

'I'm just irresponsible about gambling. Look here—'

A singer performed; Joel and Nat went forward with the others to listen.

II

The singing reached Joel vaguely; he felt happy and friendly towards all the people gathered there, people of bravery and industry, superior to bourgeoisie that outdid them in ignorance and loose living, risen to a position of the highest prominence in a nation that for a decade had wanted only to be entertained. He liked them – he loved them. Great waves of good feeling flowed through him.

As the singer finished his number and there was a drift towards the hostess to say good-bye, Joel had an idea. He would give them *Building It Up*, his own composition. It was his only parlour trick, it had amused several parties and it might please Stella Walker. Possessed by the hunch, his blood throbbing with the scarlet corpuscles of exhibitionism, he sought her.

'Of course,' she cried. 'Please! Do you need anything?'

'Someone has to be the secretary that I'm supposed to be dictating to.'

'I'll be her.'

As the word spread, the guests in the hall, already putting on their coats to leave, drifted back and Joel faced the eyes of many strangers. He had a dim foreboding, realizing that the man who had just performed was a famous radio entertainer. Then someone said 'Sh!' and he was alone with Stella, the centre of a sinister Indian-like half-circle. Stella smiled up at him expectantly – he began.

His burlesque was based upon the cultural limitations of Mr Dave Silverstein, an independent producer; Silverstein was presumed to be dictating a letter outlining a treatment of a story he had bought.

'—a story of divorce, the younger generation, and the Foreign Legion,' he heard his voice saying, with the intonations of Mr Silverstein. 'But we got to build it up, see?'

A sharp pang of doubt struck through him. The faces surrounding him in the gently moulded light were intent and curious, but there was no ghost of a smile anywhere; directly in front the Great Lover of the screen glared at him with an eye as keen as the eye of a potato. Only Stella Walker looked up at him with a radiant, never faltering smile.

'If we make him a Menjou type, then we get a sort of Michael Arlen only with a Honolulu atmosphere.'

Still not a ripple in front, but in the rear a rustling, a perceptible shift towards the left, towards the front door.

'—then she says she feels this sex appil for him and he burns out and says, "Oh, go on destroy yourself—"'

At some point he heard Nat Keogh snicker and here and there were a few encouraging faces, but as he finished he had the sickening realization that he had made a fool of himself in view of an important section of the picture world, upon whose favour depended his career.

For a moment he existed in the midst of a confused silence, broken by a general trek for the door. He felt the undercurrent of derision that rolled through the gossip; then – all this was in the space of ten seconds – the Great Lover, his eye hard and empty as the eye of a needle, shouted 'Boo! Boo!' voicing in an overtone what he felt was the mood of the crowd. It was the resentment of the professional towards the amateur, of the community towards the stranger, the thumbs-down of the clan.

Only Stella Walker was still standing near and thanking him as if he had been an unparalleled success, as if it hadn't occurred to her that anyone hadn't liked it. As Nat Keogh helped him into his overcoat, a great wave of self disgust swept over him and he clung desperately to his rule of never betraying an inferior emotion until he no longer felt it.

'I was a flop,' he said lightly, to Stella. 'Never mind, it's a good number when appreciated. Thanks for your cooperation.'

The smile did not leave her face – he bowed rather drunkenly and Nat drew him towards the door . . .

The arrival of his breakfast awakened him into a broken and ruined world. Yesterday he was himself, a point of fire against an industry, today he felt that he was pitted under an enormous disadvantage, against those faces, against individual contempt and collective sneer. Worse than that, to Miles Calman he was become one of those rummies, stripped of dignity, whom Calman regretted he was compelled to use. To Stella Walker on whom he had forced a martyrdom to preserve the courtesy of her house – her opinion he did not dare to guess. His gastric juices ceased to flow and he set his poached eggs back on the telephone table. He wrote:

DEAR MILES: *You can imagine my profound self-disgust. I confess to a taint of exhibitionism, but at six o'clock in the afternoon, in broad*

daylight! Good God! My apologies to your wife. Yours ever,
  JOEL COLES

Joel emerged from his office on the lot only to slink like a male-factor to the tobacco store. So suspicious was his manner that one of the studio police asked to see his admission card. He had decided to eat lunch outside when Nat Keogh, confident and cheerful, overtook him.

'What do you mean you're in permanent retirement? What if that Three-Piece Suit did boo you?

'Why, listen,' he continued, drawing Joel into the studio restaurant. 'The night of one of his premières at Grauman's, Joe Squires kicked his tail while he was bowing to the crowd. The ham said Joe'd hear from him later but when Joe called him up at eight o'clock next day and said, 'I thought I was going to hear from you,' he hung up the phone.'

The preposterous story cheered Joel, and he found a gloomy consolation in staring at the group at the next table, the sad, lovely Siamese twins, the mean dwarfs, the proud giant from the circus picture. But looking beyond at the yellow-stained faces of pretty women, their eyes all melancholy and startling with mascara, their ball gowns garish in full day, he saw a group who had been at Calman's and winced.

'Never again,' he exclaimed aloud, 'absolutely my last social appearance in Hollywood!'

The following morning a telegram was waiting for him at his office:

You were one of the most agreeable people at our party. Expect you at my sister June's buffet supper next Sunday.
  STELLA WALKER CALMAN

The blood rushed fast through his veins for a feverish minute. Incredulously he read the telegram over.

'Well, that's the sweetest thing I ever heard of in my life!'

III

Crazy Sunday again. Joel slept until eleven, then he read a newspaper to catch up with the past week. He lunched in his room on trout, avocado salad, and a pint of California wine. Dressing for the tea, he selected a pin-check suit, a blue shirt, a burnt orange tie. There were dark circles of fatigue under his eyes. In his second-hand car he drove to the Riviera apartments. As he was introducing himself to Stella's sister, Miles and Stella arrived in riding clothes – they had been quarrelling fiercely most of the afternoon on all the dirt roads back of Beverly Hills.

Miles Calman, tall, nervous, with a desperate humour and the unhappiest eyes Joel ever saw, was an artist from the top of his curiously shaped head to his niggerish feet. Upon these last he stood firmly – he had never made a cheap picture though he had sometimes paid heavily for the luxury of making experimental flops. In spite of his excellent company, one could not be with him long without realizing that he was not a well man.

From the moment of their entrance Joel's day bound itself up inextricably with theirs. As he joined the group around them Stella turned away from it with an impatient little tongue click – and Miles Calman said to the man who happened to be next to him:

'Go easy on Eva Goebel. There's hell to pay about her at home.' Miles turned to Joel, 'I'm sorry I missed you at the office yesterday. I spent the afternoon at the analyst's.'

'You being psychoanalyzed?'

'I have been for months. First I went for claustrophobia, now I'm trying to get my whole life cleared up. They say it'll take over a year.'

'There's nothing the matter with your life,' Joel assured him.

'Oh, no? Well, Stella seems to think so. Ask anybody – they can all tell you about it,' he said bitterly.

A girl perched herself on the arm of Miles's chair; Joel crossed to Stella, who stood disconsolately by the fire.

'Thank you for your telegram,' he said. 'It was darn sweet. I can't imagine anybody as good-looking as you are being so good-humoured.'

She was a little lovelier than he had ever seen her and perhaps the unstinted admiration in his eyes prompted her to unload on him – it did not take long, for she was obviously at the emotional bursting point.

'—and Miles has been carrying on this thing for two years, and I never knew. Why, she was one of my best friends, always in the house. Finally when people began to come to me, Miles had to admit it.'

She sat down vehemently on the arm of Joel's chair. Her riding breeches were the colour of the chair and Joel saw that the mass of her hair was made up of some strands of red gold and some of pale gold, so that it could not be dyed and that she had on no make-up. She was that good-looking –

Still quivering with the shock of her discovery, Stella found unbear-able the spectacle of a new girl hovering over Miles; she led Joel into a bedroom, and seated at either end of a big bed they went on talking. People on their way to the washroom glanced in and made wise-cracks, but Stella, emptying out her story, paid no atten-tion. After a while Miles stuck his head in the door and said, 'There's no use trying to explain something to Joel in half an hour that I don't understand myself and the psychoanalyst says will take a whole year to understand.'

She talked on as if Miles were not there. She loved Miles, she said – under considerable difficulties she had always been faithful to him.

'The psychoanalyst told Miles that he had a mother complex. In his first marriage he transferred his mother complex to his wife, you see – and then his sex turned to me. But when we married the thing repeated itself – he transferred his mother complex to me and all his libido turned towards this other woman.'

Joel knew that this probably wasn't gibberish – yet it sounded like gibberish. He knew Eva Goebel; she was a motherly person, older and probably wiser than Stella, who was a golden child.

Miles now suggested impatiently that Joel come back with them since Stella had so much to say, so they drove out to the mansion in Beverly Hills. Under the high ceilings the situation seemed more dignified and tragic. It was an eerie bright night with the dark very clear outside of all the windows and Stella all rose-gold raging and crying around the room. Joel did not quite believe in picture actresses' grief. They have other preoccupations – they are beautiful rose-gold figures blown full of life by writers and directors, and after hours they sit around and talk in whispers and giggle innuendoes, and the ends of many adventures flow through them.

Sometimes he pretended to listen and instead thought how well she was got up – sleek breeches with a matched set of legs in them, an Italian-coloured sweater with a little high neck, and a short brown chamois coat. He couldn't decide whether she was an imitation of an English lady or an English lady was an imitation of her. She hovered somewhere between the realest of realities and the most blatant of impersonations.

'Miles is so jealous of me that he questions everything I do,' she cried scornfully. 'When I was in New York I wrote him that I'd been to the theatre with Eddie Baker. Miles was so jealous he phoned me ten times in one day.'

'I was wild,' Miles snuffled sharply, a habit he had in times of stress. 'The analyst couldn't get any results for a week.'

Stella shook her head despairingly. 'Did you expect me just to sit in the hotel for three weeks?'

'I don't expect anything. I admit that I'm jealous. I try not to be. I worked on that with Dr Bridgebane, but it didn't go any good. I was jealous of Joel this afternoon when you sat on the arm of his chair.'

'You were?' She started up. 'You were! Wasn't there somebody on the arm of your chair? And did you speak to me for two hours?'

'You were telling your troubles to Joel in the bedroom.'

'When I think that that woman' – she seemed to believe that to omit Eva Goebel's name would be to lessen her reality – 'used to come here—'

'All right – all right,' said Miles wearily. 'I've admitted everything and I feel as bad about it as you do.' Turning to Joel he began talking about pictures, while Stella moved restlessly along the far walls, her hands in her breeches pockets.

'They've treated Miles terribly,' she said, coming suddenly back into the conversation as if they'd never discussed her personal affairs. 'Dear, tell him about old Beltzer trying to change your picture.'

As she stood hovering protectively over Miles, her eyes flashing with indignation in his behalf, Joel realized that he was in love with her. Stifled with excitement he got up to say good night.

With Monday the week resumed its workaday rhythm, in sharp contrast to the theoretical discussions, the gossip and scandal of Sunday; there was the endless detail of script revision – 'Instead of a lousy dissolve, we can leave her voice on the sound track and cut to a medium shot of the taxi from Bell's angle or we can simply pull the camera back to include the station, hold it a minute, and then pan to the row of taxis' – by Monday afternoon Joel had again forgotten that people whose business was to provide entertainment were ever privileged to be entertained. In the evening he phoned Miles's house. He asked for Miles but Stella came to the phone.

'Do things seem better?'

'Not particularly. What are you doing next Saturday evening?'

'Nothing.'

'The Perrys are giving a dinner and theatre party and Miles won't be here – he's flying to South Bend to see the Notre Dame–California game. I thought you might go with me in his place.'

After a long moment Joel said, 'Why – surely. If there's a conference I can't make dinner but I can get to the theatre.'

'Then I'll say we can come.'

Joel walked his office. In view of the strained relations of the Calmans, would Miles be pleased, or did she intend that Miles shouldn't know of it? That would be out of the question – if Miles didn't mention it Joel would. But it was an hour or more before he could get down to work again.

Wednesday there was a four-hour wrangle in a conference room crowded with planets and nebulae of cigarette smoke. Three men and a woman paced the carpet in turn, suggesting or condemning,

speaking sharply or persuasively, confidently or despairingly. At the
end Joel lingered to talk to Miles.

The man was tired – not with the exaltation of fatigue but life-
tired, with his lids sagging and his beard prominent over the blue
shadows near his mouth.

'I hear you're flying to the Notre Dame game.'

Miles looked beyond him and shook his head.

'I've given up the idea.'

'Why?'

'On account of you.' Still he did not look at Joel.

'What the hell, Miles?'

'That's why I've given it up.' He broke into a perfunctory laugh
at himself. 'I can't tell what Stella might do just out of spite – she's
invited you to take her to the Perrys', hasn't she? I wouldn't enjoy
the game.'

The fine instinct that moved swiftly and confidently on the set,
muddled so weakly and helplessly through his personal life.

'Look, Miles,' Joel said frowning. 'I've never made any passes
whatsoever at Stella. If you're really seriously cancelling your trip
on account of me, I won't go to the Perrys' with her. I won't see
her. You can trust me absolutely.'

Miles looked at him, carefully now.

'Maybe.' He shrugged his shoulders. 'Anyhow there'd just be
somebody else. I wouldn't have any fun.'

'You don't seem to have much confidence in Stella. She told me
she'd always been true to you.'

'Maybe she has.' In the last few minutes several more muscles
had sagged around Miles's mouth. 'But how can I ask anything of
her after what's happened? How can I expect her— ' He broke off
and his face grew harder as he said, 'I'll tell you one thing, right or
wrong and no matter what I've done, if I ever had anything on her
I'd divorce her. I can't have my pride hurt – that would be the last
straw.'

His tone annoyed Joel, but he said:

'Hasn't she calmed down about the Eva Goebel thing?'

'No.' Miles snuffled pessimistically. 'I can't get over it either.'

'I thought it was finished.'

'I'm trying not to see Eva again, but you know it isn't easy just to drop something like that – it isn't some girl I kissed last night in a taxi. The psychoanalyst says—'

'I know,' Joel interrupted. 'Stella told me.' This was depressing. 'Well, as far as I'm concerned if you go to the game I won't see Stella. And I'm sure Stella has nothing on her conscience about anybody.'

'Maybe not,' Miles repeated listlessly. 'Anyhow I'll stay and take her to the party. Say,' he said suddenly, 'I wish you'd come too. I've got to have somebody sympathetic to talk to. That's the trouble – I've influenced Stella in everything. Especially I've influenced her so that she likes all the men I like – it's very difficult.'

'It must be,' Joel agreed.

IV

Joel could not get to the dinner. Self-conscious in his silk hat against the unemployment, he waited for the others in front of the Hollywood Theatre and watched the evening parade: obscure replicas of bright, particular picture stars, spavined men in polo coats, a stomping dervish with the beard and staff of an apostle, a pair of chic Filipinos in collegiate clothes, reminder that this corner of the Republic opened to the seven seas, a long fantastic carnival of young shouts which proved to be a fraternity initiation. The line split to pass two smart limousines that stopped at the kerb.

There she was, in a dress like ice-water, made in a thousand pale-blue pieces, with icicles trickling at the throat. He started forward.

'So you like my dress?'

'Where's Miles?'

'He flew to the game after all. He left yesterday morning – at least I think—' She broke off. 'I just got a telegram from South Bend saying that he's starting back. I forgot – you know all these people?'

The party of eight moved into the theatre.

Miles had gone after all and Joel wondered if he should have come. But during the performance, with Stella a profile under the pure grain of light hair, he thought no more about Miles. Once he turned and looked at her and she looked back at him, smiling and meeting his eyes for as long as he wanted. Between the acts they smoked in the lobby and she whispered:

'They're all going to the opening of Jack Johnson's night club – I don't want to go, do you?'

'Do we have to?'

'I suppose not.' She hesitated. 'I'd like to talk to you. I suppose we could go to our house – if I were only sure—'

Again she hesitated and Joel asked:

'Sure of what?'

'Sure that – oh, I'm haywire I know, but how can I be sure Miles went to the game?'

'You mean you think he's with Eva Goebel?'

'No, not so much that – but supposing he was here watching everything I do. You know Miles does odd things sometimes. Once he wanted a man with a long beard to drink tea with him and he sent down to the casting agency for one, and drank tea with him all afternoon.'

'That's different. He sent you a wire from South Bend – that proves he's at the game.'

After the play they said good night to the others at the kerb and were answered by looks of amusement. They slid off along the golden garish thoroughfare through the crowd that had gathered around Stella.

'You see he could arrange the telegrams,' Stella said, 'very easily.'

That was true. And with the idea that perhaps her uneasiness was justified, Joel grew angry: if Miles had trained a camera on them he felt no obligations towards Miles. Aloud he said:

'That's nonsense.'

There were Christmas trees already in the shop windows and the full moon over the boulevard was only a prop, as scenic as the giant boudoir lamps of the corners. On into the dark foliage of Beverly

Hills that flamed as eucalyptus by day, Joel saw only the flash of a white face under his own, the arc of her shoulder. She pulled away suddenly and looked up at him.

'Your eyes are like your mother's,' she said. 'I used to have a scrap-book full of pictures of her.'

'Your eyes are like your own and not a bit like any other eyes,' he answered.

Something made Joel look out into the grounds as they went into the house, as if Miles were lurking in the shrubbery. A telegram waited on the hall table. She read aloud:

CHICAGO
Home tomorrow night. Thinking of you. Love.
MILES

'You see,' she said, throwing the slip back on the table, 'he could easily have faked that.' She asked the butler for drinks and sandwiches and ran upstairs, while Joel walked into the empty reception rooms. Strolling about he wandered to the piano where he had stood in disgrace two Sundays before.

'Then we could put over,' he said aloud, 'a story of divorce, the younger generation, and the Foreign Legion.'

His thoughts jumped to another telegram.

'You were one of the most agreeable people at our party –'

An idea occurred to him. If Stella's telegram had been purely a gesture of courtesy then it was likely that Miles had inspired it, for it was Miles who had invited him. Probably Miles had said:

'Send him a wire – he's miserable – he thinks he's queered himself.'

It fitted in with 'I've influenced Stella in everything. Especially I've influenced her so that she likes all the men I like.' A woman would do a thing like that because she felt sympathetic – only a man would do it because he felt responsible.

When Stella came back into the room he took both her hands.

'I have a strange feeling that I'm a sort of pawn in a spite game you're playing against Miles,' he said.

'Help yourself to a drink.'

'And the odd thing is that I'm in love with you anyhow.'

The telephone rang and she freed herself to answer it.

'Another wire from Miles,' she announced. 'He dropped it, or it says he dropped it, from the aeroplane at Kansas City.'

'I suppose he asked to be remembered to me.'

'No, he just said he loved me. I believe he does. He's so very weak.'

'Come sit beside me,' Joel urged her.

It was early. And it was still a few minutes short of midnight a half-hour later, when Joel walked to the cold hearth, and said tersely:

'Meaning that you haven't any curiosity about me?'

'Not at all. You attract me a lot and you know it. The point is that I suppose I really do love Miles.'

'Obviously.'

'And tonight I feel uneasy about everything.'

He wasn't angry – he was even faintly relieved that a possible entanglement was avoided. Still as he looked at her, the warmth and softness of her body thawing her cold blue costume, he knew she was one of the things he would always regret.

'I've got to go,' he said. 'I'll phone a taxi.'

'Nonsense – there's a chauffeur on duty.'

He winced at her readiness to have him go, and seeing this she kissed him lightly and said, 'You're sweet, Joel.' Then suddenly three things happened: he took down his drink at a gulp, the phone rang loud through the house, and a clock in the hall struck in trumpet notes.

Nine – ten – eleven – twelve –

V

It was Sunday again. Joel realized that he had come to the theatre this evening with the work of the week still hanging about him like cerements. He had made love to Stella as he might attack some matter to be cleaned up hurriedly before the day's end. But this was Sunday – the lovely, lazy perspective of the next twenty-four hours unrolled before him – every minute was something to be approached with lulling indirection, every moment held the germ of innumerable possibilities. Nothing was impossible – everything was just beginning. He poured himself another drink.

With a sharp moan, Stella slipped forward inertly by the telephone. Joel picked her up and laid her on the sofa. He squirted soda-water on a handkerchief and slapped it over her face. The telephone mouthpiece was still grinding and he put it to his ear.

'—the plane fell just this side of Kansas City. The body of Miles Calman has been identified and—'

He hung up the receiver.

'Lie still,' he said, stalling, as Stella opened her eyes.

'Oh, what's happened?' she whispered. 'Call them back. Oh, what's happened?'

'I'll call them right away. What's your doctor's name?'

'Did they say Miles was dead?'

'Lie quiet – is there a servant still up?'

'Hold me – I'm frightened.'

He put his arm around her.

'I want the name of your doctor,' he said sternly. 'It may be a mistake but I want someone here.'

'It's Dr – Oh, God, is Miles dead?'

Joel ran upstairs and searched through strange medicine cabinets for spirits of ammonia. When he came down Stella cried:

'He isn't dead – I know he isn't. This is part of his scheme. He's torturing me. I know he's alive. I can feel he's alive.'

'I want to get hold of some close friend of yours, Stella. You can't stay here alone tonight.'

'Oh, no,' she cried. 'I can't see anybody. You stay, I haven't got any friend.' She got up, tears streaming down her face. 'Oh, Miles is my only friend. He's not dead – he can't be dead. I'm going there right away and see. Get a train. You'll have to come with me.'

'You can't. There's nothing to do tonight. I want you to tell me the name of some woman I can call: Lois? Joan? Carmel? Isn't there somebody?'

Stella stared at him blindly.

'Eva Goebel was my best friend,' she said.

Joel thought of Miles, his sad and desperate face in the office two days before. In the awful silence of his death all was clear about him. He was the only American-born director with both an interesting temperament and an artistic conscience. Meshed in an industry, he had paid with his ruined nerves for having no resilience, no healthy cynicism, no refuge – only a pitiful and precarious escape.

There was a sound at the outer door – it opened suddenly, and there were footsteps in the hall.

'Miles!' Stella screamed. 'Is it you, Miles? Oh, it's Miles.'

A telegraph boy appeared in the doorway.

'I couldn't find the bell. I heard you talking inside.'

The telegram was a duplicate of the one that had been phoned. While Stella read it over and over, as though it were a black lie, Joel telephoned. It was still early and he had difficulty getting anyone; when finally he succeeded in finding some friends he made Stella take a stiff drink.

'You'll stay here, Joel,' she whispered, as though she were half-asleep. 'You won't go away. Miles liked you – he said you—' She shivered violently, 'Oh, my God, you don't know how alone I feel.' Her eyes closed, 'Put your arms around me. Miles had a suit like that.' She started bolt upright. 'Think of what he must have felt. He was afraid of almost everything, anyhow.'

She shook her head dazedly. Suddenly she seized Joel's face and held it close to hers.

'You won't go. You like me – you love me, don't you? Don't call up anybody. Tomorrow's time enough. You stay here with me tonight.'

He stared at her, at first incredulously, and then with shocked understanding. In her dark groping Stella was trying to keep Miles alive by sustaining a situation in which he had figured – as if Miles's mind could not die so long as the possibilities that had worried him still existed. It was a distraught and tortured effort to stave off the realization that he was dead.

Resolutely Joel went to the phone and called a doctor.

'Don't, oh, don't call anybody!' Stella cried. 'Come back here and put your arms around me.'

'Is Dr Bales in?'

'Joel,' Stella cried. 'I thought I could count on you. Miles liked you. He was jealous of you – Joel, come here.'

Ah then – if he betrayed Miles she would be keeping him alive – for if he were really dead how could he be betrayed?

'—has just had a very severe shock. Can you come at once, and get hold of a nurse?'

'Joel!'

Now the door-bell and the telephone began to ring intermittently, and automobiles were stopping in front of the door.

'But you're not going,' Stella begged him. 'You're going to stay, aren't you?'

'No,' he answered. 'But I'll be back, if you need me.'

Standing on the steps of the house which now hummed and palpitated with the life that flutters around death like protective leaves, he began to sob a little in his throat.

'Everything he touched he did something magical to,' he thought. 'He even brought that little gamin alive and made her a sort of masterpiece.'

And then:

'What a hell of a hole he leaves in this damn wilderness – already!'

And then with a certain bitterness, 'Oh, yes, I'll be back – I'll be back!'